IN HIS HANDS

Short Stories

A.J. CORK

LifeRich
PUBLISHING

Scripture taken from the New King James Version. Copyright © 1979, 1980, 1982 by Thomas Nelson, Inc. Used by permission. All rights reserved.

Scripture taken from the Holy Bible, NEW INTERNATIONAL VERSION®. Copyright © 1973, 1978, 1984, 2011 by Biblica, Inc. All rights reserved worldwide. Used by permission. NEW INTERNATIONAL VERSION® and NIV® are registered trademarks of Biblica, Inc. Use of either trademark for the offering of goods or services requires the prior written consent of Biblica US, Inc.

Scripture taken from The Living Bible copyright © 1971 by Tyndale House Foundation. Used by permission of Tyndale House Publishers Inc., Carol Stream, Illinois 60188. All rights reserved. The Living Bible, TLB, and the The Living Bible logo are registered trademarks of Tyndale House Publishers.

LifeRich Publishing is a registered trademark of The Reader's Digest Association, Inc.

LifeRich Publishing books may be ordered through booksellers or by contacting:

LifeRich Publishing
1663 Liberty Drive
Bloomington, IN 47403
www.liferichpublishing.com
1 (888) 238-8637

Because of the dynamic nature of the Internet, any web addresses or links contained in this book may have changed since publication and may no longer be valid. The views expressed in this work are solely those of the author and do not necessarily reflect the views of the publisher, and the publisher hereby disclaims any responsibility for them.

Any people depicted in stock imagery provided by Thinkstock are models, and such images are being used for illustrative purposes only. Certain stock imagery © Thinkstock.

ISBN: 978-1-4897-0853-3 (sc)
ISBN: 978-1-4897-0854-0 (hc)
ISBN: 978-1-4897-0852-6 (e)

Library of Congress Control Number: 2016909351

Print information available on the last page.

LifeRich Publishing rev. date: 07/26/2016

CONTENTS

NEW TESTAMENT STORIES

FOREWORD

Dear friends and readers

I AM SURE YOU WILL notice I've written a lot of the same background history, on purpose. I realize many of you will be new to Biblical history, as this book will probably not be a book that appeals to the masses of serious Bible students. This is only to place the characters in a timeline you will easily be able to find in Bible history.

My efforts here have been a joy to write. My aim is to write stories that put flesh and blood on the bare bones of the people we've been taught about in Sunday School. They were real people just like you and me. They all have their own story that we don't know anything about. Why they were where they were, at that time in history where we find them. What made them tick? What circumstances in life forged their personalities? What made them sad or happy? Inquisitive, or just plain misunderstood? We don't know, so I have given them a personal story out of my imagination.

I have come to love these people as I have given them a story, just as Jesus loved them. We were all created a one of a kind child of God! He must have loved variety or we'd all be clones. Psalms 139:1-18 tells it beautifully. It is a story of each one of us. "He knew us before we were!" Isn't that amazing?

Look at verse 17-18. "How precious are your thoughts toward me!" "O God! How great is the sum of them!"

"If I could count them, they are more than I can number. They would out number the sand of the sea shore:"

"When I awake you are still with me!"

We are no surprise to God. He saw it all and loves us anyway! There is nothing bad enough He will not forgive, or so good we can save ourselves. He will not remove his love from us. Our own proclaimed, self-righteousness does not impress Him.. He knows us much better than we know ourselves.

Isn't that the way we are as parents? When no one else loves us, our mother/father/ grandmother does!

I've studied these people and imagined a story line for each one. It soon became clear, "Jesus love for the least of these," shines through.

It was the people who thought they had all the answers that gave him trouble. In their self-righteousness they planned to kill him, thinking they were doing God a favor.

The sick, the lame, the blind; the deaf and dumb, sinful and demon possessed. It was the nobodies of this world that came to him. They knew they needed a Savior. He touched them with healing or whatever they needed, and they followed him.

The fishermen Jesus called to be his disciples were rough talking, loud, uneducated and unrefined: A dishonest tax collector, who robbed the Jews and the Romans to enrich himself. Thomas was a doubter, and Judas a dishonest treasurer that carried the community money bag. Not a one of them was a surprise to Him. He chose them on purpose. And guess what? They set out to change the world.

Since Jesus chose them. It is not such a stretch to imagine he could use you and me? We don't seem so out of place in the company of these.

I have asked several people what they knew about Barabbas. They answered: "A riot causing rabble- rouser/murderer." And that was the crime for which he was awaiting execution for. What we don't know is, why?

The characters I picked to write about were mostly obscure, with not much written about them in the Word. As you read their stories, imagine yourself in that story line. Each of us has a story written in His book of life. He still loves them and He still loves us too. He died for each of us. Paid the ultimate price to satisfy our death sentence and set us free!

It is my intent to bring these people to life, as someone in your family: Your next door neighbor. Someone you can identify with. The ones who might ask you to pray for them in their hour of need. Someone we might sit down with and have that cup of morning coffee. We see ourselves in these.

If you enjoy their stories, pick up your Bible and begin to read. As soon as you see one of these people not much is said about, imagine yourself into their story: Telling the world your story and how you came to be who you are. Or, someone you know; there is more too them than the gossip told about them. I believe everyone is worthy of redemption. Jesus came to save that lost sheep. That lost coin. And that prodigal son. To that grieving mother or father; Peter wrote (2Peter 3:8-9), "He was not willing that any should perish, but all come to repentance" How blessed we will be when we see all people through this lens..

AJCork

OLD TESTAMENT STORIES

ADAM, WHERE ARE YOU?

I T IS FOOD FOR THOUGHT: How much we are still so much like Adam and Eve.

Truth is, "all have sinned and fallen short of the glory of God." Each and everyone of us. We have all fallen short and made bad choices of our own free will.

Many would say, "the Bible doesn't fit our culture." What really doesn't fit, is man's attempt to make the Word fit his culture. Sin isn't just a problem for the ax murdered, or the king-pin of the drug cartel, but all of us. "There is none righteous, no not one!" He will never force us to do his will by his demands. It is by the choices we make.

Jesus told his listeners, "I have food you know not of." As food feeds our physical bodies and sustains life, our spirit being is sustained and fed with God's Word. "In you we live and move and have our being." This is what we are created to be.

You enlighten me daily. You expound the Word with deeper meaning of things I thought I knew. There is no end to your wisdom. I will never know it all. Praise God! Proverbs 1:7. "The fear of the Lord is the beginning of wisdom, but fools despise wisdom and discipline."

We are created in God's image! We are created to be like Him! Example Proverbs 3:5-6 tells us "to trust the Lord and lean not on our own understanding. (The natural man's, understanding.) Proverbs 14:12 tells us "there is a way that seems right to a man, (the natural man) but in the end it leads to death."

When God completed His fourth day of creation, this place we call home, He said, "and it is good!"

Then God said, "Let the waters be filled with fish and other life. Let the skies be filled with birds of every kind. So God created it all, sea creatures, and every kind of fish and birds. They so pleased God! He blessed them and told them to multiply. He stocked the oceans and the sky. This was the fifth day, and it was good.

Then God said, let the earth bring forth every kind if animal-cattle and reptile and the wildlife of every kind. He made all sorts of wild animals, cattle, and reptiles, yes, even that snake. He whole of creation pleased God. I was good. Nothing surprised God. Each of creation was perfect in his eyes. (I notice God specifically mentioned wildlife, cattle and reptile twice.) God said, "It is good."

So God said, "Let us make man; in our image to have dominion of all life upon the earth and in the sky and in the seas." Notice : God gave Adam dominion over all this. Even that serpent in the Garden, but Adam chose not to do it!

"Our", speaks of the Triune God: God the Father, God the Son, and God the Holy Spirit. All three facets of God's Triune being was involved in the process. He created them male and female, God blessed them and told all mankind and animal life to be fruitful and multiply. He provided all the seed bearing plants, I have given you seed bearing plants throughout the earth, and all the fruit trees for man's food, and all the grasses and plants to the animals and birds for their food. Then God looked out over all he made and saw that it was very good. The evening and the morning was the sixth day.

It was a beautiful paradise with nothing lacking. Adam had the run of the place. God took him to the tree in the middle of the garden, showed him exactly the one he was speaking of and said, "Adam, my son, this is the only tree I am withholding from you. You may eat of all the trees, of every sort, except this one. It is the tree of good and evil and in the day you eat of it you shall die. This is the only one! All others are yours and they are wonderful. Eat to your hearts delight!"

Shortly after the garden tour, Almighty God said. "It is not good for man to be alone, so I will make him a mate. She will be a loving helper to him." The story goes into detail of the creation of Eve. And she was a masterpiece! When God awaken Adam from the deep sleep Father God had put him in for the surgery, He presented this beautiful creature He had made just for him. Every translation uses different words to describe Adams reaction, but all let us know he was wonderfully surprised and pleased! I can imagine he whooped it up in excitement and said, "For me?"

"Yes son, for you!"

Can't you just picture Adam falling to his knees thanking and praising God? (This could very well be the first praise and worship service!) "Love at first sight!" perfect relationship, in the perfect paradise. (All spoiled by "sin at first bite.)

Chapter 3:, describes the fall. This fall affecting all mankind; every person down through the centuries, even to us, today.

Was there some mistake which tree God was speaking of? No! He took Adams to the tree, so there could be no mistake. Adams showed Eve; as she knew the story. The serpent knew, as he called it the tree of good and evil. There was no mistake, they all knew which tree. God told Adam, "You can have all of the things in this place except this one. This is the only thing I am withholding from you." God even told him the consequences. Nothing could be mistaken.

One day in that beautiful place, they encountered that devil possessed serpent.

"Good morning Eve. Beautiful day isn't it?""Did you notice this beautiful tree in the middle of the garden?" The serpent said.

"Yes, it is most beautiful," Eve responded.

"Have you tasted it?"Ask the serpent. "It is the most delicious of the all trees in the garden."

She eyed it longingly. "No, we are forbidden to eat of it." "We are free to eat of all the others, but not this one."

"Did God really say, 'you must not eat of this tree?'"

"Yes he did. He told us the day you touch it you shall die."(I am thinking she should have checked the exact wording with Adam.) So like us, every time a story gets told we add our own little twist. (She adlibbed a bit; which is never a good idea.) As she added "when you touch it you shall die"

The serpent: "You shall not surely die!" "Doesn't this fruit look delicious?" "It appeals to your senses doesn't it?" (Her natural senses wanted it!)

"God knows that when you eat of it, your eyes will be opened and you will know all things and be as powerful as he is! You will truly know good and evil." "He is holding out on you!"(This would have been a good place for them to have a

4

conference and refresh Adam's memory as to what God had said; his exact words, and taken the dominion, but they didn't.) But, as is said; "She didn't, and the rest is history!"

She not only ate, she turned to Adam and said; "O Adam, this is wonderful! Have a bite." He didn't protest; he took the fruit and took a BIG bite!

Sin is deceiving. Just as it was for Eve. When Adam and Eve listened to that deceiver/accuser; that serpent, the devil in the garden; he appealed to her natural being of flesh and blood. She allowed herself to be deceived. They knew that tree was off limits. God had not kept this a secret from them. The deceiver was who she chose to listen too.

They listened, heard the lie, they ate, and saw they were naked. They felt shame! Emotions they had never before encountered. Thoughts of lust. Nakedness, shame and guilt; lies! Excuses, blame, sorrow; and all the disturbing thoughts shame brings. They made coverings of fig leaves to cover their nakedness and shame. Then they hid from God in the bushes.

As it was their appointed time; their afternoon stroll in the garden with their Father; He came, and they were in hiding. They had once communed with God daily: A perfect relationship with their maker. A time they always looked forward to. Now their shame had separated them.

"Adam. Where are you?" God knew very well where they were. He had seen it all. The temptation, eating the forbidden fruit, the juice still dripping off their chins. He saw their shame. He knew where they were and what they had done. But he was giving them room for repentance. Their own free will of choice, to repent and be free and blessed; or hiding in the dirty covering of fig leaves.

The leaves, cut off from the plant will wither and die, falling to the ground as dust, leaving them exposed, naked and ashamed.

They knew they were separated from God. That most wonderful relationship with the Father was gone! "Abba," Daddy, Creator, maker of all things. That relationship gone!" Now, they were hiding in fear.

The blame game begins.

"Adam, where are you and why are you hiding?"

"I heard you in the garden and I was afraid."

"Why are you afraid?"

"I heard you walking and I did not want you to see me naked."

"Who told you, you were naked?" "Have you eaten from the tree I warned you about?"

"Yes, but it wasn't my fault." "That woman you gave me made me do it?""She brought it to me and forced me to me to eat it!""Why did you bring her to me, anyway?" "It's not my fault!"

"Eve," God said, "what do you have to say?"

"It wasn't my fault either." "It was Adam's fault." "You told him which tree it was and he didn't tell me. And besides, that snake you created deceived me." "He told me it would be good for me!"

As they quarreled, no one admitting their failure; they would not repent and ask forgiveness. The choice and the opportunity was there, but they refused to take it. Notice: God did not ask the serpent his side of the story. He knew who he was, the devil. He handed him down his sentence!

To Adam, God said, "your punishment will be, You will be driven from the garden where the soil will be poor and you will toil to grow just enough food to eat, all the days of your life. It will be difficult and drudgery."

To Eve, God said, "Your husband will rule over you, and in child bearing you will be in great pain, suffering and distress. There will be little joy in your life."

To the serpent. "You shall crawl on your belly and eat dust all the days of your life, and woman forever will be at war with you. You will strike the heel of her offspring, and he shall crush your head!"

They were banished from the garden of paradise and angels with flaming swords guarded the entrance so they could not return.

Isn't that what we still do? When we know we have sinned we hide from God and others who love us. We make garments of our good works. Busy ourselves with cares; busy, so busy we have no time to meet with God. "Not enough hours in the day." "I have nothing to wear." "Those people are so judgmental and hypocrites!" On and On. Hiding behind our own creation of leaves! Hiding behind all sorts of leaves and bushes. Seems we are all busy; watching our neighbors with a critical eye. We notice all his wrong doings; saying," well, I am better than he is!" We hide behind our family, our denomination, our nation/political party. It is all smoke and mirrors, an illusion.

We are like the prodigal son. When we come to ourselves, look at our own desperate situation and say. "I will go home to my Father and ask him for forgiveness. There I will have a place to sleep and have food, as one of his hired men. I don't deserve to called his son, not after all I have done.(When we come out of hiding and say, "Father, I have sinned against you. It is my fault. I am the one who disobeyed you. I cannot bear

7

to be without you. Be my Lord and My God again! Restore to me the joy of your Salvation.") All these thing the sons has prepared to say.

But guess what? His Father has been waiting and watching, with tears in his eyes, to see one small move toward home. When he sees him, he runs with outstretched arms to meet his son. Tears of joy running down his cheeks! Before the son can finish his prepared speech, The Father calls out. "Bring the Royal Robe! Bring the Ring of Authority with the Royal crest and put it on his finger! Bring him the sandals of peace, fit for the Royal family!

When we come to that place we get so much more than we can imagine. We are received! Restored! He takes our garments of filth and covers us with the garment of the Kingdom; His righteousness! What a trade His Grace is!

How long does He offer His Grace? Remember the thief hanging on the cross next to Jesus? He was down to his final few breaths and said, "Jesus remember me when you come into your Kingdom." Jesus in his last few moments of life said, "This day you will be with me in paradise". Grace greater than all of our sin!

CAIN AND ABEL

THE BOYS FOUGHT AND QUARRELED continuously. We got so tired of all the grumbling, bickering, and running in to tattle on the other. Eve yelled at them, "get outside and play and don't come in here again unless there is blood!" "Are you two trying to drive me crazy?!" (She was probably the first mother to speak those words!)

Angrily, she snapped the tent flap closed and furiously began; Slamming and banging the clay cooking pots and pans together as she started to make something for the evening meal. Grumbling at the lack of things she had to use. Adam could barely scratch out enough to make a thin soup! Her attitude was anything but grateful.

Somehow those boys grew up!

One day as Adam came in from the drudgery of his toil, and found them fighting again. "It is time you two got a job and went to work! It is about time you started contributing something around here besides complaining!"

Cain went to work tilling the ground as his father, And Abel started to grow a herd and a flock. He took a couple of cows; a couple of ewes, a bull and a ram to begin with. It was astounding to realize how slow it would be before he saw any return for his work. Of course, all the while Cain taunted him for not contributing anything to the family welfare.

As the herd and flock grew and somewhat flourished he found satisfaction in his work. For the first time in his life he felt some worth. He began seeing the wonder of God's creation in the plan of reproduction.

So exciting he didn't even mind the heat and humidity. Nor the humiliation of having to ask his brother to trade some meat for the grain he needed to feed his livestock. Cain complied but kept a very detailed account of every grain of wheat. He stacked the books in his own favor.

After awhile it came time to make an offering. God was gracious enough to give them time to have something to offer.

Cain offered, with a bad attitude some of his grain and a few poor vegetables. Abel offered the best lamb he had raised.

The Lord did not accept Cain's offering, but he did accept Abel's lamb!

Cain had furious! Inside he was raging! The Lord said "Cain, why are you so down cast and angry?" "Had you truly offer your best with a grateful heart. I would have smiled on it." "Perhaps you could have traded some of your harvest for a lamb; then your offering would have pleased me also." "Be forgiving and Grateful Cain, instead of angry and hateful!" "You have the power to do this. The choice is yours."

All of this made Cain more enraged. And he took it out on Abel. His mind set on revenge.

He put his game face on, as if he had changed, but in his heart was a murderous rage. He began devising how he could do away with his brother!

He began to reason with himself.

"Since I have no respect for God; since he does not have any favor for me; what does it matter how I settle the score?" He never examined his own heart, coming to the truth. Sin always has way of justifying its own actions.

Well, he would show them all! "I am my own god and I will take my own revenge!"

One day when he had been unusually peaceful toward his brother he suggested they play some horseshoes. (Well actually it was more ring toss with a braided strip of leather; rock-toss into a clay pot.) Or the best three out of five wrestling match.

Cain said; "Hey Bro, how about we go out into the fields, have some fun and games, topped off with a picnic?"

"Good idea Bro. I'll barbeque some burgers and dogs and you bring some buns from your ground wheat!"

Abel was all in! This was a great break through to an overdue friendship!

Cain made sure their place of this outing was far enough from their folks, so they could not see or hear what was going on.(Cain was plotted the perfect crime.)

Cain brought salad fixing's and burger buns, and Abel brought the burgers and dogs from his range feed beef and lambs. No pesticides or MSG.

The played a few games in their muscle shirts, showing off their highly- developed biceps, from all the hard work and wrestling with each other in the outdoors, to escape their mothers wrath. Yes, they had plenty of time outdoors releasing all of their pent up anger.

"Let me get the fire started so the coals will be just right for the grilling."

"Good idea!" "We can play a few more games awhile we are waiting."

Cain thinking; "I'll let him get the burgers on before I do him in." "Those burgers sound pretty tasty." Then thinking; "I could almost like this guy!" "No, tomorrow I'll hate him again."

Abel got the meat started and the buns laid out for toasting, his back turned to Cain, not guessing what was about to happen. Cain came up behind him with a large rock and crushed his brothers' skull with a mighty blow. Calmly and without remorse, fixed a burger,as he sat watching to make sure his brother was dead.

Cain took his tools, dug a grave in the hard soil and buried his brother and all the bloody soil deep, so his folks could not see it.

Cain gathered up his tools, the extra burgers and buns and went to the patch he was farming, as if nothing had happened.

The only thing he didn't count on; God was watching! The God he had no respect for!

"Cain."

"Yes."

"Cain, where is you bother?"

"How would I know?" "I am not my brother's keeper!" "You are so smart; where do you think he is?"

"Cain, Cain!" "Your brother's blood cries out to me from the ground!" "I know what you have done." "I saw it all." "You have refused to confess your sin and be grieved over what you have done." "I would have forgiven you, but you would not allow it.""

"You are forever banished from this place and your family." "You will wander this earth as a vagabond forever. The soil will no longer yield a crop for you."

"My punishment is more than I can bear!" "You have driven me from my land and every man that sees me will try to kill me!"

The Lord replied, "Men will not kill you." "I will a put a mark on you and anyone who tries to kill you will be punished seven times over."

So Cain went out from the presence of the Lord and settled in the land of Nod, east of Eden.

Cain found a wife and she conceived and bore him a son they named Enoch, and Cain named his city after his son.

It seems as at least five generation passed, and the history of Cain fades from view.

In the mean time, Adam and Eve had another son they named Seth. The line of Adam descended many generations down to the days of Noah from Seth's lineage.

NOAH

N OAH WAS THE ONLY MAN of faith living after about 1000 years has passed between Seth, the third child of Adam and Eve, to Noah. The first couple had fell and refused to repent. They had lost their blessed position in that wonderful place God had created for them. Sin was passed down from generation after generation. In this time span there was a population explosion, but so had sin.

They had degraded into such a state of depravity: God was grieved; he would wipe them all out and start over. "I will blot them all from the face of the earth. Everything that has breath! I will blot out every man, woman, child; and every animal!"

There was one man, in all that humanity who pleased God, Noah. He pleased God, because he continuously lived a righteous life, even when all around him had become vile. "Noah found grace in the sigh of the Lord."

The Lord spoke to Noah. "Noah, I have taken notice of all the depravity and violence, of all mankind, except for you. I am going to bring disaster in the form of a flood to wipe out all these people. You, your wife, your three sons and their wives will be spared."

"I am about to send such rain, as the world has never seen to accomplish this." "I will give you the blue print for a very large boat you are to construct."

"I will give you detailed plans, to prepare a place for your family, a pair of all animals, that they may reproduce and repopulate the earth. I will give you instructions for the building materials; the food stuffs to feed all these creatures and your family." "You must begin to stock pile all of these materials soon."

"This large vessel will be constructed of a resinous wood that is water-proof, with tar to seal it. It will be fitted with 3 decks of stalls to separate the animals; to feed and care for their needs in an orderly fashion."

"The dimensions of this ship will be 450 ft. in length; 75 ft. wide; 45 ft. high. You will build a sky light 18 inches from the roof line, all around the ship. The interior will consist of 3 decks, bottom, middle, and upper, filled with stalls. Put a door in the side. A large door that opens from the top, that serves as a ramp to load this vessel."

"I am going to cover this earth with a flood that will destroy every living thing that has breath. All will die!"

"Only you, your family and the animals I have instructed you to take, will be spared." "The pairs of all these species: Male and female, to reproduce after its kind."

"Of the ones used for food and sacrifice, bring 7of those."

"Store all the food and supplies needed for this very long vogue." "I will lead, guide and direct you all the way."

His neighbors must have taunted him, as they already felt Noah a strange man. "They did not participate in all the things they felt was normal. They were always speaking of a "God" we do not know. Now, here they are building this big monstrous building, whatever it was, in the desert. Maybe it is a resort hotel? Who knows?

That makes more sense than a boat. He says the rain is coming that will flood the earth. We have never seen such rain. What little we get is soon evaporated or quickly disappears into the sand.

"Hey, Noah, what is this thing you are building?"

"It is a boat."

"Noah,why would you build such a thing?"

"It will save us, when the rains come."

"What! Who told you that?"

"Jehovah God has told me."

"That is nonsense, and you know it!"

"Are you going to start preaching that crazy stuff again?" "You are crazy you know?"

"We will see."

"Noah. You are so out so step with society. You dress differently, and even eat differently. You don't enter into any of the community fun. You think you are better than we are. So much so, that you are insulting."

"You expect us to believe in this God of yours and then you say ours are not gods at all, but evil." "Who do you think you are?"

Noah went right on with his work to complete this boat on schedule.

He had gathered and stored stock piles of building material; bales of hay and bags of grains and other animal feeds. It looked like a mountain of supplies.

The community children even came out to watch and taunt him. They sang and danced around this construction site, singing. "Crazy man; crazy man; come and see the crazy man!" But he would not resort to arguments with any of them.

He had told them over and over about the God of creation, but they had no interest, except to entertain themselves, taunting him. It was a hard thing to see them refuse God.

Especially how they were deceiving the little children, but all he could do was live a life he knew God had instructed him to live, and he had been blessed because he chose to follow God.

The day came when this boat was completed and God told him to get his belongings and move into the family quarters in the vessel. Stow all the provisions of food for yourselves and all the animals. Begin to guide all the animals into their proper stalls. Starting with the lighter animals for the top deck, The medium sized ones on the second deck and heaviest on the bottom deck for stability.

The next week, all secured and ready, it began to rain. And God closed the door!

At first, small drops, then becoming heavier, until it was a torrent.

Noah could hear the people beating on the door, begging to come in, but it was too late.

Noah was 600 years, 2 months, and 17 days old when the floods came. The torrents from the sky and fountains of water burst forth from the ground. It rained 40 days and 40 nights, until the whole of earth was covered to 20 ft. above the tallest mountain peaks.

As the waters began to recede, the ark came to rest of Mont Ararat.

It took sometime before the earth was stabilized, as the waters drained away.

When Father God told Noah they could go out upon dry ground. He opened the door, let down the ramp and Noah and his sons guided the animals outside. They seemed to instinctively know where to go.

The first thing Noah and his family wanted to do was built an altar and make a sacrifice of thanksgiving to the Lord. What a journey it had been, and true to his word, the Lord had fulfilled his promise to them. When others had tried to persuade him to disbelieve God, he would not be tempted.

The Lord told Noah and his family to reproduce and fill the earth again. All the animal life would begin to reproduce after its kind also.

God said, "I will never again destroy the earth with a flood. I will set a sign in the sky to seal my promise."

God set a beautiful rainbow above the earth for all to see as a promise. After a rain, the sun will come out, and a rainbow arch in the clouds as a reminder. God said, "As long as the earth remains, there will be springtime and harvest, cold and heat, day and night."

Noah planted a vineyard and when it produced, he made wine, got drunk and passed out naked in his tent. OOPS!

His son, Ham, seeing his father's nakedness, went out and told his brothers, "come take a look!" Shem and Japheth, knew this was a shameful thing, and would not, but they placed a blanket on their shoulders, backed into the tent, so as not to look, and dropped the blanket on their father's naked body. Ham had dishonored his father.

When Noah awoke from his drunken stupor, he was told the shameful thing Ham had done. Noah spoke a curse on Ham's descendants. "They will forever be servants to their two brother's family lines.

The line of Shem's descendants would eventually be the line of "Abraham, Isaac and Jacob; the people of the promise."

ABRAHAM AND LOT

FIRST, LET'S GET SOME BACKGROUND. Noah the boat builder lived in a place that had become so wicked God sent a flood that destroyed all except Noah, his wife, his three sons and their wives, the animals, two by two and seven's of those that were for sacrifices, and enough to care for them all until the earth, covered by water, had receded so they were securely on dry ground. The three sons, Shem, Ham and Japheth started over, repopulating the earth.

The people of that day had began a downward spiral almost immediately. Shem was the best of the lot, and many generations later came down to Terah.

Terah was 70, had 3 sons. Abram, Nahor and Haran, but Haran died young, leaving a son, Lot. His father, Terah, out lived his son. They lived in Ur of the Chaldeans. Abram married his half-sister, Sarai. While his brother Nahor married their orphaned niece, who was the daughter of their brother Haran. Teran took this family and left Ur to go to the land of Canaan. They stopped in a city called Haran and lived in that city for some time.

When Terah, Abram's father and Lot grandfather, died at 205, God spoke to Abram. "Leave your country and relatives behind you, and go to a land I will guide you too. I will cause you to become a great nation. I will bless you. I will bless all those who bless you and I will cruse those who cruse you. Abram was 75; when the Lord spoke to him. And Sarai, his wife was barren.

Abram was the only one of his time, just as Noah, that believed God, and he was taunted by his community. Now that is faith; leaving all to follow God.

I can hear the community's laughter as they sit around the fire taunting him.

"Hey Abe, where are you going?"

"I don't know."

"Then why are you doing such a thing?"

"Because God told me to."

"He told you but didn't tell you where?"

"Nope!"

"Are you sure you didn't eat too much goat pizza last night?"

As they sat around the fire laughing and scoffing, old Abe continued to gather up his belongings.

"What was it God told you?"

"He said he would make of me a great nation and all the families of the earth would be blessed by me."

At this a great uproar of laughter erupted around the campfire. I can imagine a few fell off their log perch and rolled around in the dust with hysterical laughter. (When God tells us something it always seems like foolishness.)

Then as they whispered around the fire, the talk turned to Abe's mental state.

"After all, Abe is 75 and has no children, his wife is barren and he believes a great nation will come from him?" "Do you think he has dementia, or Alzheimer's?" "May-be we ought to tie him for his own good."

(I see a clue here. God, you tell him to leave these people, just as you called Noah to build the boat and separate him and his family, from their wickedness.)

Abram was living in Ur of the Chaldeans and his people had picked up their wicked ways. As in the days of Noah, God saw that the wickedness of man was great in the earth and that every imagination of the thoughts of his heart was only evil continually. Noah found grace in the eyes of the Lord and, so did Abram. God was calling out the only man of that generation that followed and worshipped Him.

The book of Hebrews list Noah and Abraham, in order, as men of faith that honored God. Hebrews 11:7-12. James 2:23 "and God called him a friend of God."

I've noticed throughout history, each country over the years, falls from its own pride and self importance. Even whole nations start with such vigor and when they are at ease, they begin "thinking of themselves more highly then they ought". Counties, nations, cities and individuals all fit into this same category of prodigal sons. The son who walked away and squandered the family fortune, to hit rock bottom in the pig pen. He took a good look at himself, swallowed his pride and started for home: Received by his father in great joy. The other son was so filled with pride at what a righteous man he was, he wouldn't even come into the house and celebrate with his father, that the lost son had come home. (Wasn't that the Pharisees problem?) Even the same attitude we can fall into after we've been saved awhile?

Matthew 25:31-46 tells us whole nations will be judged by the way we treat the least off these. "The Judgment of the

Nations." I don't think I have noticed that before. V. 31 says:
When the Son of man comes, he will judge. He will gather
the nations and judge. I think some how I had the idea it was
speaking of us as individuals, and it is also that. Before him
shall be gathered all the nations, and he shall separate the people
one from the other, as a shepherd divides his sheep from the
goats. Wow! This surprised me! I guess I've always started this
study from V. 33. "Judged individually." Whole nations will be
judged by how we treat the least of these." Seems we are judged
more on our compassion, as individuals, countries, nations, and
etc. by this standard, than on how beautifully we pray and sing
and so on within the four walls of our church home..

So here we are....Abram, 75 with his old wife and Lot his
nephew and all his possessions, wandering off, having heard
from God. Believing God was faithful and would lead him
step by step.

Even though he had not exactly followed orders, he took
his nephew Lot, along.

They went forth into the land of Canaan. They took quite a
journey, as they also went to Egypt because of famine. (That's
another story.)

The next time we hear the name of Lot, they were back
in Canaan and they had been so blessed, the land was not big
enough to support the flocks and herds. Abram and Lot's
herdsmen were quarrelling over pasture.

Then Abram said: "Lot, we cannot remain together, as
there is not enough pasture here to support all the Lord has
blessed us with. We are family, we must not quarrel. This
whole country is before us. Let us separate. You choose the
land you want. If you choose the right, I will go to the left. If
you choose the left I will go to the right."

Lot looked out over the land and saw the whole Jordan valley. He saw how lush and green the pastures were. It was well watered. Here lay the cities of Sodom and Gomorrah in this lush valley and said: "I will take that!"Greed had seized his heart. It seems he could have told Abram; "I'll share the water rights with you." Do you think may-be that is why God told him to leave his kin and family in Haran?

Lot took all he had, and made his way to this green valley and settled among the people.

"But the men of Sodom were wicked sinners before the Lord."

Abram's herds and flock multiplied and he prospered. Time had passed, and God was blessing him mightily.

About this time Lot had moved his tent closer to the city of Sodom. He liked this city life.

Five kings of the area went to battle against four other kings, and in the process the people of Sodom were over run and taken captive. Along with Lot, his family and all he had included!

Abram called his herdsmen and his shepherds and put together a somewhat rag tag fighting force. They went to the rescue; and rescued Lot, his family and all he had, which was substantial.

Good old uncle Abe!

Abe said to himself: "I need to have a talk with that boy!"

"Lot, I hope you can see the hand of Almighty God' is on me." "See how he has prospered me and all he has put into my hands?"When you were with me, He prospered you as well, and we dwelt in safety."

"Uncle Abe, I've done alright since I left you and moved to the Jordan Valley."

"But look, Lot, you were taken captive, with all you had. Can you imagine what would have happened to you, had God not rescued you through me?"

"Oh, they would have probably turned me loose."

"The Lord caused me to prevail against 9 kings and their armies. I don't have an army, yet the Lord took a bunch of herdsmen, shepherds and household servants, and made a mighty fighting force of them and we prevailed! Only the Lord God Almighty could do that! Don't you see it?"

"Now Uncle Abe, you are being over emotional!"

"Lot, you know I love you, and I took you along as an honor to my dead brother. I disobeyed God to do it! I pleaded with God to allow you to come along! I feel very responsible for your welfare, and all of your family."

"I know, I know, Uncle Abe, and I appreciate all you've done for me. But I need some freedom to live my own life. You are so straight and narrow! You live by some old rules that no one else does. Even what you eat! Uncle Abe, people don't live like that anymore." "The people I live among have none of these rules and they have the most delicious meals I've even eaten"

"O Lot, Gods rules are not to harms us but do us good. He does not deny us anything that is good for us. It is his loving way to protect us" "Why don't you move up the Jordan Valley away from all this wickedness?"

"No! My wife and my daughters are descendants of these people! I like it there! We live in a house not in tents! Nothing is withheld from us. Their gods are not rigid and restrictive! We are free to do what pleases us."

With tears, Abram allows him to go where he chose.

Over the years Abram has many encounters with God. The promises are still the same, and Abram and Sarai are getting older and older.

Sarai decided to take matters into her own hands.

Here we must enter the story of Hagar, Sarai's Egyptian handmaid.

The story of Hagar is purely of my imagination, but there must have been some circumstances that brought her into these people's lives. She was a real person. We are told little about her and her thoughts as she fulfilled her part in God's plan.

(Perhaps she was acquired on that trip to Egypt.)

Abram and Sarai had gone to Egypt because of famine, and they pre-planned what they would say and do if Pharaoh should desire Sarai as one of his concubine. They would say. "She is my sister." "Else he will slay me and take you," Abram said.(Technically it was a half truth, but deceit.)

Sarai was still a beautiful woman and yes, Pharaoh did take her to his home.

Pharaoh was warned in a dream not to touch this woman as she was Abram's wife. Out of fear Pharaoh demanded they leave his country and take all his belongings with him. And this must have included Hagar. Anyway, when the story of Abram and Sarai pick up, Hagar is in the picture. (This story is actually before Abraham and Lot separate; Lot going to the Jordan Valley.)

God had promised Abram he would have a son, an heir that would be the seed that populated this chosen people to become a great nation; as many as the sands on the seashore, and the stars in the sky.

(Sarai takes matters into her own hands!)

Since they weren't getting younger and she was well past childbearing years, Sarai decided God needed a little help or this wasn't going to happen.

She saw how beautiful this Egyptian girl named Hagar was. Sarai sized her up. "hummmm."She is young, beautiful, strong and a loyal servant. She was healthy and would bear healthy children." This woman would not dare disobey her. She would do anything I ask! A servant of Abram wife was the best job in the camp!

Now, Abram might take some convincing!

The next time Abram and Sarai were alone, she fixed his favorite meal, pampered him. Massaged his feet and put his favorite sheep wool slippers on his feet. Cuddled up close to him and said sweetly, "Abraham, the Lord has kept me from having that son you have been promised. A son, of your own body." " I am old and you know I love you, right?" "Will you do something for me?"

"Of course, Sarai. You know I would do anything for you!"

"You promise! You would Vow it?" Do as I ask?'

"Yes! Yes! I vow it! What is it?" "Anything!" (This is getting pretty interesting!)

"Will you lay with my handmaid, Hagar, and she will be a surrogate for me and that child would be yours! Your bloodline!"

Well he did! (I didn't notice him putting up any argument. Do you suppose he had already thought of that?) He was so willing. I guess a vow is a vow! Surely he had not prayed about this.

Two women and one man is trouble brewing! Contentions building! Sarai was the boss but Hagar was carrying his child. (This is not going to turn out well.)

As soon as the pregnancy was confirmed the atmosphere changed. Sarai became extremely jealous and Hagar played the pretty young thing that had replaced her perfectly. She flaunted the blossoming pregnancy to the max!

Hagar would jump into helping Sarai do everything, not because she really needed help, but to make her look as old and helpless as possible. Sarai had once been young and beautiful too. Strong and able, an adoring wife and life partner.

When Abram came home at night Hagar arose gracefully, even with her rounding belly, with the energy of youth. Ran to bring him his sheep wool slippers before ever so slow Sarai, could make a move. Hagar handed him his goat's milk smoothie before Sarai could struggle to her feet. Sarai had to roll over, get on her hands and knees, pull herself up to something, straighten up, gather her balance and by then the task was done. Hagar would give her a look of pity to try to hide the smirk. How could Sarai compete with that?

Hagar enjoyed showing her up and Abram enjoyed all of the attention.

When Hagar delivered it was Sarai who was expected to wait on Hagar. Hand and foot! Tending her baby that Abram radically adored. He had a descendant and he was beautiful! He had that long awaited heir! That baby had the very good looks, of his Egyptian mother. Olive skin, eyes almost black and tuffs of black hair. Abram adored him! The most beautiful baby he had ever seen. He couldn't take his eyes off this child. He spent every minute he could cooing and cuddling this baby. Sarai hated that baby and hated Hagar even more.

Again, Abram had visitations with God. The promise is still the same. God makes it clear that Ishmael is not the one the inheritance will come through. It will come through Sarai!

About this time next year Sarai will give birth to a son, the promised heir!

The Lord gave Abram a new name. Abraham, father of many nations. Sarai also got a new name. She is now Sarah, princess. Abraham will father a baby at 100 and Sarah at 90? He fell before the Lord laughing.

But, old hatreds die hard and Sarah's jealousy blazed hot. Hagar's attitude toward Sarah keep it fueled. Two women in one kitchen is not good news. It was a war zone! The most powerful and blessed man of God's chosen people caught in the middle!

He loved his wife of many years so much; but he also loved Ishmael. He loved God and God had told him plainly his heir would come through Sarah!

He was promised his descendants would outnumber the stars of the sky and the sands on the seashore. The people of promise!

He and Sarah did have that son as promised and he was healthy and robust also. The one they had been promised and so long awaited! They named him Isaac.

But still there was this slave girls and her child. Hagar and Ishmael taunted Sarah and her child.

Sarah gave Abraham an ultimatum! Get rid of this slave girl and her child or else! We are not sure what her "or else" was, but it seems Abraham did, as he sent them away with a heavy heart. After all, Ishmael was his son also. Sadly, the old man sent them away with water and provisions.

When their resources were gone, they were in an arid desert wilderness. Death seemed so close. Hagar could not bear to watch the young man die, so she left him in the sparse shade of a bush, and went a bit farther and wept.

She prayed. Whether she prayed to Abraham's God, we don't know. She had lived among these people and had witnessed many amazing things. Such as, Sarah, giving birth, well past her child bearing years, and many other unexplainable things. Hagar was Egyptian most likely was brought up too believe in many different and assorted gods.

As she lay weeping and praying, God spoke to her.

"Hagar, why are you so sick at heart?" "I am making a great nation of Ishmael also." "You nor your son will die!"

"Arise and look around you!" When she did, there was a water well she knew was not there before! "Yes, this God of Abraham was real and he cared for her and her son."

She filled the wineskin with water and took it to Ishmael, kneeled down and gave him water and he revived.

Hagar and Ishmael had been sent away with a promise too! He will become a great nation! God was with the lad!

Ishmael dwelled in the wilderness in Paran and became an archer. His mother got him a bride out of Egypt.

(Paran is in the Sinai Desert close to Egypt.)

(Back to the story of Lot in Sodom.)

The visitors from God had told Abraham, they were going to Sodom to see if it was as wicked as they were told. If so, it would be destroyed! Good old Uncle Abe. He began pleading and bargaining for some to be spared. It finally got down to, "if they could find 10 righteous people it would be spared.

When they got to Sodom, it was even more wicked than any could imagine. The men had no interest in women at all. Men seeking only men in the most perverted way.

Lot rescued those heavenly visitors and took them into his own house to protect them. The men surrounded the house and beat on the door. Lot even went so far as to offer them his own daughters! But they did not want them!

The angels told Lot to gather his family and run for the hills. Only four were spared. Lot, his wife and two daughters. These heavenly visitors caused a blindness to come over the citizens of Sodom so they could escape. They told them to "run, run for the mountains! Don't stop and don't look back!" This city would be destroyed by fire and brimstone raining down from heaven. Lots wife could not resist looking back with longing for her home city and she was burned into a heap of salt.

Lot and his daughters fled to the mountains. They escaped the city, but not their evil upbringing.

Lot's daughters had no moral compass. These people they came from were all involved in moral depravity. It was their way of life.

After escaping with their lives from the fire and brimstone, that destroyed Sodom. Their thought was, how will we have children, since we cannot find a husband here. They made a plan. They would get their father drunk, and each went into Lot his tent, lay with him, and each was pregnant by their father.

The oldest of the daughters had a son named Moab, and was the ancestor of the Moabites. The younger named her son Benammi, and he became the ancestor of the nation of the Ammonites.

Sarah died at age 127 and Abraham buried her in a field he bought from Epron for 400 pieces of silver, as his family burial plot at Mach-pelah near Mamre.

In his very old age he called his household administrator, his oldest servant and made him to vow, he would seek a wife for his son Isaac, from the people of his homeland and not allow him to marries any of these Canannites.

Isaac and Rebekah

S ARAH DIED AT 127 YEARS of age, so that would have made Abraham 137.

Before he died, he must find Isaac a wife. He called in his most trusted servant, who was his administrator. You must go to my family homeland, and bloodline and find Isaac a wife:

He bound his servant with an oath to do as he asked.

"But suppose I cannot find a young lady among them, or perhaps none be willing to come back with me, un-sight and un-seen?" "Shall I then return and get Isaac and bring him to meet them?"

"Absolutely not!" "Not under any circumstances shall you do that!" "For the Lord God of heaven told me to leave that land and my people and he would give me a land and a people; descendants that will make a great nation; that the whole earth would be blessed through them."

"He will send his angel before you.""He will see to it that you will find the one among those people."

"What if I do not succeed?" "If you don't, I will release you from the oath." "I have no doubt you will succeed!"

This loyal servant followed his instructions and set out on his journey with 10 camels loaded with gifts for the young lady and her family, among the descendents of Nahor in Iraq. (Is this the early day equivalent of a mail order bride or an internet match?)

Outside of Nahor's village was the water-well. Where the people of the village came to draw house-hold water, and where water was drawn into troughs for the live stock;

Abraham's servant stopped to pray.

"Show kindness to Abraham, O Lord God, Jehovah." "I need your help.""By this way, show me the one you have chosen." "I will ask the young lady, would you be so kind as to give me a cup of cold water?" "Then she would answer, 'yes and I will draw water for you camels also.'" "May that be the one".

The young women of the village came at this time of day to draw their household water. While the servant of Abraham was still at prayer, they came. A very beautiful girl named Rebekah, with her water jug on her shoulder, let it down and filled it; the servant of Abraham spoke the words he had prayed.

(He looked as if he was a wealthy man, but dusty and tired from his travels)

"Certainly sir". She immediately replied, pouring him a cup of cold water from her jug. "I will also draw some water for you camels too."

"O Lord, that must be the one!"

She filled the troughs, over and over until the camels all had their fill.

Abraham's servant watched in amazement. He must have been silently thanking God!

When the camels had all been watered, he brought out a gift of earrings, made of a quarter ounce of gold, and two bracelets of five ounces of gold each, and gave them to the young lady.

He asked, "Whose, daughter are you?"

"My father is Bethuel, son of Nahor."

"Would your father have room enough to put me up for the night?"

"O we have plenty of room, and food and straw for your camels too."

Rebekah ran on ahead to tell her family.

The servant bowed his head and thanked Jehovah, the God of Abraham.

"You have blessed me Lord! You have led me to the appointed one." "I know Abraham and Isaac will be pleased with her."

Rebekah met her brother, Laban on the way. "Look! See what a man I met at the well gave me!" She showed him the gold gifts. She told him all about their conversation.

Laban ran to meet this man. "Come, we have room ready for you and a place to stall your camels and care for their needs too."

Laban took him to their family compound, fed and watered the camels again, and gave the servants who drove the camels, water to wash up and rest. They were made to feel right at home.

"Dinner will be soon be ready."

The servant said to Laban, "I must tell you before we eat. I am here on a errand. (He did not want to be deceiving.)

"All right, what is your errand?"

"I am the servant of Abraham." "Jehovah has blessed him greatly. Above and beyond imagination, with much silver and gold. With many slaves, cattle, sheep, goats and camels. In his old age the Lord has given him a son, an heir to it all. Abraham made me vow not to allow his son to marry any of the local girls, but to get him a bride from his own people; to bring this young lady back with me to marry Isaac."

"I ask him, what if she will not come with me?"

"She will", Abraham said, "for the Lord has told me she will."

"The Lords angels have come before me and prepared the way, making this a successful mission."

"This afternoon I prayed and ask the Lord to show me the one, and he showed me Rebekah, and confirmed it in the word and deeds."

The servant of Abraham, his traveling companions, Rebekah and all the family sat down to a feast. All agreed, Rebekah would go to marry Abraham's son Isaac.

The servant brought out all the valuable gifts and gave all of this to the family of Bethuel, son of Nahor.

They spent the night as Bethuel's guests. Saying they would start the return journey in the morning.

In the morning the family asked for 10 days. (I can imagine It was a time of saying good-by to their loved one and preparing her for the journey.)

"Let us call in Rebekah and ask her how she feels on this matter."

"Yes, I will go!" She said without hesitation. "But I will need a time to prepare for this journey."

So after she was ready they departed, with the family blessing. Rebakah and her servant girls, all on their camels went gladly with Abraham's servant.

As the neared home in the Negev, Rebakah raised her eye and saw a man working in the fields and ask the servant who this might be. The servant replied, "This is Isaac, your intended." (She was pleased!) She dismounted her camel and covered her face with the proper veil, as was the custom.

As Isaac neared, the servant introduced Isaac; and he was very pleased! Genesis 24:67 tells us he brought her into his mother's tent, and the marriage was consummated. (Well, actually it says, and she became his wife and he was comforted after the loss of this mother.)

(Their story picks up sometime later, as Genesis 25:21, we learn they had been married a long time and she had been unable to get pregnant.)

Before I can go on into Isaac's story I must comment on "the in between." The in between Genesis 24:67 and 25:18.

This seems sandwiched in between sending the servant to find a wife for Isaac and their return: to some 20 years later in the life of Isaac and Rebekah.

During this gap, old Abe has remarried a wife named Keturah and they have several children. We don't know how many, but there were six sons. By this time he is ageing on. He is said to have died at 175.

I assumed, he was old and near death when he sent his servant off to find a wife for Isaac. I was obviously mistaken. He was at least 137 when Sarah died. Isaac, forty when he married. Given the numbers, He and Ketura must have started a family shortly after Sarah death.

Also Ishmael, Abraham and Hagar's son was still in the picture. I had assumed he and his mother stayed in the desert of Paran. But, at Abraham's burial he is mentioned. He is also mentioned as receiving gifts as children of Abraham's concubines. In Genesis 25:17, it says Ishmael dies at 137 years of age.

Taking all these ages into account, Ketura and Abraham didn't waste much time getting started on a family after Sarah's death.

So you see, I am not quite sure where to put this story. I am thinking it makes more sense to assume life went on and Ketura was bearing children when the servant went to find a wife for Isaac. They returned with Rebkah, and this story was inserted as a bi-line.

On with the story of Isaac and Rebekah

Abraham is now gone and Ishmael too has died. Rebekah to this point had not been able to get pregnant. It is now Isaac pleading with Jehovah God to give a son to Rebekah. It was then God allowed her to have children.

When at last she was pregnant, it was with twins! It seemed as if they were fighting with each other in the womb. She was miserable and said "I cannot endure this", and asked the Lord about it.

"Yes, Rebekah, the two in your womb will become rival nations. One will be stronger than the other and the older shall be ruled by the younger!"

When she delivered them, the first was covered with reddish hair as if he was wearing a red fur coat. They named him Esau because he was so hairy. Then the younger delivered having a hold of the older brothers heel. So they named him Jacob, which means "Grabber".

Isaac was 60 by this time. It seems he and Rebekah must have been married 20 years. (Considering he was 40 when the servant went to fetch him a wife from their ancestors.)

These boys grew up and Esau was a skilled hunter, and Isaac favored him because of the venison and wild game he brought home. Rebekah favored Jacob because he stayed close by; probably a Mama's boy. Esau the hunter, the man of action, and Jacob was a dreamer and a schemer.

Isaac and Rebekah,
Esau and Jacob

S OME TIME HAS PASSED AND the sons are grown.
One day Jacob was preparing some of his vegetarian red
bean stew. Esau returned from a long day in the field hunting,
with no success, and was famished. "I am starved!"Give me a
bowl of that stew you are cooking."

"Alright! If you will trade me your first born birthright
for it!"

"When a man is dying of starvation, what good is his
birthright" Esau said.

"Will you vow it before God, that it is mine?" Jacob asked.

Esau vowed it, giving away his oldest son birthright to his
younger brother.

Jacob served his brother a meal of veggie stew, bread and
peas. Esau ate and drank, indifferent to the rights he had
thrown away, and took a needed rest.

Time went on!

(It seem there was a time span between Esau selling his
birthright; and Isaac's old age. As their story picks up during
a severe famine, where they left their home and went to Gerar

where Abimelech was king of the Philistines. Since the boys are not mentioned, they were probably grown and did not want to go with them.)

Isaac and Rebekah left. Their intention was to go to Egypt, but God warned them in a dream not to go there. Again God reminded them of the promise He made to Abraham, Isaac's father. "Do as I say and I will be with you and bless you, and make of you a great nation. I will cause your descendants to out-number the stars of the sky and the sands of the seashore. I will give them all of these lands and they shall bless all the nations of the earth. I will do these things because Abraham obeyed my commandments and laws."

So, Isaac stayed in Gerar of the Philistines where Abimelech was king. Isaac had warned Rebekah his wife, when asked; tell these people you are my sister.(Which, if you go back a generations, they closely followed the scheme Abraham and Sarah had used in Egypt.)

The same scenario. Not exactly a lie, but not quite true either. It may have had some merit. "If these men know you are my wife, they may kill me and take you."

Perhaps it was the customary practice of these people. It was not considered bad to kill a man. Yet, it was considered bad to take her if her husband was living. Maybe to kill him first was considered a sacrifice to their gods. Who knows?

Well, they did tell the king the story; but one day he was looking out his window and saw Isaac and Rebekah in an embrace, that was not a brotherly/sisterly embrace, and their cover was blown!

In anger the king called Isaac to come before him! He had some explaining to do!

"Why have you lied to me?" "She is your wife!"

"Isaac confessed the truth. "I was afraid you would kill me and take her, as she is a beautiful woman."

Abimelech stormed! "Someone might have raped her, not knowing she was your wife and that would have doomed us!"

"Anyone harming this man or woman shall die!"

That year Isaac crops yielded 100 times the grain he had sown. Jehovah God was certainly true to his word, promising he would be blessed. His flocks enlarged greatly; producing great gain in grain, sheep, goats, cattle and servants. Isaac was blessed above and beyond all Imagination.

At all these obvious blessings, the people surrounding him became jealous, filling his wells with debris, even those his father Abraham had dug many years before. Those people demanded Isaac leave their territory.

King Ablimelech demanded. "Take your wife and go!" "You are too rich and powerful for us!"

So Isaac withdrew a way up the valley and settled there. Here in this place was another well dug many years ago by Abraham's servants. After Abrahams death, the Philistine herdsmen stopped up this well with debris also. There they re-dug the ancient well.

Isaac's shepherds also dug a new well and hit an artesian spring gushing forth with good cold water!

All of this did not come without cost. The Philistine herdsmen came and claimed this one too.

Again, they moved and dug another. "The well of Room Enough for Us." "At last, the Lord has made room for us and we thrive."

It seems he may have moved one more time. As Genesis 26:23 says he went to Beer-Sheba, and Jehovah appeared to him on the night of his arrival, saying; "I am the God of Abraham, your father." "Fear not for I am with you and will bless you and give you so many descendants they will become a great nation. Because of my promise to Abraham, who obeyed me." Then and there Isaac built an altar and worshipped Jehovah; and he settled there, and his servants dug another well."

One day King Abimelech visited him, with his advisor Ahuzzath and Phicol, his army commander.

"Why are you visiting me here?" "This is obviously no social call, since you so unceremoniously kicked me out of your country, in such an uncivilized way."

"Well," they replied. "We can see how your God, Jehovah, is blessing you. We have come to seek a treaty with you." "Promise that you will not harm us, nor will we harm you." "In fact, you must realize we have not harmed you, but we have done you good, and sent you away in peace; we bless you in the name of the Lord."

(Here again, I am not sure what authority they had, blessing in the name of the Lord. Maybe they simply feared using the name of their puny gods.)

The story goes; Isaac prepared a great feast, and they ate and drank in preparations for the treaty ceremony. The next morning they took a solemn oath to seal the nonaggression treaty. Isaac sent them happily on their way home.

That same day Isaac's servants came with the news, they had again dug and found water and they named that well, "Oath."

Time had passed and they returned to their own home land, very wealthy.

When they arrived home, they were old. Esau, the oldest son, now 40, has married a girl named Judith, the daughter of Be-eri the Hittite, and he also married Basemath, the daughter of Elon the Hittite. This was a bitter pill to swallow for Isaac and Rebekah. Now they are home and Isaac it old and nearly blind.

A few days later, Isaac called his first born to his side. Esau was his favorite because of his hunting skills and the tasty game he brought home. (Jacob was Rebekah's favorite. He hung around home. Most likely tied to mama's apron strings.)

Esau answered, "Yes, I am here father."

"Go into the field and get me the game you know I so dearly love." "Cook some of that food you know is my favorite, that I may eat, then I can give you my blessing before I die."

Rebekah was eves-dropping close by the entrance to Isaac's tent. As soon as Esau had departed for the hunt, she hurried off to find Jacob. She related to him the conversation she had overheard. Esau has gone to hunt, bringing back the game food he will serve your father and receive the blessing of the first born."

"We have no time to waste!" "My son, listen to me! Do what I say!" "I will tell you what to do."

"Go at once to the flock and bring me two young goats so I may prepare your father's favorite dishes." "You take it to him and he will give you that blessing."

"But Mom, my brother is a hairy man and I am smooth skinned man. If he touches me he will know the difference, and he will know I am deceiving him."

"My son, let the curse fall upon me, if he figures it out!" "You let me worry about that!"

The deception is set in motion.

Jacob brought the young goats to his mother. He still had his doubts, but Rebekah had already thought this out. Bring me some of your brother's hunting clothes, those with the smell of the woods and game on them. Dress yourself in those clothes" "Now put on these hairy gloves and the goats hair scarf I have made, covering your neck and shoulders." "We will take advantage of his blind old eyes."

Jacob did as his mother directed and took the meat dish to his father.

"My father," Jacob said.

"Yes, who are you?"

Jacob answered, "It is I, Esau, bringing you the meat dish you so love."Please eat some and give me your blessing of the first born."

"How did you find the game so quickly my son?"

Jacob said, "The Lord your God gave me quick success."

Isaac, even in his old age and blindness, felt something was amiss.

"Come near my son, so I may touch you once again and feel your hairy skin, then I will be satisfied it is you."

About this time Jacob must have felt like running as fast as his feet could carry him, but he was in way too deep for that! He hoped and prayed his father's hearing was even worse than his eye sight. He said in a quivering voice, "father, it is I, Esau."

"Your hands are hairy as Esau's, but your voice is as Jacob."

"Well father, I have a bit of a cold and it is effecting my voice."

Isaac ate, being spoon fed by Jacob, and his father gave him the blessing of the first born.

In that culture and faith; the blessing was speaking life over his first son. They were given a much larger share of blessing.

The blessing Isaac, still a bit suspicious, prayed over Jacob, thinking it was Esau.

"O the smell of my son is like the smell of the field that the Lord has blessed."

"May nations serve you, and the people bow down to you. Be Lord over your brother and sons of your mother's family will bow before you."

"May those who curse you be cursed and those who bless you be blessed."

Shortly after Jacob received the blessing, he ran! And just in time!

Esau came in from the field with the meat dish he had brought his father.

"My father, here is you favorite. Sit up, eat and bless me!"

Confused, Isaac said, "who are you?""I am Esau, your first born!"

At this Isaac was stunned and trembling. "Then who was it that brought in the meat stew, fed me and I blessed?"

The old man in tears sobbing said. "I have given him my blessing of the first born!" "I cannot reverse it!" "I have pronounced him Lord over you and all his relatives. I have proclaimed all his substance blessed and with great bounty in grain and new wine."

"So what can I do?" "What can I possibly do now?" The old man wailed.

"Do you not have any blessing left for me?" "O my father, do you not have any blessing left for me?

Isaac, with tears running down his cheeks, prayed.

"Your dwellings will be far away from the world's richness. The dew from heaven will be scarce."

"You will live by the sword and you will have strife with your brother. When you grow restless with all this oppression, you will throw his yoke off your neck."

(Esau could envision that last one!)

Esau held a grudge against his brother, even though he remembered he had sold his birthright to Jacob years before.

He justified his actions by telling himself, "I was under the age of accountability" Or, "I had my fingers crossed behind my back." (Or, whatever the equivalent was in those days.)

He did plan his revenge! As soon as my father dies and the mourning has passed, I will do Jacob in!" "Mother will not be able to save him then!"

Rebekah told her youngest son what his brother was planning as soon as Isaac was dead. This is a household full of turmoil! Isaac way laying near death, and his family was thinking little of him. Esau's mind was on revenge, and his wife and youngest son's mind was on a quick disappearing act!

Rebekah said, "Jacob your brother is planning to kill you."

This wasn't exactly news to Jacob, but now it was urgent. "Your father can be only hours away from death, so we must hurry." "I won't tell Esau how close death is until you have gone. That will give you a head start."

"You must be ready to flee as soon as I tell you!" "Get ready!"

"You must go to my brother in Haran and seek a wife amidst his people." "Stay there until I see Esau's anger has waned and then I will send for you.""Why should I lose both of my sons?" She wailed. (She seems to have forgotten all this was her doing.)

Rebekah went in to see Isaac and said, "I am so disgusted with these Hittite women Esau has married. I think I will die if Jacob married one also!" (She was most convincing.) She truly did not want another Hittite daughter-in-law, but her primary objective was protecting Jacob from Esau.

Isaac called Jacob in to speak with him. The old man blessed him and made him promise he would go to Haran and seek a wife from Laban's family in Paddan Aram. Laban, or one of the families of Abraham and Sarah must have a young woman of marriageable age by now.

"Go there at once, find a wife, that the family line of Abraham will continue to grow vast; that they will out-number the stars in the sky and the sands of the seashore."

Jacob could see the old man was failing fast, and time was of the essence.

Jacob skedaddled! He was putting miles between himself and Esau. When Rebekah felt he had made a safe distance, she called Esau in saying, "you need to go in, sit by your father and tell him good-bye. His time is short." "He loves you. Do not leave his side until he is gone." (Buying Jacob a little more time.)

It was at his father's bedside he learned his father had sent Jacob away to Paddan Aram to find a suitable wife. Esau was even more enraged! Thinking, "well, I will show them!" He later went to find himself another wife even more detestable, among the family of Ishmael's foreign wives.

Rebekah's scheming and Jacob's fleeing worked again! She had managed to get Isaac to unknowingly send Jacob away with his blessing.

Jacob made good time getting out of Esau's reach, so he stopped for the night and lay down on the ground to sleep a bit before traveling on come daylight. Laying his head on a rock for a pillow, fell asleep and began dreaming.

The dream was most vivid. He saw a stairway that seemed to start from this place where he was sleeping, and ascending into heaven. He saw the angels of God moving, ascending and descending this stairway. At the top of the stairs he saw God himself, who spoke to him. "I am the Lord God of your grandfather Abraham. I am the God of your father, Isaac. I will give you the descendants I promised your forefathers. This very ground you are lying on is but a small portion of the land I am giving you and your descendants. You will become a great and mighty nation, that will bless all the earth." "I will do what I have promised Abraham, Isaac, so will I extend to you; as numerous as the dust on the ground, the sands on the seashore, and the stars of the sky."

Jacob awoke from the dream, that was still so fresh he knew he had a visitation from the Lord. Jacob exclaimed.""Surely the Lord is in this place, and I was unaware of it when I lay down!"

Jacob set up a pillar of remembrance there and anointed it with oil, and there he called it Bethel. The House of God.

There Jacob's life was changed. He had met God and believed. There Jacob made his first vow to God. "Now I believe." "You are my own God, not just the God of my fathers."

The vow: "If you, Father God, will be with me, and watch over me; protecting and providing me with food to eat, clothes to wear, then returning me to my father's house after a successful trip, I will give you a tenth of all I receive."

Jacob traveled on toward his mother and father's ancient home land and it was beautiful. "Maybe, now my vision has changed and I see things through the eyes of God." Now he began looking for his God in all things, and finding him everywhere.

Jacob and Rachel and Leah, and Zilpah, and Bilhah.

J ACOB CONTINUED HIS JOURNEY WITH a new attitude. He has met God! He traveled on until he had reached Paddan Aram. He could see a well in a field, with flocks of sheep and goats at rest. A beautiful sight.

This was the routine: When all the flocks were gathered, a shepherd would remove the rock cover from the well, the troughs were filled, and the animals watered. Each flock had it own shepherd to move them in and out.

What Jacob saw next made his heart skip a beat! A most beautiful young woman tended one of the flocks. The only girl among them.

Jacob asked one of the men shepherds, "Whose flocks are these?" The young man answered, "These belong to Laban, Nahor's grandson." "We are originally from Haran. We've been with our master for many generations." "Do you know him?"

Then Jacob asked, "is he well?"

"Yes he is well. And here comes his daughter Rachel with the flock she shepherds."

When he saw her, he was moved. He rolled the stone away from the well and watered the livestock for her. Then he wept and kissed her, telling her he was a relative. "My mother is your father's sister."

At this she ran on ahead to tell her father of Jacob's arrival. At the news, Laban ran quickly to meet him. Laban kissed him and took him to their home, saying "you are my flesh and blood!"

Jacob lived with Laban's family for a month.

Laban telling Jacob, "it is not right for you to work for me or nothing."

"Name your wages and I will pay whatever you ask."

By this time Jacob was madly in love with Rachel and he knew the feeling was mutual.

He answered Laban, "I will work for you for seven years for your daughter Rachel to be my wife."

"It is better to give her to you than a man we do not know," Laban replied.

At this Laban set about gathering all the relatives and friends for the wedding feast. It was a great affair with an abundance of good food and the wine flowed freely. (A wedding feast is an elaborate affair and not over quickly.) By the time it was over, Jacob had way too much to drink.

By the time he reached his tent it was dark and his senses were not all that sharp.

When morning came he awakened, to what must have been a great shock! The woman he had slept with was not Rachel! It was her not so pretty sister!

Jacob confronted Laban: "You did not give me the wife you promised!" "What are you doing?" "I kept my end of the bargain and you have not kept yours!" "You have deceived me!"

Laban told Jacob. "It is not our custom for the younger sister to be married before her older sister."

(Truth of the matter was, no one was going to marry Leah. This was Laban's ways of fixing the problem.)

"I tell you what!" "Finish your obligated wedding week with her and I will give your Rachel, and you work for another seven years and we will call it even."

Deception runs deep in this family gene pool. Jacob and his mother Rebekah had their issues also.

Jacob got two wives. The beautiful one he loved and the older sister that had a face only a mother could love.

Leah was awkward, and stumbled about. Shy, not wanting attention, knowing it was usually a joke at her expense. Her eye sight was poor, so she had a perpetual squint and a frown. For a native of that area her skin was sallow and blemished. Her hair was thin, flighty and unmanageable, besides a dull brown color. Because of all these things, she had learned no social graces. Laban was probably right. The only way to get her married was deceit. He needed to find a way to gain some heirs through her. The chance of him finding her a husband was small.

The Lord had compassion of Leah, because she was not loved and her womb was quickly opened. She bore Jacob his first son and named him Ruben. She said "The Lord's sees my sorrow. Now my husband will love me."

Rachel was barren.

Now we have the beginning of a family feud; population explosion! Each wife believing, "be fruitful and multiply was a direct command to them."

Leah bore him number two. She named him Simeon saying, "I am still not loved, so the Lord has given me another son."

She conceived again and had Levi, saying now my husband will have respect of me.

Still Rachel was barren.

Leah bore him number four and named his Judah, saying "I will praise the Lord." At least if she didn't have Jacob's love she did have children she would love.

Rachel is so grieved. Her sister has given her husband four strong sons and she could not give him a one! She snapped at Jacob. "If you do not give me a son I will die!" Jacob said, "am I God? Is it I who have kept you from having children?" "NO! It is not me who is barren, the fault is yours!" He stormed out.

Rachel did what Sarah did, she gave Jacob her servant girl Bilhah: "Give me a son through her, so I can build a family!" She did, and they did, and Bilhah had a son. Rachel named him Dan.

Bilhah got pregnant again, this time Rachel said, "I have had a great struggle with my sister and I have won." "So she named him Naphtali."

About this time Leah noticed she had stopped baring children, so she got into the act and gave Zilpah her servant girl to Jacob, and she very quickly produced another son for him and she named him Gad. "What good fortune I have had"

Leah's servant girl bore him a second son and Leah said, "I am a happy woman! All the women will call me happy!" Leah named this one Asher.

During the harvest, Ruben, Leah's son was in the field and found some mandrake plants growing. This "natural foods" plant was known for its aphrodisiac properties.

Rachel said to Leah. "Please give me some of your son's mandrakes."

"Wasn't it enough you took my husband, now you want my son's mandrakes too?"Leah fumed.

"Very well," "If you give me some of the mandrakes, Jacob can sleep with you tonight."

So when Leah saw Jacob coming in from the fields she ran to meet him. "You must sleep with me tonight. I have hired you with my sons mandrakes" Jacob didn't know what kind of game these women were playing, but he was game. Again Leah got pregnant and gave Jacob his 5th son with her, and she named him Issachar. Then she said."God has rewarded me. She then gave Jacob another son and she named him Zebulun. Leah then gave him a beautiful daughter, she named Dinah

The mandrake tea was working for Leah but not so with Rachel.

Rachel was drinking mandrake tea by the gallons. The greens in her salads were of mandrake. She even made a mandrake dip and a creamed mandrake/goat cheese casserole.

Jacob had planned to give his full attention to Rachel, but well, he needed descendants! Soon it mattered little who gave him the sons. Since Rachel wasn't producing, it got easier and easier have children with the other three.

Rachel loved him fiercely and she was his real love, but all these women were loyal and loving.

The Lord looked upon Rachel and opened her womb and she had that beloved son of her husband. She named him Joseph. "God has taken away my disgrace." "May the Lord give me another son."

Not only did Rachel have that longed for child, but Joseph was Jacob's favorite. The son of the love of his life!

After Rachel had given birth to Joseph, Jacob had a serious talk with his father-in-law. "Send me away with my wives and children that I may go back to my own homeland." I served you many years for this family I have acquired. You know how much work I have done for you."

But Laban said, "I have learned by divination, that I have been blessed by all the things under your hands. The grain fields, the livestock have increased mightily." "Name you price and I will pay you whatever you ask."

"You know how hard I have worked and you have changed my wages ten times." "When then shall I get something for my household?"

"What then shall I give you?"

"I don't want you to give me anything. I will earn what I am asking." "I will go on tending your livestock, but let me go through the herds and flocks and remove all the sheep that are specked or spotted; every dark colored lamb; all the goats that are streaked or spotted." "They will be my wages." "They will testify to my honesty." "If you find any pure in color in my flocks, it will be considered stolen."

This sounded like a good deal, as the pure colored were the most valuable, and brought a higher price.

Again Laban had a plan to deceive Jacob. He had his sons go through the flocks and removed all those that he to promised Jacob and had them put hidden in pens. Then he took a three days journey to set a space between him and Jacob, while Jacob was tending Laban's flocks.

His brother-in-laws grew angry, as they felt, all of Jacobs wealth belonged to them. Laban and his sons attitude toward him had darkened.

Jacob heard all of these rumors his brother-in-laws were spreading about. Revenge was in the air.

The Lord spoke to Jacob. "Go back to your father's land, taking all of your family and possessions you have gained." "I promised you, I would be with you, and I will do it!"

Jacob quickly sent a message to his wives. "Come quickly! Meet me in the fields where I pasture the livestock. I have had instructions from the Lord."

He told them the situations. Their brothers were plotting revenge because they were jealous because the Lord had prospered me."

"I see your father and his sons are resenting me, but the God of my father's has been with me." "My God has spoken to me, telling me to go back to my father country." "My God has told me, I will be with you."

"You know how your father has deceived me and changed my wages ten times.""My God will not allow Laban to harm us."

"When Laban promised me all the streaked, spotted, speckled and dark animals as my wages, he had his herdsmen steal them and take them to another pasture."

"In a dream the Lord has shown me what to do. At the mating season you must take branches of the poplar, almond, and plane trees. Peel the bark in a stripped pattern, exposing the white." "As strong males from Laban's herd come to drink, only allow the strongest of the females to come." "All the sickly and weak will not be there when these branches are in the troughs. Then when the gestation period has ended, all of the strongest, healthy of the new born will be speckled, spotted, stripped. They will be mine." "All the weak, and sick will be of the pure color, and they will belong to Laban."

"So God has taken away your father's livestock and given them to me as my wages."

The wives approved. "Our father has treated us as foreigners." "Surely all the wealth our father has taken from you would never reach us.""We will do as you say."

Much later.

As Laban was a three days journey away shearing sheep. Jacob put his wives, servants, and children on camels and all the wealth he had gained in Paddan Aram and stole away without telling Laban.

Rachel had stolen her father's household idol, and Jacob did not know it.

When Laban returned and realized Jacob and all he had gained had fled. They immediately started out after them; but again the Lord intervened; in a dream He told Laban not to harm Jacob, or say anything good or bad to him. Having seen the things this God of Jacob's did, he was afraid to disobey.

Within seven days they caught up with Jacob's caravan.

When Laban had overtaken them he asked. "What have you done to me?" "You have stolen away my daughters and my grandchildren and took them away like captives in a war!" "Why did you steal away like thieves in the night?" "Why didn't you tell me, so I could have thrown a feast with joy, music and dancing, and kissed them good-by?""I have the power to harm you for such a thing, but last night in a dream, your God told me not to harm you." "But why did you steal my household idol?"

Jacob answered. "I left because you have been dishonest with me, and I knew you would find reason to harm me." "As for your household idol, we did not steal it." "But if anyone has stolen it, he shall not live!" "Go ahead and search; see for yourself." "If you find anything that is stolen take it and go."(Jacob did not know Rachel had taken it.)

Laban searched Jacob's tent first. Not there. Next he searched Leah's tent. Not there either. Then he searched the two maid servants tents. Nothing. As he went into Rachel's, she was sitting of her camel's saddle. She said, "Father forgive me if I do not stand. I am unclean, as it is the time of my monthly flow." She had hidden the idol in her saddle bag she was sitting on. Laban searched the rest of her tent and found nothing.

Jacob was angry! "You have searched our belongings and treated us as criminals."

"I worked for you twenty years and you changed my wages ten times.""You know very well you have been blessed because my God has blessed everything you have?" "In all these years not a one of your female animals has miscarried. Nor have I eaten any of your rams." "I did not bring you any of your animals torn by wild beast, but I bore the cost myself." "Whenever any of your herds and flocks was stolen, I bore that cost also."

"I toiled day and night. In the scorching heat of the sun, and the freezing of the night, not ever did I leave your herds and flock unattended." "It has been like this all the twenty years I worked for you." "Had it not been for the God of Abraham, Isaac and Jacob, you would have sent me way empty handed!"

At that Laban wanted to make a treaty. (Probably fearing Jacob's God might strike him dead.)

"Let us make a treaty," Laban said. "We will set up a pile of stones as a pillar of witness." "I will not come past this place to come after you, and you will not come past this pillar after me.""I make this vow, in the name of the God of Abraham, Isaac, and Nahor." (This is interesting; he said Nahor's God, he did not claim as his.) It appears he had allegiance to another: The household idol Rachel had stolen) Early the next morning they had a feast, Laban kissed his daughters and grandchildren good-by and left for home.

Now the next challenge was Jacob's brother whom he had deceived.

Jacob and Esau, many years later

Jacob is meeting his brother after a long absence. Hoping and praying his anger had subsided.

Not knowing how the meeting might go, he devised a plan.

First he sent a couple of messengers ahead into his brother's territory; Instructing them to say. "We have come from your brother Jacob, your servant.

Jacob has been living in Paddan Aram until now." "I am sending this message to my Lord that I might find favor in your eyes."

When the messengers returned, they said, "We have done as you asked. We met with Esau and he is on his way to meet you with 400 men."

This caused Jacob some angst, not known if these men were servants or an armed force.

Not knowing what all this meant, he wanted to be as prepared as possible; he divided all his herds and flocks into two large droves. Thinking, if Esau attacks one, the other can perhaps escape.

Jacob did what he now believed: He prayed! "O God of my grandfather Abraham, my father Issac and now the one who speaks to me; You told me to go back to my country, and You would be with me. I will prosper you." And you have. "O Lord, I am so unworthy of all the kindness and faithfulness you have shown me."

"When I first crossed the Jordan, as I was fleeing from my brother, all I had was my staff." "Here I am today with all this wealth I have accumulated in livestock, family and every good thing." "Save me once again from my brother's wrath."

"I fear he will attack and me and the mothers, and these children." "You have told me I will make your descendants as numerous as the sands of the seashore, that cannot be numbered."

Jacob spent that night in the place he called Mahanaim; the place he camped earlier and the angels of God met him."

There he chose a gift to send from his large herds and flocks, to give his brother, hoping to appease him.

He selected 200 female goats and 20 male goats.

200 ewes and 20 rams,

30 female milk camels, with their young.

40 cows and 10 bulls

20 female donkeys, and 10 male donkeys.

He put them all in the care of his servants. "Go on ahead of me, and I will come behind."""When he stops you to asks, "where are you going and whose animals are these?" "You will say 'my master Jacob's, and he is coming behind.'"

He divided his massive droves in two equal groups.

Setting one forth; leave some space.

Then Zilpah and Bilhah, the maidservants and their children, and entourage.

The second division of the massive drove.

Some space.

Leah, her children, and entourage.

Further back, Rachel and Joseph, with their entourage. Then, Jacob.

Then, when Esau meets me, I can seek his favor and ask forgiveness. Perhaps he will be moved to receive us, and I can reason with him.

You can see Jacob's heart is still for Rachel land Joseph. If trouble came, perhaps he could save them.

Jacob was still praying and reminding God of His promises. Jacob is standing on those promises.

I can imagine his heart was still in his throat with that enemy of God whispering in his ear, trying to flood his mind with doubt. It seems Jacob had learned he could take those thoughts captive and cast them down, as he praised God loudly. He was doing battle and that enemy was getting weaker and less threatening! Spiritual warfare, and the Lord God assured Jacob he had won!

By the time the estranged brothers met, Jacob had seen in the distance, the dust of Esau and his 400 men arising; coming closer and closer. Jacob had the choice. Flight or fight, or wait and see what the Lord has done! He chose that one! Bowing down before Esau, and most likely in a bit of fear and trembling. He bowed seven times as was the custom, especially when asking forgiveness.

He needed not fear. Esau had run to greet him. Embracing him and kissing him on both cheeks, and said, "Who are all these with you?"

"They are the children God has given me so graciously, your servant."

Jacob motioned the groups come forward to meet his brother. The maidservants and their children; Leah his wife and her family; Rachel, his beloved wife his favorite son, Joseph."Each family group bowing to Esau in respect.

"What are these droves your servants have brought to me?"

Jacob said, "They are gifts, my brother, an offering from the goodness of God I have received."

Esau, "You need not do this." "I have plenty." "I too have been blessed.""Keep what you have gained for yourself."

"No, my brother. Please receive these from my hand, that I may know I have found your favor.""For to me, just to see your face is as to see the face of God." (I am not quite buying the sincerity of that!) This burley man with the wild red hair and that bushy unkempt beard, is not my imagined image of God.

Because Jacob was so insistent, Esau received the gift.

Esau suggested they travel on toward home together, but Jacob told him it wasn't necessary. They would be moving at a snail's pace because of the children, and if the livestock should be pushed too hard they would die.

"Well, at least let me leave some of my servants to assist you."

"No, you go on head. We will come along at our own pace." "We stop often, make camp and rest pretty often." "I am most humbled and grateful for your kindness." "We will be along as soon as possible."

Essau left in the direction of Seir, but as soon as he was out of sight, Jacob headed his family and all he owned toward Succoth. Still, a bit of deception left in the old boy.

There they rested and built a shelter for the animals.

Over all, they had come far. All the way from Paddan Aram to Succoth, then on to Shechem and camped there.

For a hundred pieces of silver Jacob bought a plot of land and they pitched their community there. Set up an altar to worship his God and named that place El Elohe Israel.

One day when Jacob was absent, his daughter Dinah went to Shechem to make acquaintance with some of the neighbor ladies.

Shechem, the son of Hamor; the Hivite, ruler of that area, saw Dinah and her beauty, took her by force and raped her. Yet his heart was so enamored of her, he went to his father Hamor and told him, "Go to these people, speak with her father Jacob and get her for me as my wife!"

Jacob had heard the terrible thing that had been done to his daughter, buy didn't speak of it until her brothers came in from the fields. They were enraged! They would take revenge! Hamor did come seeking Dinah hand in marriage for his son, thinking. "How could they refuse? Shechem was a good looking dude!" "We are the most important people in these parts."

"LET THE WEDDING BELLS RING!"

Hamor said the Jacob. "My handsome son wants to marry your daughter Dinah." "He is quite a catch you know?" "Intermarrying with us would be a good thing." "We would marry your daughters and your daughters would marry our sons."

"This would be a great advantage to you." "Our land would be open to you." "You can live on it, farm it, graze your herds and flocks. Trade with us, and all the peoples around us in safety."

"We will give you whatever bride price you ask for Dinah." "I will pay whatever you ask! Name it, and I will pay it!"

Jacob wanted a few days to think about it. He told his sons, the brother's of Leah what was said and left for a few days.

What happened next was probably the first dirty trick recorded in the Bible!

Taking advantage of their father's absence, they would act. They met with Shechem and the men.

"Tell you what guys." "We cannot do this, as it is against our religion to marry into a people or clan of uncircumcised people." "If you will all agree to be circumcised, we will do this."

"Otherwise, it is impossible; A no go!" "We will take our sister and move on."

The men of Shechem thought it a good idea and quickly agreed. Shechem, the man who desired to marry Dinah was the first in line!

Dinah brothers, Simeon and Levi set up the ceremonial site in the city gate, and did the deed; as serious as a judges and keeping straight faces.

Three days later as the men lay in the gate in great agony and pain, Simeon and Levi put them to the sword, leaving them where they fell.

Not a man of that place survived.

Other sons of Jacob came upon the grizzle scene, seeing the dead, went into the city of Shechem, looted the place, and took all of their flocks and herds, and they also took all the women and girls captive.

Who knows, Maybe they let the women go before Jacob returned from Bethel. Nothing more is said about them.

All of this done while Jacob was away meeting with His God in Bethel. When he returned he was enraged with these children of his! "What have you done to me?" "Don't you know you have made us a stench in the nostrils of the Canaanites and the Perizzites?" "Should all the peoples of this land join forces against us, we will be out numbered and die!"

His sons lamely replied, "What were we to do?" "Don't you care they treated our sister as a prostitute?"

God again spoke to Jacob."Get up! Go to Bethel and settle there." "Build and altar to Me, Your God, who appeared to you when you were fleeing from your brother Esau."

By now, Jacob is hearing so naturally form God, he is looking forward to these times; not just when he was trouble, crying out to God for help."

Jacob built the altar and called his people to purify themselves, change their clothes and come before the altar I have build to worship God. The God of Abraham, Isaac, and Jacob." "The God who has answered me in our distress. Who has been with me; every step of the way. Just as He has promised."

There he told them to bring out all of their idols and jewelry of gold and silver they might be tempted to worship. There they buried it all beneath a great oak."

It seems, some where in all the travels, Rachel's prayer for another son was answered, and God had opened her womb. She was pregnant!

They moved some distance toward Bethlehem. (Ephrath, at that time.) Rachel went into labor. It was a most difficult labor and things not going well at all. Her maid told her "do not to fear, you have delivered a beautiful son."

With Rachel's dying breath she named him Ben-Oni. But Jacob called him Benjamin."Son of my right hand."

They lay her to rest along the road to Bethlehem.

This was around 1876 B.C. Here Rachel dies in childbirth on her way to Bethlehem, and some 1800+ years later, Mary delivered the Son of God, after an arduous trip to Bethlehem!

JOSEPH'S STORY

TIME HAS PASSED. THE SONS of Jacob are now well grown. Joseph and Benjamin, sons of his dearly loved dead wife, are his favorites. They all knew it.

Jealousy and hatred fuel each other in a vicious circle and they were circling! Faster and faster. It was not as if they had nothing. Their father was a very wealthy man, and he was a man of faith. This leads me to believe he loved them all. It was his deep love for Rachel that he could see in Joseph and Benjamin.

Joseph was a dreamer. Even as a teenager, and no one could deny it was a God given gift; as the things he dreamed had meaning and they came to be. Of course the things he dreamed did not please his jealous brothers, and they took offense.

One such example: Joseph told them this dream: "We were binding sheaves of grain out in the fields when suddenly my sheaf arose and stood upright, while your sheaves," (nodding toward his brothers so they didn't miss the meaning.) "gathered around mine and bowed down to it."

His brothers said in anger, "Do you intend to rule over us?" They hated him all the more.

Then he had another dream and told this one to his brothers also.

"Listen, I have had another dream, and this time, the sun and the moon and eleven stars were bowing down to me."

Even Jacob could see this is one he should have kept to himself! Jacob said "What is this!" "Do you say, your mother and father, as well as your brothers will actually come and bow down to you!" His brother's were so angry, but Jacob pondered all these things in his mind.

Jacob was saying to himself: "Maybe my giving him that special coat of many colors wasn't such a good idea either. I can see contentions building."

His brothers had gone out to graze their fathers flocks near Shechem, so Jacob said, "Son, go out and check on your brothers, then return and report to me"

This was a job Joseph liked. To be able to report their bad behavior and he didn't usually have to embellish the truth. Joseph was a brash but honest young man.

After looking were his brothers were suppose to be, and they weren't: He asked a shepherd grazing his flocks in the area. "Have you seen where the sons of Jacob are grazing his flocks?"

"I heard them say there were going to Dothan." so Joseph followed them and sure enough, he saw them in the distance lazing around their campfire. They saw him too!

"Here comes that dreamer, flaunting that outrageous coat!"

"He has come to spy on us, and carry the tale back to Dad!"

"Let us kill him and see what becomes of those dreams!"

"Let us kill him and toss his body down that dry well shaft."

Ruben was not there when the plan was made to kill him. When he arrived and heard it, he cried out,""NO! His blood will forever be on our hands!" Let us simple toss his down into the well shaft where he will starve and die of thirst!" "That way his blood won't actually be on our hands."

When Joseph arrived, they arose as one, tore that precious coat off him and tossed him down the well shaft.

"We will tell our father, all we found was this ripped coat, covered in dried blood and nothing more was found of Joseph." "Wild animal must have devoured him!"

"Let us kill a lamb, and use the blood to make the evidence more realistic?" "After that we can put the lamb on the spit and have it for our dinner!"

Joseph screamed and screamed, to let him out; but they sat about casually, enjoying the evening meal. As they sat devoid of conscience, they saw dust arising in the distance. As it neared they could see it was the Ishmaelite traders, making their regular trip to Egypt. They recognized them and said among themselves, "Why not make a profit from this?" "We can sell him and tell our father he has been killed by wild animals."

Well, that was what they did. They rehearsed the story, and how they would wail as they told their father that story.

They went home and playing their roll very convincingly, said, "Father, is not this the coat you gave to Joseph?"

"This is all we found of him! The wild beast must have torn him into pieces and eaten him!" "Oh how sorry we are to be the bearer of such bad news." (More weeping and wailing and mourning.) It really wasn't necessary, because by this time, it was Jacob who was loudly weeping and wailing and mourning. Tearing his clothing and throwing dust in the air. Jacob thought he would surely die! "O my son, my son, my dear son of my beloved Rachel."It went on for days.

These 10, by now were worried that the old man would die! It was the sight of his younger son Benjamin, who gave Jacob the courage to go on. This son also of his beloved, who had died giving him birth! He still had that part of her.

Life went on.

(Here is where the story of Judah and Tamar happened. That will be told later. But it was in this time frame in the life of Jacob.)

Joseph has arrived in Egypt, at 17 years old. Sold on the auction block to Potiphar, one of Pharaoh's high officials, as a household servant. Potiphar was an important man. Captain of the guard, and chief executioner."

The Lord greatly blessed Joseph and all he put his hand too. This Potiphar noticed and was so impressed, he put him over the entire household, and made him administrator over all of his affairs. Joseph ran Potiphar's affairs so smoothly, all things multiplied to him a handsome profit.

Joseph was not only intelligent, hardworking but handsome as well. Potiphar wife took notice of that. She was infatuated with this handsome young Hebrew, and even though she was old enough to be his mother. She was without scruples and usually took what she wanted.

She began flirting with him, but he would give her no notice! Joseph wasn't stupid and tried to stay out of her reach.

One day when she knew there were no other servants close by, she dressed in her most provocative nighty and brazenly said, "Joseph come lie with me."

He refused her, and said. "How could I do such a thing against my master" "He has put everything he has into my hands expect you." "I could not do such a thing against him, nor I could do such a thing against my God!"

In anger she lunged at him, ripping off his shirt as he fled from her. She was not used to being said "no" to by any servant, especially by a Hebrew!

She screamed loudly after ripping her clothes. As she heard the servants come running, she began weeping and screaming all the louder. "Go get my husband quickly!" "That Hebrew slave he brought into this house has tried to rape me!" She kept up the act telling and retelling the story, with great emotion. Poitphar came in and she began screaming, "kill him, kill him!"

Telling her story again, with sobs and showing Potipar, Joseph's torn shirt in her hand. (Potiphar must have shown little emotion.) "Don't you see, how that slave you brought into this house has treated me?" At this he had Joseph arrested and thrown into prison.

Deep down, Potiphar must have been an intelligent man; to have risen so high in Pharaoh's government; he was not likely fooled. This probably was not the first indiscretion his wife had pulled off. This was more a matter of saving face on his part.

While Joseph was in prison the Lord was with him there also. Everything put in his hand was blessed. At this his jailers took notice and began assigning him tasks that made them look good.

In jail, at this same time, was Pharaoh's baker and his cup bearer. Their crime is not noted, so we just have to guess. Maybe Pharaoh was in a bad mood or a temper tantrum! Who knows?

One night, each had a dream that troubled them. A dream so vivid, it didn't fade when they awoke. Joseph saw they were troubled and ask "Why?" When he learned they had these dreams, he told them his God held the key to dreams and interpretations.

The cup bearer, and wine taster of Pharaoh. A rather dignified looking fellow. Tallish, thin and balding, with the air of a first class butler about him, was the first to tell Joseph his dream.

"In my dream, I saw a vine with 3 branches and they sprouted, budded, and blossomed. I looked again, and there were clusters of plump, ripe grapes." "I was holding Pharaoh's wine goblet in my hand, so I squeezed the ripened grapes, and the succulent juice ran into the goblet and I presented it to Pharaoh."

"I know what your dream means.' "My God has made it known to me!"

"In three days you will called for by Pharaoh, and you will be restored to your former position."

At this good news the baker could hardly wait to tell his dream. This man was portly, and looked as if he cared little as to his appearance. Wild bushy hair and beard, greasy and unkempt: But he could bake. (Most of us wouldn't want him in our kitchen.)

"My dream is this." "I was carrying three baskets of all sort of baked goodies on my head, to take to Pharaoh" "Birds swooped down, devouring and wasting all these delicious baked goods from the top basket."

In sadness, Joseph said, "I know what your dream means also." "In three days Pharaoh will sent for you, and you will be executed." "Your impaled body will be exposed, and the birds of the air will pick at your flesh."

Just as Joseph had foretold, both were called from prison. The cup bearer restored to his place, and the baker was executed in a most horrible fashion.

Joseph had told the cup bearer, to speak on his behalf, that he might be released. The man promised, but soon forgot all about Joseph and the promise.

Two more years passed.

A birthday party was given for Pharaoh and on the third night of the party, Pharaoh had a disturbing dream. He called for his magicians and soothsayers, and they could not tell it.

Then the chief cup bearer remembered his promise to Joseph and was ashamed.

"O King Pharaoh, while I was in prison, there was a Hebrew young man there, who interpreted correctly a dream I had, and it was so. I was restored to your service." "I am sorry to say, I had promised I would bring his case before you, as he was wrongfully imprisoned." "I forgot that promise until now."

Pharaoh immediately called for Joseph to come!

The jailers bathed him, washed and combed his hair and made him presentable in clean clothes to stand before Pharaoh.

"I have called for you because I have been told you can tell the meaning of dreams."

"I cannot do this by myself. It is my God who gives dreams and makes the interpretations known."

"Very well." "This is my dream." I was standing by the river bank and there arose from the river 7 beautiful, fat and sleek cows and as they were crazing, 7 gaunt and ugly cows arose from the same river and devoured the fat cows. Yet the gaunt cows were still gaunt and ugly." "The second dream I saw, 7 heads of grain on a single stalk, strong and healthy. Producing fat heads, each grain of wheat plump and perfect."

"After these came up 7 withered and thin heads of grain, swallowing up the 7 good, full heads, and yet the thin still look poor and withered."

"In the morning I was troubled and my magicians and soothsayers could not tell me what it all meant." "That is why I have sent for you."

"Your dreams are one and the same." "The 7 fat seek cows and the 7 good heads of wheat are 7 years of plenty." "The 7 gaunt cows and the thin withered grain are 7 years of severe famine." "My God is telling you what is about to be, so you can prepare." "If you do not prepare, your prosperity will be forgotten and the land will suffer, as all of your surplus will be eaten up"

"Since this is a double dream foretelling the same trouble, means this is sure to happen! Doubly sure!" "The impact will be double!" "It is certain, God has decreed it!"

"My suggestion to you; appoint a very wise man to visit all the regions of Egypt, and put him in charge of administrating a national farm policy. Divide the land into 5 districts, and build great silo's in each district to hold all the excess grain. In the good years each farmer will give to Pharaoh 5% of all these abundant 7 years of this grain, and keep the other 95%. Each responsible for his own household needs, seed, and keeping his livestock fed."

Joseph went into great detail how this should work.

Pharaoh and his council spoke together and came to the conclusion; that wise man should be Joseph!

After all, it was he who had told them all these things, to save them from disaster.

So it was. Joseph went from the Dungeon to the Penthouse, in one day! All the doing of his God!

Pharaoh made him second in command only to himself.

Joseph was given a make-over. Joseph's imaged was changed to look as a rulers of Egypt. His hair, and his face, with the black lines under and around his eye. His royal clothing of fine Linen, and the elaborate robes of royalty. Gold chains about his neck. He was given a royal chariot to travel about, into all the 5 districts. The most impressive honor, was the royal signet ring, to seal into any law, all Joseph was to administer. He was also given his Egyptian name. Zaphnath Paneah. Truly Joseph was second only to Pharaoh. Joseph continually gave his God all the credit and the glory.

A very special gift to Joseph was the daughter of Potiphera, the priest of On, to him for his wife. A beautiful young lady, Asenath. They were devoted to each other, as she allowed their two sons be raised in Joseph's faith. It seems she could very well have adopted his faith also.

All the things done as planned, and Joseph well settled into his Egyptian way of life and it was good. They were respected and they had no needs.

The 7 years of plenety passed quickly it seemed, and Joseph oversaw the rationing and allocating to meet the needs. It was well with Egypt, but all the surrounding countries suffered the famine, but without such good planning. Joseph's family, by birth among them.

People began to look to Egypt to buy grain.

TAMAR

M Y NAME IS TAMAR AND I actually show up in the story of Judah, Jacob's fourth born son of Leah.

During the time of Jacobs travels, the family had settled in Canaan. Judah was of the ten brothers who treated Joseph cruelly, sold him to the Ishmaelite traders going to Egypt. They told their father Jacob, wild animals had torn him to bits and they all they found was the fragments of his blood stained coat of many colors.

The old man bought the story hook, line and sinker. He mourned and grieved over the death of his son. This son of his beloved wife Rachel.

Judah, now a grown man, took his leave for a time, and went to Adullam to spend some time with his friend named Hirah. There he met and married a woman and she gave him a son they named Er. Then a second son, Onan, and a third son Shelah.

Judah took a wife for Er, named Tamar. But Er was wicked in the sight of God, so he put him to death. They had no children. As the Israelite law commands, the next brother is to marry the widow to bear sons for the dead man's inheritance, so Judah gave Tamar to Onan as a wife, to produce a son of Er's line. But because of his disobedience, he died. Tamar still childless.

Judah told Tamar to live as a widow until Shelah is grown. (Truth of the matter, Judah thought, "to marry Tamar, he too would die.") Tamar had gone to live in her father's house in Adullam, while waiting.

Years passed.

Judah went up to the town of Timnah, where his men were shearing his sheep and to visit his old friend Hirah once again.

It was told Tamar, her father-in-law was there to shear sheep. Hearing this she thought, "Judah has no intention of giving his son Shelah to me as a husband. He is a grown man by now and I am not getting any younger.

She took off her widow's garments, covered herself with a veil, to disguise herself, and sat down at the entrance of Enaim next to the road to Timnah; where a harlot might sit and wait. When she saw Judah approaching, she made advances toward him, and he took the bait.

When Judah saw her, he thought she was a prostitute, for her face was covered. Not realizing it was his daughter-in-law, propositioned her to sleep with him.

"What will you give me?" she asked.

"I will send you a young goat from my flock."

"Will you give me something as a pledge that you will sent the young goat?"

"What do you want as a pledge?" He asked.

"Your signet ring, your bracelets, the staff in your hand." "You are an honorable business man, so I am sure your word can be trusted" (A little flattery goes along way!)

So he gave her what she asked for and he slept with her.

After he was gone, she returned to her father's house and put on her widow's clothing.

Meanwhile Judah sent the young goat by his friend the Adulamite. He returned saying there was no prostitute there. Asking around of the men, they told him there has never been a prostitute there we know of.

So Judah said to himself, "Let her keep the things I gave in pledge, or I will become the laughing stock of all the men of that area." With that he went back home to his brother's people.

Sometime later, it was told him, "your widow daughter-in-law is pregnant. She has been seen by many, and she is with child." "She has played the harlot and is pregnant by her whoredom!"

At this Judah was enraged! "Bring her to me!" "She will pay the penalty and be burned to death!"

Tamar send word back to Judah, "Yes, I am pregnant by the man who owns these things." "This signet ring, these bracelets, and this staff!"

When Judah saw the evidence, he acknowledged the things belonged to him. In much shame he declared, "She is more righteous than I, because I did not honor my word and give her my youngest son as a husband." Judah never again troubled her.

Tamar gave birth to twins.(Do you suppose one represented Er and the other Onan?) There was conflict between them even in the womb. The first hand to come out; a red thread was tied around his wrist. But during the struggle of delivery, his hand was withdrawn and the other came out first. The one first delivered was Pharez and the second, with the threat still tied to his wrist was named Zarah.

According to the lineage of King David, Pharez, whose father was Judah and whose mother was Tamar; going forward many generations; Boaz, the father of Obed. The father of Jesse, who was the father of King David.

There you have it. The thread running through time, all leading to Jesus. The most seemingly undeserving, in the line of his heritage. People we would not expect. Those were the ones Jesus appealed to through-out his walk here. The ones we would deem as important thought they had it all figured out and didn't need him.

JOSEPH MEETS HIS BROTHERS

J OSEPH HAS LIVED THROUGH THE most extreme highs and lows, but no less a very adventuresome life as he could not have imagined. From the bottom of that dry well pit, even to his days in prison would have seemed a bright spot from there. In that pit, it seemed the only way out was death by starvation. Being traded to the Ishmaelite merchants didn't seem all that rosy. This brings meaning to the saying, "What doesn't kill you, makes you stronger."

Jacob's family has come down, to near the end of their food supply, for themselves and their animals. There is no end in sight to this draught. Calling his family together to discuss the matter; the only answer seemed to be, the sons would go to Egypt and buy grain; hopefully enough to last until this draught ended. All, that is, except Benjamin! He would not risk losing him too. The other ten loaded up their donkey's for the trip and enough money to purchase the grain.

The brother's, son's of Jacob, reached Egypt and inquired where they might register to buy grain? They were ushered into a large empty room to wait. They were tired and dusty from the trip, so the resting seemed good.

In due time, in walked a middle aged looking man who wore the bearings of a man of stern authority, with what seemed to be an interpreter. This man Looked, dressed, and spoke as an Egyptian. Little did they know it was Joseph! He recognized them, but they had no clue this was Joseph the dreamer.

The interpreter spoke first. "Who are you and why have you come?" Ruben, the oldest was the spokesman. "We are brothers from Canaan who have come to secure grain for the survival of our family."

This interpreter turned to the official and repeated the request in Egyptian. They had a back and forth, then the man turned to them and said. "No, you are spies!" "You have come to inspect the security of our boarders and spy out how to overcome us!"

What a great surprise this was. They had not heard of such an interrogation from their neighbors who had come to Egypt to buy food. Each side put up their best efforts to convince the other and it came to an impasse.

In the process of trying to convince these people they said. "We are all brothers of one man, our Father Jacob. We have yet one younger brother at home, and one is dead."

"It is just as I told you, you are spies!" "In this way you will be tried to prove your truthfulness." "One of your shall go and get this younger brother and if he comes, I will believe you."

At this, the official ordered them jailed, turned his back on them and walked away. Leaving them jailed three days.

Later he returned with a revised plan. "One of you shall be held in custody, while the others of you shall return to Canaan to bring your younger brother back to me. If he comes, then I will believe you." "If he doesn't, your brother held here will be executed!"

At this the official turned his back on them and walked away.

When the man returned he demanded: "Chose which one will remain here, until you return from Canaan. Take the grain to your starving family, but if you do not return with your younger brother, this brother here in jail, will be executed!"

Thinking this man could not understand Hebrew, they began lamenting over their sin. "We are being punished for what we did to our brother Joseph, and the grief we have caused our father." Ruben wailed,""didn't I tell you not to harm the boy and you would not listen?"

Joseph wept as soon as he was out of their sight. He was weeping for their pain. He was weeping for his loss. He was weeping for the pain of his dear father. But most of all these were tears of joy, that only comes when there is forgiveness. His God was orchestrating it all: Just as He had done all along this long, long road.

Suddenly this official reappeared and with a surprise, pointed out Simeon. He did the choosing! Simeon would stay! Simeon was arrested and bound before their eyes. This was for real!

In the Egyptian tongue, Joseph ordered their grain sacks filled, and to put each man's money they had paid, hidden in their grain sacks, unbeknown to them.

They were released from custody, loaded their grain onto their donkey's and headed home. I can imagine they were in a hurry to get away from that place, yet conflicted about having to leave Simeon. Also, not all that anxious to face their father with the terrible plan this official had demanded. If Benjamin did not come, Simeon would die, if this man's word was to be trusted, Simeon would die! It all depended on what Jacob said. He was an old man and either way he might die of sorrow.

They could well remember the mourning for Rachel, and at the terrible grief at the news of losing Joseph.

That night as they stopped to rest and feed their donkey's. There, in the mouth of each bag of grain was all the money they had paid the Egyptians for the purchase! They fell into fear, saying "What does this mean?" "God is punishing us for our sin against Joseph and our father!"

They returned home, hands clammy, hearts pounding, and their thoughts trying to unravel all their scrambled thoughts as to how to tell their father this turn of events.

How can they explain Simeon's absence? This will not be easy!

It took Jacob about 2 minutes to notice Simeon was not among them! "Where is Simeon?"

"Father, the Egyptians treated us sharply, as if we were common criminals, telling us, "You are spies!" "But we said to him. 'Sir we are honest men, come to buy grain here for our starving families!'"

"NO!" "You are spies, come to check out the security of our boarders, to seek any weakness you could breach to attack us!" "You are spies!"

We replied; "we are all the sons of one father, not spies!"

Then he asked us, "Is your father living and do you have other brothers?"

"We told him the truth. Our aged father is still living and we have one younger brother with him. We had one other brother, who has died."""We were 12 now we are 11."

The man demanded us to take the grain and go home, leaving Simeon in custody until we return with our younger brother. Should we not return, Simeon will be executed as a spy!" "Returning with Benjamin will confirm our story and Simon will not be harmed," they told him.

"A strange thing happened. When we stopped for the first night to rest and feed our donkeys, we found our money that we had paid the Egyptians for the purchase of our grain. Each man's sack had the silver in the mouth of each bag. We did not know what this meant, but it frightened us, considering all that has happened."

At this news, Jacob went into loud wailing and lamenting. "Joseph is no more! Simeon is no more! And now my Benjamin is to be required of me also!" "I cannot bear it!" "Why has everything come against me?" "Woe is me! Woe is me!"This went on until the old man was spent.

After he had calmed a bit, he said, "I will not allow Benjamin to go! If I did let him go, I would go to my grave in sorrow."

The famine continued and still no sign of rain. This grain nearly gone, facing starvation once again. Jacob now admitting their dire need said, "you must make another trip to Egypt, lest we all starve. All of our children, grandchildren and all the animals."

Judah arose, "father, you do not understand." "If we return to Egypt without Benjamin, Simeon will die and we will never see this man's face again! We would never ever be able to buy grain." "Then all the family would surely starve!"

"Why did you bring all this trouble upon me by telling the man you had another brother?" "Why?"

"This man grilled us unmercifully!" He demanded to know, "is your father living and do you have any more brothers." "We were all jailed three days, and if we lied to this man, we would all have been executed!" "The grain we were able to bring home, would not have been, and all this family would have already starved." "Even if this famine ended tomorrow, you would never have known what happened to us." "That is the reality of our situation!"

Judah spoke calmly. "Father, send Benjamin with me. That we may leave at once, so that all of our children survive."

At this the old man relented. There was no other option. Jacob kissed Benjamin good-bye and sent him off with his brothers, their caravan of donkeys with gifts for this Egyptian, and double the grain money. Paying the going price of the grain they had used and the fresh supply.

I can see the old man watching as the trail of dust disappears into the distance, with tears in his eyes. Wondering, would he ever see his sons again?

Recalling all his God had brought him through, all he could say was: "No matter what happens, I will still praise you!"

This time as they reached Egypt, they were treated much better. Simeon was sent to them and he looked no worse for the wear. A servant of this Egyptian official, who spoke fluent Hebrew, told them. "You will dine this evening with my master, Zaphenath Paneah, in his house." Now that is a surprising turn of events!

After allowing us to clean up and make ourselves presentable, we were ushered into the grand dining room of this man's personal mansion. This must be a dream or some illusion!

The first thing they noticed was the table had been set beautifully. The seating arrangement by their order of birth! How did they know these things? Perhaps Simeon had told them.

Zaphenath Paneah walked in, dressed in his royal finest. Looked them over and asked, through his interrupter" "Is this your youngest brother?"

"Yes it is Sir."

How is your aged father you spoke of? Is he still living?"

"Yes Sir, he is."

This man looked straight at Benjamin, as if blessing him. "May God be gracious to you, my son."

This man hurried from the room. He found a private place where he could not be seen or heard and wept loudly.

After a time, he wiped tears, washed his face and freshened his Egyptian make up all officials wore in those days. Then he rejoined the others.

Since Egyptians see it as detestable to eat with people from other lands, a separate table was set for him alone.

The servants served copious portions to the ten, but 5 times the amount to Benjamin! The food wonderful; the fare fit for a king. There was much wondering what in the world was happening? Was this some kind of a last super thing? Would executioners seize then and drag them off?

All of this was wonderful, yet terrifying!

Joseph had given instructions to his steward to have the donkey's loaded with the grain; and with surplus. Put their money into each man's sack again, and have his own silver cup put in the sack of Benjamin. The steward did as he was asked.

At dawn the next morning they set out for Canaan and home.

Joseph had told his steward to let these men travel a short distance and then halt them. Saying, "Why have you repaid us evil for good?" "My master's silver cup for divination is missing. Why have you stolen it?" "We will search you until it is found!"

The brother's said, "We did not do such a thing. We are honest men." "Go ahead and search and if you find that cup among us. That man shall surely die!" "And we will make ourselves your slaves forever more."

(A side note here: just as I wrote this, I realized they had just spoken their 400 years of slavery into existence. What we speak out of our mouth will be, even then, as now!)

The Steward said: "Let it be as you have said."

When the cup was found, it was in Benjamin's sack! Planted by Joseph, but they had no idea. They began to object and wail in disbelief! The steward over saw their turn to Joseph's house.

When they returned, the 11 threw themselves at Joseph's feet, pleading for mercy on Benjamin's behalf.

Joseph said, "What is this you have done?" "Don't you know a man such as I can find all these things out by divination?"

"What can we say, my Lord? Let your servant speak a word with you." "Do not be angry, even though you are an equal to Pharaoh himself." "Do you have a father or a brother?" "We are answering truthfully." "We have an aged father and this younger son was born unto him in his old age. His older brother is dead and Benjamin is this brother's, full brother, by our father's most beloved wife, who died in childbirth during delivery."

"You said to me bring this son down to me so I can see for myself, then I will surely believe you?"

"Did I not say, if anything happens to this old man's youngest son, he will surely die?" "Please let me remain here and serve his sentence as your slave, only let Benjamin return to his father."

"When we returned with the first caravan of food, our father would still not allow Benjamin to travel with us." "It was when that food was nearly gone, we convinced him, this is our only option." "It was then I vowed to my father, upon my life, if Benjamin did not return, I would bear the punishment, even unto death."

At this Joseph could no longer control his emotions. He cried out for all his attendants to leave the room. They did, as he wept so loudly, it was heard, even to Pharaoh's palace.

Joseph turned to his stunned brothers, who were too terrified to speak. Then Joseph beckoned them to come close to him. He said. "Come close, I am your brother Joseph!" "Come tell be about my father!" He embraced Benjamin, tears of joy streaming down his cheeks and unto his brother's neck.

"I am your brother you sold into slavery, but do not be afraid, God has sent me here before you, that you will all survive. To preserve that remnant that will bless the whole earth." "The God of Abraham, Isaac and Jacob has done this." "What you meant for evil, God has meant for good. It is his purpose!" "Now go, bring your father, all the family and the livestock, I will give to you the best of all the land of Goshen and you will be saved."

At this he drew close and kissed all of his brothers, weeping. With the full blessing of Pharaoh and his assistance, they returned to their father with the good news: "Joseph is alive!"

Before Jacob died in his old age, he did get to bless all these grandchildren and great grandchildren the Lord had blessed him with. Even the two sons of Joseph. He also made his sons promise they would carry his bones back to his home land for burial. And that they did.

Some 400 years they flourished in the land of Goshen, but now no one remembered Joseph, the famine or the Pharaoh that ruled Egypt at that time.

They had become so numerous the Egyptians were afraid of them, so they made them slaves under harsh task masters. It was the only life they knew and settled into it as a normal state of affairs.

How many of us remember any to the toil of our forefathers 400 years back? Not many. We do what needs to be done to survive. So it was with the Hebrews in Egypt. But that is our next story.

THE RISE OF MOSES

(Joseph sends for his father.)

S UCH AND EMOTIONAL REUNION THEY had! The brother's still not fully understanding how this ruler in Egypt can possibly be the brother they so despised, and could have forgiven them so easily. They were seeing it and hearing it, but somehow it felt like a dream they would awaken from at any moment. Such a mix of emotions: Running back and forth; between guilt, remorse and full forgiveness. How could it be?

Pharaoh so trusted Joseph, believing the dream interpretation, knew this draught was not ending for awhile, invited all of Joseph's family to move to Egypt where they would be provided for. He offered all the assistance they would need to make the move.

Jacob hearing his son was alive, was willing to go anywhere and do anything to be with his son again.

The plans made and put into action; the move began. Joseph and Pharaoh waiting in joyful expectation for their arrival, was beyond trying to explain.

News of their caravan nearing Egypt brought Joseph and many dignitaries out to greet them. Pharaoh told Joseph to relay to his father and the families, "The land of Egypt is before them." "Settle them in the land of Goshen." "You may tell them they can also be in charge of all my livestock." "They are welcome here." There Jacob blessed Pharaoh and went from his presence.

Jacob lived in Egypt 17 years, and as he was nearing his death, made Joseph vow to carry his body back to be buried in his homeland.

Jacob blessed Joseph's two sons, and his own 12 sons. He died at the age to 147.

Joseph had the body embalmed, as was the custom of Egypt, and the seventy days of mourning had passed. As promised, Joseph took his father back to Cannan to the burial spot Jacob had purchased many years ago.

Joseph would live to be 110 and saw grandchildren to the third generation.

The family of Jacob made Goshen in the land of Egypt home for some 400 years.

The Egyptians flourished under Joseph and the Pharaoh that reigned at that time; but that time had passed and no one remember them any more. Now the Hebrew have become slaves in captivity, as hundreds of years have passed.

These foreigners grew quickly in numbers until the Egyptians were afraid of them. The Egyptian population growth had not kept up with the Hebrews. The Egyptians thinking; more and more difficult labor would slow this growth, they put them under harsh task-masters.

Near the end of this 400 year captivity, the Egyptians were in such an extensive building program, as the world had never seen. They built it all on the backs of these slaves. They built the cities of Pithom and Ramases; great storehouse cities, and many of the other wonders of the world. The crumbling remains of which are still standing today. A cruel and harsh life and still these people flourished.

These Hebrews had never known anything else. To them is was a way of life. About the extent of their knowledge was, "We are Hebrews!" (I can see a great comparison between these people and many of our ancestors.)

When these tactics failed to curb the growth, an order went out from Pharaoh. "All Hebrew baby boys would be thrown into the Nile to drown!"

A Hebrew man and his wife from the tribe of Levi had older children, (Aaron and Miriam), but she was pregnant at time of this order. Somehow, she was hidden from the eyes of Pharaoh's soldiers. This couple managed and to keep hidden the beautiful boy they had delivered, for about three months. Knowing their deception would soon be found out, his mother made a basket of papyrus, coating it inside and out with pitch and tar, making it tight and water proof. She lay her precious son in it with his favorite, "bankie." (Didn't all of our children have one?) Then she placed him in his "arc of survival," in the reeds near the shore. His sister, Miriam, keeping watch, and supplying him with all his needs. A very covert operation I am sure.

This being close to the palace of Pharaoh, was the favorite place of his daughter and her attendants to come bathe and play in the water.

One day as they enjoyed this place, they heard a baby's cry. There they saw the basket among the reeds, took the child, and "ooed and awed," as women do. Immediately they all fell in love with this beautiful child.

When Miriam saw they meant the child no harm, she ran to ask, "would you like me to find this baby a Hebrew woman to nurse him?" Of course they did. All recognized he was a Hebrew by birth.

(His own mother was able to nurse and care for him until he was weaned. Which, in that culture is a long time. Long past the time we wean babies today. Today we would have them sent off to nursery school or pre-school, and mostly likely day care, long before this age. He may have been 5 or 6 years old. (I am going to pick 7, as it is the number of completeness.) It was God's gift to this family, and the eternal plan of God.

Pharaoh's daughter named him Moses, as she said.""I drew him out of the water"

Pharaoh's daughter had the same power over her daddy, most little girls get figured out very quickly! It is hard for Daddy to say "no." Pharaoh must have thought. "What harm can it do?" "One little boy?" As it turned out, the entire family loved him and he became more of a son to Pharaoh, and a brother to Pharaoh's own son.

Moses had all the privileges of that class of Egyptians. Spoiled, educated in all manner of learning. All the protocol of the royal family.

Everyone knew he was a Hebrew. He knew it, Pharaoh knew, as did his daughter and her maids. All the families of the royal palace and of course, the Hebrews. (Just as the much earlier, Pharaoh and all his people, knew Joseph was as Hebrew.)

One day, as a grown man of 40, he went down to see how his Hebrew relatives were doing. He came upon a task-master beating near to death, a Hebrew slave. Seized with anger, Moses, after looking to see who might be watching, killed the Egyptian and hid his body in the sand.

A few days later as he was visiting his Hebrew people again, he came upon two Hebrews in a terrible fight. Stepping in between them said."Why are you fighting among yourselves?" The man who was in the wrong, said, "who made you our judge and jury?""What are you going to do, kill me as you did the Egyptian, and hide my body?"

"What I did is now known," Moses thought, "and when this reaches Pharaoh's ears, I will face capital punishment!"

Moses did what most of us would have done! He ran, and ran and ran. Hoping to have put enough distance between himself and the Egyptians, before they knew he was missing.

They gave up looking for him, as the desert is a formidable place and it would claim anyone there without provision and shelter. Moses was without either.

He was now 40 and in the desolate desert of the nomad Midianites, and they were sparse. Tired, dusty, hungry and thirsty Moses found an old well and sat down to rest. A group of 7 young women came, bringing their flocks to water. Before they could accomplish this, a group of scoundrel shepherds came, running the women away. Moses intercepted them. Ran the ruffians off, and watered the flocks for these women.

It so happened, these were the daughters of Jethro, a priest of Midian.

When the young ladies, returned their father ask, "How are you done so quickly?" They told him the story of the stranger who had confronted the shepherds and ran them away; then he watered our flocks himself.

"Well, why didn't you at least bring him home and offer him a meal?" They went back and found him, expressed their thanks and brought him home with them.

As it turned out Moses was invited to live and work with them. Jethro gave his daughter Zipporah, to Moses for a wife.

This was a blessing for Jethro too, as good husbands were a scarce commodity in these parts. Jethro needed a son as well as a husband for his daughter. She gave Moses a son he named Gershom, saying, "God has made me an alien in a foreign land."

In the meantime, the Hebrews had finally began to cry out to the God of their forefathers for help, and he was listening.

Forty years have passed and Moses traveled, shepherding the sheep to the area of Horeb, "The mountain of God." While resting, watching the sheep graze, he saw a strange sight! There close by, was a bush, on fire but not being consumed! "How can this be!" he said to himself. He drew near to see this sight!

As Moses came near, God called to him from the burning bush! "Moses! Moses!"

Moses replied in fear. "Here I am Lord!"

"Take off your shoes. You are standing on Holy Ground!"

Moses fell on his face to the ground in fear.

The Lord continued. "I AM the God of your fathers. The God of Abraham, Isaac and Jacob!" "I have heard the cry of your people because of their hard labor and misery." "I have come to rescue them from the Egyptians and bring them to a good land flowing with milk and honey."

"I AM sending you to Pharaoh to bring your people out of Egypt!"

"But Lord, who am I that they would listen to me?"

"I will be with you!" "I will bring my people to this very mountain to worship me." "That will be a sign to you!"

"Suppose they say 'what is this God's name?'" "What shall I tell them?"

"Tell them. I AM who I AM!" "Tell them I AM has sent me!"

"This is my name forever." "I AM the God of Abraham. I AM the God of Isaac. I AM the God of Jacob." "I AM who I AM and will be remembered through-out all generations, forever!"

"I have already assembled the elders of Israel and said to them, I AM the Lord God of Abraham, Isaac and Jacob; telling them I have seen their slavery and misery and I am bringing you out, into a land of promise, flowing with milk and honey."

The elders will listen to you, and you and the elders will go to speak with Pharaoh saying, "The Lord has spoken to us, telling us to go a three days journey into the wilderness to a make a sacrifice to the Lord our God." But, his heart will be hardened and he will not let you go. (All the requests, he will not do, until the mighty hand of God compels him. After much refusal he will be glad to get rid of this people.)

You will not go empty handed! Your women will ask their neighbors, and they will give them gold, silver, and precious stones. Beautiful clothing for their children. In this way, the Egyptians will be plundered.

Moses asked the Lord. "What if they do not believe me?" "What if they say; "The Lord did not sent you!"

The Lord said, "Moses, what is that in your hand?"

"It is my staff, Lord."

"Moses, throw it to the ground."

When he did it became a fierce looking snake, that Moses feared!

"Moses, reach out your hand and pick up that snake by the tail."

Moses did as the Lord said, with much trembling. When he touched that aggressively irritated, deadly creature, it immediately became his staff again."

"This is one of the signs you will show them in front of Pharaoh and they will believe. They will believe I AM has sent you!"

"Moses, put your hand into your shirt. Now withdraw it." As Moses did his hand was leprous, white as snow and diseased.

"Now, Moses, put your hand back into your shirt and pull it out again."

This time it was fully restored and healthy!

"These and many other signs and wonders I will demonstrate through you."

Even after all these convincing sign, Moses was still dragging his feet.

"Lord I not an eloquent speaker." "I have always been slow of speech. You know that." Moses was afraid and making excuses and they both knew it.

"Moses, who made your mouth, your hearing and sight?" "Did not I do it?" "Moses, I AM able to teach you and help you."

Still resisting and rebelling, "O Lord, send someone else!"

This angered the Lord. "What about your brother Aaron? I know he can speak well." "He is on his way to meet us now, even as we speak!" "He will be glad to see you, and he will speak for you." "You will speak to him and he will speak for you, as he will obey me!"

"Take you staff in your hand, as you will perform my sign and wonders by it."

A stunned Moses, returned to Jethro's camp, telling him all things the Lord had done. "He has called me back to deliver His people by my hand, as I am obedient to Him." "I must go back to Egypt, as all the men who sought my life have died."

Jethro agreed firmly, so Moses took his wife and his child, headed back to Egypt with his staff in his hand.

Along the way the Lord continued to instruct Moses."Moses, be sure to do all the signs and wonders I will tell you." Do not be surprised that Pharaoh's heart will be hardened and he will resist you." "I have a purpose in all of this." "It will bring about the deliverance I have promised."

Moses and his family stopped for the night to rest. There he was confronted by the Lord Jehova, who threatened his life. It was in regard to his son not being circumcised. Zipporah, in anger took a flint knife and circumcised her son, throwing the bloody foreskin at Moses feet. "You are a bloody husband to me!"

I must say, this last paragraph has always puzzled me. Not only did it puzzle me, I had no clue why it would have been included in the scripture. For this story I felt some research was in order. As near as I can concluded, and it makes sense, the Hebrew ordinance and the ordinance of Midians differed. The circumcision practiced according to the one true God of the Hebrews: Male babies were circumcised on the 8th day. The people of Midian preformed this rite just prior to marriage. Those commentaries suggest Moses had purposely chosen to not follow this Hebrew rite for his son, to appease the god's of Jethor's faith. Make peace, so to speak. This was why Zipporah was so angry. I suppose she felt Moses had broken his promise. Yet to save her husband's life, she did this herself, hating every minute of it!

Many others may have a better understanding. This seems to answer my questions.

MOSES AND AARON
CONFRONT PHARAOH

THE LORD SAID; "I WILL speak to you all the things I want you to tell Pharaoh. You will seem as God to him and Aaron as a prophet. Be sure to do all I tell you to do."

"Go!" said the Lord. "I AM the Lord." "I appeared to Abraham, Isaac and Jacob." "I made my covenant with them, to give them the land of Canaan, where they will live as aliens."

"I have heard the cry of my Hebrew people and I have come to deliver them from this Egyptians slavery." "I AM, my covenant, I will deliver them and bring them out to the land of promise."

"Go, tell them, I AM will redeem them and deliver with an outstretched arm." "They will witness mighty things of signs and wonders that they may believe it is I who have sent to them Moses and Aaron."

'I will take you as my own. I will be your God and you shall be my people. I will give you the land I promised your forefathers, Abraham, Isaac and Jacob." "I AM the Lord!"

Moses reported all these things to the Israelites, but they did not listen because in their discouragement, and cruel treatment as they had endured.

Moses and Aaron did as the Lord spoke to them and went to Pharaoh, and made their request known to him. Pharaoh quickly rejected these requests, so the Lord commanded Aaron to throw down the staff of Moses to the floor. He did, and just as in the desert, it became a snake.

Pharaoh called for his sorcerers and magicians and they immediately produced the same. They threw down they staffs and they became snakes, but the snake of Moses devoured the other snakes.

Since Pharaoh did not listen. The Lord told Moses return in the morning as Pharaoh goes to the river to draw water. Simply wait and watch. Then I will tell you what to do.

Say to Pharaoh, "This is what the Lord says; 'by this you will know that the Lord has sent me.' "Strike the river with your staff!" Aaron did, and all the water in the river, ponds, streams and even in the clay water jars became blood. The sorcerers and the magicians did the same, so Pharaoh disregarded them and ordered some wells dug. All the fish in the Nile died and from the rotting fish flesh and the decaying blood, a terrible stench went up, still Pharaoh did not listen.

Seven days later the Lord instructed Moses and Aaron to go and stand before Pharaoh again, saying, "let my people go into the desert to worship me." Pharaoh thinking, "Who is this god that I should listen to him?" So Pharaoh refused, and Aaron did as the Lord had instructed Moses. He stretched his hand, holding Moses staff toward and river and frogs came out of the Nile and covered all things. The royal palace, houses, their beds, the kneading troughs, where they made their bread: Everything was covered with these detestable things! They filled their bedroom, their kitchens, covering all their food, until all of Pharaoh's people began to cry out to him to have

Moses stop these things. This plague Pharaoh's men could not duplicate.

Moses left Pharaoh, saying, "I will leave you to decide if you will ask this curse be lifted."

The next day Pharaoh sent for them again. Crying out. "Lift this curse! We cannot endure it."

Moses said, "It will be as you say. Tomorrow the frogs will leave your land and return to the river." Moses left his presence.

The stench of all the dead frogs that covered the land was sickening. These were gathered into great heaps until they could be disposed of, and it was unbearable. The people suffered. When Pharaoh saw there was relief, his heart was hardened even more. Just as the Lord had told Moses it would be.

Next God directed Moses and Aaron to stretch out the staff over the dry ground. When Aaron did, the dust of the earth became swarms of gnats. They covered the ground, the people, all the plants and animals, and all of the food too. Again, Pharaoh's men could not duplicate it. Pharaoh's sorcerers cried out, "We cannot do this! It is the finger of their God!" But Pharaoh would not listen.

The Lord again instructed Moses and Aaron to say to Pharaoh as they confronted, him saying, "Let my people go into the desert to worship our God. If you do not, swarms of flies will cover the entire land of Egypt; all of your houses, and every inch of the ground. You will be unable to put food into your mouth without flies covering it. It will be most detestable." "But I will deal differently with the land of Goshen where my people live. That you will know I have set a difference between them and you. They will suffer no harm."

At this Pharaoh relented a bit by trying to bargain with them. "You may go sacrifice and worship in this land."

Moses replied, "That would not be right." "To make our sacrifices and worship here would be detestable to the Egyptian people, and they would stone us."

"We must go a three days journey into the desert, as the Lord our God has commanded us."

Pharaoh said "I will let your people go." "Please pray for me."

Moses. "As soon as I leave I will pray to the Lord on your behalf. Tomorrow this curse will be lifted." "Only be sure you are not acting deceitfully again, by not letting my people go." Moses prayed and not a fly to be found.

Still again, Pharaoh's heart was even more hardened, and he refused them.

Pharaoh sent one of his officials out to investigate the people in Goshen. There they found, just as Moses said, not a sign of any of the plagues had touched them. God had made a distinction between his own people and the Egyptians.

The next day the Lord told Moses and Aaron to take handfuls of soot from a furnace and scatter it into the wind. They did as Pharaoh was watching. The Lord said, "Let all that fine soot cause boils to break out on all living warm blooded creatures. Man, woman, child, and every animal and beast. They suffered these grievous boils. But not in Goshen.

Still Pharaoh had a hard heart. His heart so filled with pride he would not bow to any god, not even the God of Moses and the Hebrews.

Next, at God's command came devastating hail. A few of Pharaoh's own livestock was brought into some shelters and survived, but most were destroyed. No change in Pharaoh's heart.

All these things were getting his attention though. He called for Moses and Aaron. "How long will you be gone and who will go with you?"

Moses, through Aaron responded, "We will go with all of our people and animals. The young and old; men and women, boys and girls." "We are to celebrate a festival there, unto the Lord our God."

"If I let you go with all of you people you will not return!" Then he drove Moses and Aaron from his sight. Then God sent swarms of devouring locust, that ate up every green thing the other plagues had left. This land was now barren.

Pharaoh then cried out to Moses and Aaron and asked forgiveness. Please stop this plague. But as soon as it had stopped, his heart was still as hard as flint.

Next the Lord told Moses and Aaron, stretch out your hand toward the sky. When he did, a darkness so vast it covered the entire land. So thick, it could be felt. So dark was the darkness of it, not a hand could be seen in front of their eyes. They could not see another person for three days. Frightening and dreadful!

A distressful cry went out among the people. "Stop this! Let those people go!"

Pharaoh cried out. "Go! Get out of here! Stop this terrible darkness!" "Go worship your God!"

As soon as Moses and Aaron had prayed the darkness lifted. But, the Lord made his heart harder than ever before. This time Pharaoh's heart was so enraged he demanded they go. "You will never see my face again." "I am through with you!" I am through with all of your demands!"

Moses said, "You are right. You will never see my face again."

Moses and Aaron left his presence. Again the Lord spoke to them what they must do.

"This last plaque God will cast upon them is so terrible, they will plead with you to leave. He will drive you out. After this you will go, but not empty handed." Each woman will ask her neighbor for gold and silver; for other precious things and they will gladly be given to them.

"This way the Egyptians will be plundered."

Tell all the Hebrew people to do as I say and get ready to depart on a moment's notice. These Egyptians have seen all the suffering and forced labor you have endured and they are favorably sympathetic toward you."

The officials were silently favorable to Moses and Aaron, as they could see how unjustly Pharaoh treated them. All of this suffering had been caused by the hardness and stubbornness of Pharaoh's own heart.

Moses said about midnight the Lord will send his angel of death throughout the land seeking every dwelling that is marked with the blood of a lamb, painted on the lintel and the side posts of your door; the angel sees and by-passes. He will visit the homes not so marked and the first born son of every family there will be taken."

Moses explained exactly how the Lord God told him to instruct them.

He told them, "How the sacrificial lamb was to be chosen. How the blood would be used for the marked door frames would be painted. How the lamb would be roasted and eaten, and what would be served with it. Should any anything remain of that lamb, it should be burned up. This will be the Passover, when the angel of death passes over my people. This shall be an everlasting ordinance."

That very night all these things happened just as Moses had said. There was such weeping and wailing as the world has never seen or heard, or would hear every again. From Pharaoh's own home, where his beloved son died; to the lowest of the servants who ground his wheat. All of the first born of the male animals died too. A great mourning filled the land.

While Pharaohs and all his house were in distress, the Hebrews left the land of Egypt. Headed for the desert; as God had instructed them.

When Pharaoh's head had cleared enough to realize all his slave labor was gone, in great anger he called forth his army with their horses and chariots to chase these people down and kill them.

The Hebrew's had a fair head start, but the horses and chariots could travel much faster. The Hebrew came to the bank of the Red Sea where they came to a stop, where they considered how they might cross with such a large and somewhat fragile party. In the distance they could see the dust rising from Pharaoh's army and they trembled with fear. They were no fighting force. The sea on one side of them and the advancing troops on the other.

The one thing they did not consider. They had the power of the Almighty to fight their battle. These Hebrews, most likely did not know the power of the Almighty. After all they were slaves without hope for 400 years.

CROSSING THE RED SEA

THE LORD HAD TOLD MOSES and Aaron, "fear not, I will be with you," and they took him at his word. What faith! I suppose after all they had seen the Lord do in Egypt, nothing was that much of a surprise.

To the people of the Hebrews it was probably a bit more like stepping into the unknown.

They headed for the crossing, as a massive crowd of people and animals for the land of Canaan; the land of promise God gave to their forefathers, Abraham, Isaac and Jacob. 400 hundred years have passed and they most likely didn't have any recollection of who these men were, let alone the promise Land. They were trusting Moses and Aaron, as they were trusting God.

Can you imagine the thoughts these Hebrews slaves were thinking? They didn't see, but might have heard at least some of the experiences Moses and Aaron had. I rather doubt they were excused from their hard labor so they could witness God in action.

Some may have said, "Why are we following this pied piper that has not been among us for 40 years?" It was a march on faith alone. I can almost see them and hear them thinking.

Wide eyed in disbelief, "What in the world are we doing?" "Is it too late to change our mind and turn back to Egypt?" "How did we get ourselves into such a mess?" "Yes, we were worked unbearably hard by heavy handed task-masters, but we did survive." "We had homes, not much to look at, but a place for our families." "We had gardens, and this fertile soil all along the Nile could grow anything." "We ate what we grew, and had a bed to sleep in at night." All these thoughts, they dared not utter aloud to anyone. "Who knows; this Moses may be a harder task-master than the Egyptians."

Now here they were staring at the Red Sea, with no visible way to cross. Seemingly impassable in front of them and surely by now, the army of Pharaoh's was in pursuit behind.

They are a formidable fighting force and what do we have? A few swords, bows and a few arrows, but what is that against horses and chariots? Marching troops, armed with spears, body armor, and shields? "What are we doing?" Panic was rising! Moses and Aaron praying hard!

"Lord you see all things and unless you make a way we will all be slain."

"The Egyptians will say you have brought us all out here to slay us." They will say, "Their God, was no match for the might of Pharaoh's army." Moses prayed. Again saying, "Lord I believe you and all your promises! Show the world you are the, I AM. The God I know, that I know, that I know!"

The Lord answered Moses. "Did I not tell you I would be with you?" "Did I not tell you I would lead you, a cloud by day and a fire by night?" "The cloud will lead you and shield you from the hot sun during the day and the pillar of fire will lead and warm you in the cold desert nights."

"Pharaoh will pursue you, but I will gain the glory."
"Fear not!"

As Pharaoh's dust was rising in the distance, the Hebrews fear was now more than internal thought. It was now down right terrifying fear!

They could see the evidence of the chase! They cried out loudly, "What have we done?" "Was there not enough graves in Egypt that you have brought us out to die in the forsaken place?""Didn't we say in Egypt, "leave us alone?" "Let us serve the Egyptians." "We would be so much better off to serve them than to die here in this terrible place?"

Moses cried out. "Do not be afraid! Stand and see what the lord can do!"

The Lord said, "Why are you crying out to me?" "You have seen what I can do!"

"Moses, stand firm." "Raise your staff out toward the sea with your right hand, and the left raised toward heaven. The waters will be divided so the Israelites will pass through the sea on the path of dry ground. I will provide it." "I will harden Pharaoh's heart and he will follow you." "I will gain the glory through defeating Pharaoh's army." "Then they will know that I AM the Lord your God!"

The angel of God who had been travelling with them, keeping watch over them, withdrew from the front and took up position in the rear. He was their protecting rear guard. At the angels command a dark thick cloud covered the rear, so the approaching army could not see them. The cloud so thick they could not penetrate it.

Moses did as the Lord had told him. Standing of a high rock, lifted his arms and the staff. A strong east wind began to blow, cutting a path through the sea; leaving a wall of water, standing on the right and the left, a dry roadway between: From the banks on the Egyptians side, to the Sinai Desert on the other.

The mighty arm of the Lord had done it! The Hebrews and all their possessions passed safely through. All safely to the Sinai side!

As soon as the last of them were ashore, the dark cloud lifted and Pharaoh's army saw the dry roadbed and rushed in. When they were all on that dry road, Moses again raised his staff, then dropping his arms, the walls of water came crashing down. The pursuing troops of Pharaoh's army perishing.

That day the Lord demonstrated his power to the Hebrews. It was a marvelous thing the Lord had done.

(This faith the Hebrews had gained was tested many time in this journey.)

The first thing they did, when they realized what a marvelous escape they had been through; they celebrated. Celebration broke out all over the camp. They saw with their eyes, heard with their ears and now they believed with their hearts. What went from a nightmare, to the most outlandish sight of the sea opening up making a way for them, was almost too much to take in. It was a pinch-me-I-am dreaming kind of things. "Did I really see that?"

Celebration did break out! Singing and dancing. Miriam and Moses leading in a new song Moses wrote for the occasion. Miriam led the women in dance with tambourines. They slaughtered beef and had a feast. A celebration to the Lord for their deliverance!

The euphoria was short lived. A day's journey in, they forgot all about the miracles the Lord had displayed. That was now only an image in the rear view mirror.

They came to a place where there was water, but it was contaminated and not consumable. They were tired, dusty and thirsty, and began to whine a grumble once again. Instead of trusting the Lord, they began to accuse Moses. "What are we to drink?" "Did you bring us out here to die of thirst?"

At this Moses once again cried out to the Lord God. The Lord showed him a large stick. "Throw it into the water, Moses." When he did the bitter water became sweet. So that place they named Mara, meaning "Bitter."

There the Lord gave Moses a word for the people. "If you will listen carefully to the voice of the Lord your God and do what is right in his eyes; if you pay attention to his commands and keep all his decrees. I will bring none of the diseases on you that I brought on the Egyptians." "We will believe, rejoice and obey!" They cried.

The ball is now in their court; or at least until they fall back into their old habits.

They moved on to Elim, where they had plenty of water. The place was beautiful! Twenty nine palm trees and 29 springs of water, and here they camped. Most likely they did not desire to move on.

From there they traveled deeper into the Sinai Desert. It was the second month into their journey.

Again they began to grumble loudly. "If only we had died in Egypt!" "There we had meat to eat and all the food we wanted!" "You, Moses, have brought us here to starve to death!"

The Lord spoke to Moses. "Don't fear these people or their words." "I will rain down from bread from heaven for you and all these people each day." "Enough for that day, to see if they will trust me day by day." "Each day, just enough for that day." "They are to gather only enough for that day; but I will resupply them each morning with the same." "For five days, but on that sixth day they are to gather enough for the sixth day and Sabbath day also, as no work must be done on the Sabbath. It is the day of rest!"

Moses relayed this message to the people. In the morning you will see the glory of Lord who has brought you out of Egypt." "He will give you bread in morning and meat each evening." "You are not grumbling against me, but against the Lord!"

As they raised their eyes toward the desert eastward, that evening the glory of the Lord appeared in the clouds. With an east wind quail came and covered the ground. They knew what this was, as they had eaten this bird before, but what is this other stuff? Each morning the ground was covered with dew. When the moisture dried, there was thin white flakes, like frost. Since they had never seen anything like it, they said, "What is it?" So they called it manna, which means, what is it?

It looked like coriander seed, and had the taste of honey. They were instructed to bake it, boil it, cook it however they desired, but do not keep any overnight, as it will smell bad and be covered with maggots. "Only on the sixth day can you gather enough to cook for the Sabbath also."

"You must trust me day by day for your provisions." "I AM the Lord God who delivered you from Egypt."

God command Moses and Aaron to keep one omer in a stone jar as a memorial to God for generations to come.

Those people were a trial to Moses all the way. They whined, murmured, grumbled and complained. No one seemed to remember from one miracle to the next how God had supplied them.

Now it was water they demanded again. "Did you bring us out here to die of thirst?"

Moses cried out to God. "What am I to do with these ungrateful people?" "They are ready to stone me!" "Go, stand by that Rock of Horeb and strike it with your staff. I will pour out of it a great stream of water sufficient for all these and all of their animals."

So it was, but they soon forgot this miracle too. They journeyed on.

The Amalekites came against them for war, and attack them at Rephidim. There Moses and Joshua chose some men to be an army to go out and meet their enemy in battle. As long as Moses kept his arms raised to heaven, the Israelites were winning. If he let his arms down the enemy was winning. Aaron and Ben Hur, sat Moses on a rock, as he was getting tired, and held his arms and staff toward heaven, so Joshua was able to win the battle.

Isn't that always the way? When we keep our arms raised heavenward in Praise, God wins the battle for us. When we are too weak to stand, friends and family stand in the gap and uphold us in worship and we prevail.

There Moses built an altar to the Lord and called it "The Lord, my banner."

Jethro, Moses father-in-law had heard all the Lord was doing for them, came to visit. He brought with him Moses wife, Zipporah and sons, Gershom and Eliezer. Moses went out to greet them with hugs and kisses, then Moses and Jethro went into the tent, for a discussion. I believe Moses and Jethro had a very special father/son relationship. After all they had taken him into their family all those 40 years and they formed a special bond.

As they talked, Moses caught Jethro up on all that had happened. All the trials and victories, and all the mighty miracles of God. Jethro was delighted how God had delivered them. Jethro said, "Now I know the Lord your God has done all of this and has taken great care for you, all the way. Praise the Lord!" "Now I know there is no God greater than your God!" There Jethro brought a burnt offering and sacrificed it to the God of Moses and Aaron.

Jethro watched as Moses attended one of his many duties. He heard all the cases these people brought, one against the other. From morning until evening, he had heard their cases and made judgments.

At the close of the day Jethro pulled Moses aside and said. "The thing you are doing is not good. You are wearing yourself out." "Listen to my wisdom in this matter."

"Choose good men of good reputation to be over groups of 1000, 100, 50, and 10, to hear their complaints. They will judge and settle the matter. The ones that are too difficult, they can refer on to you and you will judge those. You will be the Supreme Court, so to speak." This seemed good to Moses and satisfied the people.

They journeyed on to Mount Sinai. Arriving there three months into their journey. Israel camped at the foot of Mount Sinai. There Moses was called by God to come meet him on the mountain.

Before Moses went, he told the people how God had chosen them to be a kingdom of priest unto himself. Moses would go up the mountain and receive their instructions

The people were in awe and vowed they would do everything God said. Moses and all the people held a convocation ceremony, dedicating themselves; cleansing themselves and cleansing their clothing: A serious business before the Lord.

Three days later Moses went up the mountain after instructing the people. Not a man or animal may cross the boundary at the foot of the mountain, or they will be put to death.

On the third morning there was thunder, lightning and a thick dark cloud covering the mountain top. God called Moses to come and there they met, out of the sight of all the people. There God told Moses to go back and warm the people of the seriousness of all they had been told to do. "Be sure you do not violate the command, that no one is to come near this place, even the priest, as the anger of the Lord will break forth against you." Moses did as the Lord asked of him.

When he returned up to the mountain top, it was there the Lord gave Moses the Ten Commandments, and wrote them with his own finger on the tablets of stone. There God gave Moses all the statues with all their detailed instructions. Every decree covering all the details of everything. It would be Law unto them and exact in every way.

When the people saw that Moses had been gone for a long time and they had not heard from him. They disregarded their vow and began complaining. "We do not know what has become of this man, Moses."

"Perhaps God has struck him dead!" "Aaron, come, make us a god we can see."

(Aaron must have feared what they might do to him. So he was thrust into leadership.)

Aaron said to them, "take off all of your gold jewelry and give it to me." "Give me all the gold from your wives and children also." They did so. Aaron heated it in the fire until it melted. Then cast it into a mold they had dug in the sand in the likeness of a calf. After it had cooled, they fashioned it with their tools giving it detail: A work of their own hands.

There they worshipped it saying, "This is our god Israel, who brought us out of Egypt!" the next day they made sacrifices to this thing: Burnt offerings and fellowship offerings. Afterwards they sat down to eat and drink and party.

The Lord said to Moses; "Go down, because the people you brought out of Egypt have become corrupt!" "They have quickly broken their vow and turned from me!" "They had made themselves an idol and have bowed down to it." "I have seen this! They are a stiff necked people!" "I will destroy them in my anger; then I will make of you a great nation, Moses."

Moses cried out," "O Lord, these are your people!" "Why should your anger burn against these people?" "If you do this thing, surely the Egyptians will hear of it and say, you brought them out to kill them." They will say. "It was with evil intent you brought them out!" "O Lord, turn from your anger." The Lord listened to Moses and relented of bringing disaster upon them.

Moses went down the mountain with the stone tablets in his hands.

Joshua met him and said, "There is shouting in the camp!" "The sound of war!" Moses answered him, "It is not the sound of war or victory. It is the sound of partying and singing."

When Moses saw what the people were doing; the golden calf, the singing and dancing: Moses threw down the tablets of stone, with the words God had written, shattering them. He took the golden calf and beat it to dust and threw it into the water, then made the Hebrews to drink it!

Moses demanded of Aaron. "What did these people do to you that you would do such a thing?"

Aaron told him his pre-rehearsed speech. His excuse was an outright lie. "So, I told them, give me your gold and I threw it into the fire and this likeness of a calf came out!"(This kind of reminds me of Adam and Eve's excuses in the Garden of Eden.)

Moses demanded" "Who is on the Lord's side?" "Come stand by me!" All the Levites rallied around Moses. "Now, strap on your swords. Go through out the camp and kill all who will not stand with us, even if it is brother, sister, son or daughter, relative or friend!" This they did and 3000 people perished that day.

"You people have committed a great sin, but now I will go before the Lord for you. Perhaps I can make atonement for your sin."

Moses went before the Lord and pleaded for these people. The Lord replied. "Whoever has sinned against me, his name shall be blotted from my book!" "Now go, lead the people to the place I spoke of, and my angel will go before you. However, when the time comes to punish, I will punish them for their sins."

And the Lord struck the people with a plague, because of the golden calf idol they had made.

The remainder of their journey was pretty checkered. They would promise to believe, and then soon start whining and murmuring Over and over in a vicious unending circle.

When they came to the boarded of Canaan, Moses sent out spies to check out the land. He chose 10 men, besides Joshua and Caleb. Moses and the people waited, camped at the border. When they returned they told of a fabulous land. The things that grew there were better than they could have imagined. They brought back with them a cluster of grapes so large one man could not carry it alone. They hung this cluster on a pole between two of them. No one had ever seen anything like it.

Then Moses asked. "Did you see their people?" "Are the war like?" "What are we to expect?" The ten were fearful and said. "We are no match for them. They are giants!" "We would seem like grasshoppers in their sight!" At this report, the people feared and began crying, "we will all die at their hands!" Joshua and Caleb said. The Lord our God has promised this land to us and he will fight our battles for us!" "Don't you remember how he made a way for us at the Red Sea and all Pharaoh's army perished?" "This land is ours for the taking!"

The people, wailing loudly, "O that we had died in the desert!" "We wish we had never left Egypt!"

Moses replied: "You have spoken it!" "The words of your mouth have called your own doom." "You will not see the land we are promised."

Upon hearing this, they changed their tune. "We will go! We will go!"

"No! We will wander this land until everyone of you has died, and only the ones born after we left Egypt will go in and claim the land."

At the end of 40 years of wandering the desert, they had all died that started out from Egypt, except loyal Joshua and Caleb, and the new generation, that had came back to this border place.

Miriam, and Aaron had died, and Moses was 120 years old. The Lord took Moses and Joshua and went up on Mount Pisgah, where they could view that promised land, across the Jordan. Joshua was commissioned to now lead the people and Moses died there. His eye sight was not dimmed nor his strength spent. He was gathered unto his forefathers and buried there. He had earned his rest.

The people mourned there for the 30 days of mourning, then Joshua with the wisdom of his walk with Moses and his dependence upon God, led the people across the Jordan.

Rahab's Story

T HE HEBREWS WERE FAST APPROACHING! Moving our way as an advancing army of ants! This was the talk of the town! Stories had been drifting in from people all across the Sinai Desert.

The first thing we heard was most disturbing. The Egyptian army of Pharaoh's mighty fighting force, pursued these people, all on foot; with their belongings and animals. They were no match for Pharaoh's army; it would be a slaughter! All the tools of war; against this mass of newly released slaves. They had been worked unmercifully until they were worn and thin, yet tempered by hard work.

Over 400 years of captivity, it had become home and their dream for a better life was just a distant fairy tale.

Their history of a gloriously called people had been forgotten, or now just a tale. They had all heard the story, but it had no relevance to them. Most were so accustomed to this life, it was home. All had large families, and although the work was hard, they had a home life, and multiplied they did!

Along came this man Moses, who claimed God had spoken to him through a burning bush in the Sinai Desert. Some believed him, most didn't. They dismissed him as some kind of a nut case!

yes, we all heard the stories and we feared!

It seems not long after the Hebrews left, Pharaoh had a change of heart; his free labor to build his great empire was gone! If he enslaved his own people, they would rebel and he would go swimming in the Nile in cement boots.

No, he must over-take these escapees. If they killed most of the woman, children and all the old people; re-enslave the able workers, it would slow down their numbers for a long time.

The chase was on! All these stories were coming to us about this caravan who worshipped a powerful God!

The Hebrews were in fear of the fast approaching troops with no visible way of escape. But God had a plan of escape. The God of Moses and Aaron intervened and the entire mass escaped without lifting a finger.

I, Rahab, was a woman of "ill-repute." After the death of my husband and with no sons or daughters, I did what I had to, to stay alive. (Business was thriving.)

All I had was this big house, built into the city wall of Jericho. All the travelers who came here brought me and my girls, gifts and the latest news. We got it first.

The rumors were of such a marvelous account of this Moses and the delivery of this mass crossing the Red Sea, and the defeat of Pharaoh's mighty fighting force. The miracles we were hearing of all that had happened by their God's mighty hand this past 40 years, I could not deny. I became a believer.

If the Egyptians had no power against this God, who was I to resist him? Yes, I believed!

All of these things I had to keep to myself, lest I be accused of being a traitor and executed.

117

Anyway, as they approached, they send two spies ahead to check out how secure we were, and where our weaknesses lie. We knew the Hebrews would do this, yet so far, none could find them.

When they entered Jericho, I welcomed them. I told them I had heard the stories and I had become a believer in their God.

The soldiers of Jericho, seeking and searching for them everywhere, would eventually come to my house too. I already had a plan. I would hide them under shocks of drying flax on my roof. When the city gates were shut for the night, no one could escape without being noticed. The soldiers would be thinking the spies would be trapped within the city.

I made a bargain with the two spies who had come to my house. "I will let you down from my window, in a basket, by a rope. I will tie a scarlet cord to my window, so as the Hebrew will know where I live." "But you must promise me when you invade this city you will spare me, my mother and father, my brothers and sisters."

"Agreed!" "But if you double cross us we will be released from our oath."

Rahab let them down and they fled into the hill country for three day, while the search was on.

I tied the scarlet cord, just as I had told them.

The soldiers of Jericho searched and searched. They even re-searched my home, finding nothing. Even the scarlet cord in the window raised no suspicion. As they took it is mean this was a "house of ill repute."

The Hebrews, in obedience to the Lord's instructions, marched around the city once a day for six days, with their trumpets, before the ark of the Lord. On the seventh day they marched around the city seven times, trumpets sounding before the ark. At the end of that last circle, they gave a mighty shout and the walls fell! Crumbling and tumbling into a mighty heap. Joshua gave the order. "Advance!" "The Lord has given you the city!"

Joshua gave the two spies orders to go out and rescue the prostitute and all her family, that had helped them in a mighty way. "Bring her out and all of her family, and all the things that belong to her."

I was saved, along with my family who were with me, as we had agreed upon. And from that time on I lived among these Hebrews as a believer in the One True God!

This woman with the checkered past was forgiven, restored, and figured prominently in Jesus family tree!

We must never count anyone out. Rahab believed and traded her garments of shame for Jesus garment of righteousness. Don't ever allow anyone or committee to condemn those Jesus has pardoned by his blood. Count them all worthy!

Naomi and Ruth

NAOMI AND HER HUSBAND LEFT Bethlehem with their two sons, to temporarily go to Moab, because of the severe draught in their homeland. They heard the draught had not come upon Moab, so they went.

Moab was a foreign country that had a checkered past with the Israelites, as they were considered unclean to them.

They lived at a time when their land was ruled by a series of Judges. Some good, some not so good, to even very bad. There was not a lot of moral leadership in the country, and everyone did what seemed right in his own eyes.

Times where hard. The well had nearly gone dry, food nearly exhausted and no sign of rain. Things looked pretty bleak. They loved their home and the land, but a choice had to be made, and it seemed Moab it was. They had no thought of living there permanently, just until the rains came again.

We knew we should have no dealings with these people, but our family needed to be cared for. So, like many others we slipped off, with our two sons, to Moab where food was abundant. We arrived there with only the possessions we could carry.

The reports were true, even better than we had hoped. There was plenty in this land. Even vacant land for the taking, where we could cultivate, plant, harvest and call home.

These people held no animosity toward us. They were kind and neighborly, helping us get established.

Yes, we came to like this land. We quickly adapted and thrived; we replaced most of the things we had left behind. Soon this was home and we were settled in.

Our sons grew into manhood, and married two beautiful young Moabite women. We were very fond of them and they were fond of us in return. They were wonderful daughters-in-law. They were o.k. with our worship of Jehovah, the One true God of Israel; even though they had been raised to worship the foreign gods of Moab. They loved us and life was good!

One day it all came crashing down! Elimelech was working in the field and had a heart attack. I was devastated! Filled with grief, that seemed more than I could bear. I still had my sons and their wives: then the second blow came! My two sons were killed in a tragic accident in the marble quarries. Unimaginable sorrow overwhelmed me. I could not think, or make a plan. My two daughters-in-law took good care of me, even in the time of their own grief. They guided me through this dark valley. How grateful I was for them.

When my grief was somewhat abated, I knew I must take stock of my options and I must go home to Bethlehem. With no husband, no children, I had nothing but the land and house of our inheritance there. These were the people of our faith. Perhaps they would take pity and help me.

I could not imagine how I would farm the land or make the repairs the house must need. Surely after 10 years it would be fallen into disrepair. I will cross that bridge when I come to it. "Surely this is the judgment of the Lord for my unfaithfulness." I told myself this damaging lie.

I must return to our land in Bethlehem. I had heard how the Lord had blessed them with an abundance of rain. The crops were bountiful. This land was alive again! The land was allotted Elimelech, by the Lord, as his inheritance to be passed on forever. This land and home would still be mine. Not that I knew how I could make a living, but it was mine. It would be a start and I would take it one day at a time. Oh, how I prayed the people would take pity on me and forgive our absence and carelessness toward our God.

We left our homeland with what little we could carry. I went there so full with family, now I was returning so empty. As I started out my son's wives traveled a way with me. I stopped and told them. "You should return to your mother's house, and find rest there. "May the Lord look kindly upon you. I am old and will never have sons for you to marry." "Go back. You are young and beautiful, inside and out. Find husbands from among your people." "Marry and have the blessings of children." I kissed each one and we all wept. Orpah kissed me goodbye and returned to her family. Ruth would not leave me.

She said, "Let me go with you. I will go wherever you go, and live wherever you live! I will become one with your people and I will worship your God!" "May I be buried there also! The Lord do so unto me and more if I let anything but death separate us!" Well, when I heard that, how could I refuse her? I am blessed to be so loved!

When we arrived in Bethlehem the people saw me and said? "Can this be Naomi?" "Don't call me Naomi any longer. Call me Mara, for the Lord has dealt bitterly with me." "I went out full and I have returned empty." "Yes, we have come home to Bethlehem."

Since no crops had been plant for 10 years, it looked very bad. It was untended and the weeds had overtaken it. The well was filled with debris; the house needed a lot of repair, but I was grateful to have roots here, and a roof over our heads.

I thought of Elimelech's near kinsman, Boaz, who had much land. He had become very wealthy and he was an honorable man. It was the time of harvest when the grain was ripe and ready to cut, thrashed and stored before the winter season.

Ruth told me she wanted to take care of me, so I let her go into the fields to glean behind the harvesters.

Boaz rode out to check on the harvest of his fields and noticed Ruth. "Who is this young woman who gleans in my fields?" He was told; "She is Ruth, a daughter-in-law of Naomi, who has come home with her after Elimelech and her sons died in Moab?" "She is caring for Naomi with such love."

Boaz told his harvesters and gleaners, to let full stalks fall for her to gather. Let her drink from the water supply I bring for you. Let her eat the lunch I supply for you, as one of the workers. Do not allow anyone to mistreat her."

Boaz made himself known to Ruth. He told her to stay close with his crew as they gathered the grain, and when they moved into another of his fields, you go with them until the harvest is finished."

"Why have I found such grace in your eyes?" "Why should you take such notice of me? I am a stranger here?" Ruth asked.

Boaz told her, "It has been told to me how freely you have loved Naomi, the widow of Elimelech and the kindness you have shown her. You have dealt so kindly with her."

"May the Lord bless you, and reward you for your kindness."
"May the Lord cover you with his wings as you have come to
trust in our God." Boaz said.

"Thank you Sir, May I find favor in your sight. Your words
have comforted me."

That day she gleaned a bushel of barley grain. She carried
it home to Naomi gladly. She had also saved some of the bread
given her at lunch, and gave it to Naomi.

"Ruth, in whose field did you find such favor?" Who was
it that blessed you so?" she asked.

"This man's name was Boaz and he spoke most kindly to
me." "He told me to stay with his harvest workers until all the
crops were in." Ruth told her. "O, daughter! Blessed be this
man who has shown you such kindness!" "Blessed be the Lord,
who has not left us forsaken!" "The Lord has blessed us in the
land of the living and he has honored the dead!" "This man is
a one of our near kinsman Redeemer. He would vow to care
for this family, that it would forever benefit our family.""Our
law requires our nearest kinsman to Redeem the family, by
marrying the widow and raising up a son to carry on the family
name and inheritance."

It is good Ruth, to go with his maid servants. Go only to
his fields."

So Ruth did as I had asked of her and worked every day in
Boaz's fields, until the harvest was finished.

I said unto her, "My daughter, I will not rest until I am
sure it is well with you."

I knew the custom of the completion of the harvest. The
wheat, the barely, and of all the grains that were planted. The
grain would be separated from the chaff; and a very large

community celebration was celebrated by all. It is a day to express our joy and thankfulness to our God.

The party is loud with singing, dancing and way too much wine. It gets pretty wild.

Naomi had a plan. "Ruth, bathe; anoint yourself with sweet smelling oil; dress in your most beautiful garment and go down to the celebration."

"After all the men have celebrated and drank too much, they will lie down in their stock pile of freshly harvested grain and sleep soundly until morning."

"Watch to see where Boaz has made his bed; go quietly, lie at his feet and cover yourself with the edge of the robe he is sleeping under."

"I will do all you tell me mother."

Ruth made herself beautiful and went down to the harvest celebration and did all that Naomi had instructed her to do.

About midnight, Boaz awoke with a start and saw this woman at his feet! Startled he said. "Who are you?" Ruth answered him, "I am Ruth, your handmaiden." "Spread your garment over me for you are one of our near kinsman."

(In the custom and law of the Jews, this would be a vow of engagement. A marriage proposal.)

"Blessed are you Ruth, for you have shown me more kindness in the later end than at the beginning, in as much as you have not gone after the young handsome men." "Don't be afraid my daughter. Fear not, for I will do all that you request!" "This entire city knows you are a virtuous woman, and how you have loved and cared for Naomi.""Now it is true there is one kinsman of Elimelech that is closer than I."

"In the morning I will inform him of his duty. If he will perform the obligation of nearest kinsman, let him, but if not, I will do it."

"Lie down until morning." "Rise up early and don't let it be known that a woman has come to the threshing floor."

"Before you go bring me the veil you are wearing; hold it out so I may fill it with grain." He laid it on her shoulders and she came home to me.

Ruth told me all things he had said, and the gift of grain he sent home for us was 6 measures of barley.

"O daughter, sit still until I know how the matter falls, for the man will not rest until he has finished the matter today."

Boaz went to the city gate where all business matters were conducted. Knowing the nearest kinsman would be there, also many others to witness agreements between citizens of that city. Boaz also brought six men of the elders to sit and listen, to better judge.

He said to the kinsman, "Naomi has come to her land, and has no sons to carry on the family inheritance." "You are her husband's nearest kinsman." "I have thought to advertise to you saying, 'purchase it before all these witnesses and elders of our people.'" "If you will redeem it, tell it now, so do it. If not, I will claim the right of kinsman Redeemer. If you desire to do so, you must marry the widow of Naomi's son, Mahlon and raise up sons to his name that the land be forever the family inheritance."

The nearest kinsman said, "I cannot redeem it without jeopardizing my own inheritance: redeem it yourself, for I cannot."

The custom of such legal agreements of that day in Israel; was to have witnesses view and attest to confirm the matter.

A man would take off his shoe and give it to the other party. Witnessed as a testimony, that Boaz had purchased the rights of kinsman Redeemer of the family line of Elimelech and his sons.

All the elders and people said, "We are witnesses." "Lord, make this woman that comes into your house be as Rachel and Leah, who built the house of Israel. Worthy in Ephrath, and famous in Bethlehem. May her descendants be as numerous as those of our ancestor Perez the son of Tamar and Judah." They prayed this blessing over Ruth.

Ruth and Boaz married and the Lord gave them a son. The women of the city said to Naomi. "Bless the Lord who has given you a grandson; he restored your youth, and has taken care of you in your old age. For he is the son of your daughter-in-law you love so much, and has been kinder to you than seven sons."

Naomi took care if that baby, and the women said, "Now, at last Naomi has a son again!"

Ruth and Boaz named him Obed. He was the father of Jesse, who was the father of King David.

Little did I know the Lord had not left me at all! Even in my grief, when I was in such sorrow and emptiness, he gave me such a wonderful daughter as Ruth,and son in Boaz, and a grandchild named Obed, whose descendants would sit upon the throne of Israel. My God had bigger and better plans for me than I could ever have imagined. His way and his thoughts are always bigger and higher than mine.

"Hallelujah! O Lord. How you have blessed me. I am no longer Mara, I am Naomi, blessed of God!"

GIDEON'S FLEECE.....

THIS MORNING IS VERY SMOKY and overcast from all the wildfires to the west. Lord, I know your ways are not my ways and your thoughts are higher than mine. Whatever purpose, I know you are able to do all things. May all mankind see your power and bow before you, acknowledging, you are God!

I cannot know any of these things unless you tell me, but I can imagine it would get the attention of all, if a soaking rain fell only on those areas.

There is precedence for this in the Bible.

Judges 6: 36-40; 7:1-23. The account of Gideon, called to lead his people to do battle against their enemy, who was much greater in strength and number than they. Another impossible situation.

Gideon was surprised he would be chosen. He was a nobody; and he was the least of the least! No self confidence here. He knew his station in life and had probably been reminded of it all his life. "Who do you think you are?" "You live in shanty town, on the wrong side of the tracks." The "good people" looked down upon Gideon and all his family. Who was Gideon to argue?

God called him; and called him "a man of valor!" I can hear Gideon saying, "You talking to me?" He rehearsed all of his poor qualifications and told the Lord; "You must be thinking of someone else."

It took some persuasion, but Gideon still needed some signs. (I have heard God, and most often I put up an argument.)

Gideon: "Lord, if this is really you, tonight while I sleep make the dew fall only on this fleece and the ground all around it dry." In the morning, so it was! (Well this could be just a co-incidence.) So this great man of faith said: "Don't be angry, but I need a little more convincing." "Tonight, may the fleece be dry and all the ground around it be wet." Next morning it was exactly that!

You know us so well! Even though Gideon rose up to take the job, you knew his heart. You know all our hearts. You knew this little army of little strength needed a lot more convincing. So they would have no doubt, you put them through a series of test that made no sense to them. You pared down this army they had put together, to 300, and then divided them into three groups of 100. (When this battle came to pass, all would know is was by the powerful arm of God, and not their own strength.) They followed the directions of the Lord and the mighty army of the Midianites and the Amalekites, fell into a panic and were defeated.

Now, to me, that was a larger feat than a few good showers in those forest fire areas. Ask Gideon... and he would say. "The Lord did it...and the battle was won."

Nothing is too hard for You! It is but a small thing to rain a good soaking rain on those wild fires only! Who could deny this is an act of God?

Well, I know there will always be many who would not admit it, but many will. I would love to see it come to pass and I would say, "I ask the Lord for this! And He delivered!"

NEW TESTAMENT
STORIES

MARY'S MOTHER'S STORY

WE DON'T KNOW HER NAME. We don't know her husband's name. All we do know, she was the mother of Mary, Jesus mother.

I will call her Deborah and her husband James. He must have died previously, as he isn't mentioned in the narrative.

Deborah and James were devoted Jewish parents and raised their children carefully in all the Jewish traditions. How they loved their children. He made a good living and Deborah, a loving mother. Her family; her world! She enjoyed every minute of it.

They celebrated all the festive traditional celebrations with delight. They were saddened to see how few took it seriously. Many had drifted away from their history and the meaning of these holidays. Some would sometimes join in, but it seemed to mean little.... Just a place to go and something to do!

Deborah and James schooled their children in the faith. Not in a heavy handed way, but in love. The children responded in kind. This family lived their faith, at home, and in public with joy and humility.

Now that James had died, Mary was their only child still at home. She was the youngest and she was a delight! She woke up smiling and happy every morning. She had an infectious laugh and like a sponge soaking up the faith of her family. Other siblings had all married and living in their own homes, starting their own families. Deborah enjoyed her young daughter and their time together even more.

I will never forget the morning Mary came to me saying, "Mother, I have had a dream; a vision, I am not sure which. It was disturbing and yet peaceful." "I feel I was completely awake, as it was so very real to me."

"Please hear me out, and stay sitting. This may overwhelm you." "I believe it was so! It is still most vivid, and you know how often things I have dreamed have come to pass."

I sat there almost afraid to breathe or move. Fearing what I was about to hear. How often I had witnessed Mary's dreams come to pass! Sometimes good things; and some not so good; some bad things like, accident or a death in the family. I felt God had given her a gift, preparing us for things to come. My mind was racing!

"Mother, I know you believe Gabriel is God's messenger. He was the one who came to me." "He identified himself and told me God had sent him to speak to me." "Throughout the ages of our history Gabriel has come to deliver God's message to His people."

For a moment I just sat there stunned. Mary sat in silence for a few moments to observe my reaction. She measured her words carefully to see if she should continue. I gathered my courage and said, "Mary, please continue."

"Mother." She waited for another moment as if searching for the right words, "He said, Greetings, you are highly favored." "The Lord is with you." I was so afraid and troubled, wondering what kind of message he might have come to give me. My heart was pounding! I am sure I was very much awake!

Gabriel said. "Do not be afraid, Mary, you have found such favor with God"'

Mary said, "The next sentence startled me even more. More than anything I have ever heard in my life!"

"You will be with child and give birth to a son and you will call his name Jesus."

Deborah's eyes were wide and she could not make a sound. When she had somewhat recovered, she said, "well, that makes sense. You are engaged to be married and I am sure you will have a family. A son will be a blessing." Deborah was trying hard to rationalize this whole situation.

"No mother!" "He went on to say." 'He will be great and he will be called the Son of the Most High.' "The Lord will give him the throne of his ancestor, King David!" "He will reign over the house of Jacob forever." "His kingdom will never end!"

"Mary, how can this be?" My mind was spinning. I thought I would faint!

"Mother, that was exactly my reaction." I said: "How can this be? I am a virgin and have not known a man?" He very calmly explained, "The Holy Spirit will come upon you. " "The power of the Holy Spirit will overshadow you. The Holy One to be born will be called the Son of God."

I was stunned! Then Mary said "and there is more." "He told me our relative Elizabeth, in her old age and far beyond her child bearing years has conceived and she is in her sixth month!"

I gasped at the news! Elizabeth was old! Zachariah was old! Not just a few years old,... but ancient old! I had expected news at any moment they had died of old age! The family had been preparing for that kind of news and arranging a beautiful funeral: Not a baby shower!

"Mary, are you sure he said Elizabeth and Zachariah?" "Yes Mother, I am sure."

Mary continued. "I believed all Gabriel had told me. I believed! I fell down and worshiped, how could I refuse such an honor from my Lord and my God?" "I am the Lord's servant, and I am willing to do whatever he wants." "May everything you have said come to pass." And then the angel, Gabriel, disappeared.

The two of us sat in silence for some time, absorbing all this. We had many things to talk over, such as how to tell Joseph, and what his reaction would be. We came to the conclusion, this is of God, and he will make a way. At that moment Mary said, "I will go visit Elizabeth. She will understand, as she has had such a visit from Gabriel too." We both knew this was the course of action we should follow.

We would tell no one else, especially the women. They would think the worst and the tongues would fly. Our God is faithful and he will make a way, step by step and day by day. They would know soon enough and Joseph needs to know first.

We will simply trust God.

No wonder Mary would confide in her loving, trusting mother. She could be trusted to give her the best council and unconditional love.

There was no amount of shame or disgrace that could be spread about Deborah's daughter that would shake her faith in

Mary. She would not be budged! (It was probably Deborah's idea that Mary first visit Elizabeth.) Elizabeth and Zachariah were godly people. If anyone understood, they would! They believed in dreams and visions. They had recently had their own visitation from Gabriel!

Barren, old Elizabeth was six months pregnant. Old Zachariah had his struggles in believing Gabriel, and he was struck speechless until the child was born.

Mary stayed with them for the 3 remaining months of Elizabeth's pregnancy before returning home.

(What we do know, is... Mary was perhaps the niece or cousin of Elizabeth, on Deborah's side of the family. Elizabeth and Zachariah, were of the line of Abijah. The priestly line could come only from the Aaronic lineage. Priest could only marry within their lineage to keep the line pure. So, Elizabeth was of that line too. This priestly heritage came through the line of Abijah, a descendant of Aaron, through one of his two sons. So, Mary's mother's side descended from this line also.)

We also know Joseph was of the kingly line of David

(We all know this wonderful story of Jesus birth, but my story line here is to see it all through Deborah's eyes and thoughts. Then in Bethlehem, through the eyes of the inn-keeper.)

1Peter 2:9-10 we are called a chosen people. (We who have chosen to believe in Jesus.)"But you are a chosen people, a royal priesthood, a holy nation, a people belonging to God, that you may declare the praises of him who called you out of darkness into his wonderful light. Once you were not a people, but now you are the people of God; once you had not received mercy, but now you have received mercy."

Revelation 5:10, "and has called us unto our God, kings and priests."

What? Now the priestly and the kingly line are in one through Jesus! Through his birth it is now possible for us who believe to be kings and priest! Before Jesus, this was not possible. The Priestly line came only through the line of Aaron and the king only through the lineage of King Davis. Jesus fulfilled it all!

None of this was random or accidental. It was the plan of God from the beginning. The shepherds on the hillside; the wise-men from the east; Herod, who ruled over Judea for Rome: The no vacancy sign on the inn in Bethlehem. Jesus birth in the lowest of places: a shelter for the livestock. The lowest of circumstances, was all orchestrated in the beginning. God had a purpose for it all.

When Mary returned from her visit with Elizabeth, it was evident to all, she was pregnant! Gossip swirling about like dust! The women at the well hushed the minute they saw Deborah; Then asking, pumping for information, "and how is Mary?" "She is fine, thank you for asking." There must have been tears shed when Deborah was home, behind her doors. Tears not shed for herself, but to see her lovely daughter slandered and hurt. There is nothing like the love of a mother.

Now, how to tell Joseph!

Joseph story

He heard the gossip! He must go to see Mary, confront her. This was difficult! He loved her and in his wildest imagination he could not believe she had been unfaithful. "I can't believe it!" Rang out over and over in his mind! It tortured him!

What would he say? What would she say? What should he do? Well it had to be faced. "O Lord, may there be a reasonable explanation! Quiet my soul!"

He reached Mary's door, hat in hand, his head hung low in sorrow. He continued to pray, "Lord, put the words in my mouth and faith in my heart!"

He knocked on the door and heard her footsteps approach. It was her...he knew the soft sound of her footsteps. Everything about her was soft and loveable. The door opened slowly. Apprehension was in her eyes.

When Joseph saw Mary and her unmistakable baby-bump, shocked is probably not a strong enough word for it! Speechless and stunned! Not Mary! How could this be? He could see it was true.

In that day and age this was a disgrace, and a man of character would have the option of calling off the engagement and publicly humiliating her, even to allow death by stoning. (The men, egged on by their wives, most likely, would advise Joseph to have her publicly stoned to death. They all agreed, this is the way to go.) But this Joseph could not do. The only option open was to put her away quietly, and have the engagement annulled. His heart was broken.

Yes, it was true! She was with child! She noticed that I noticed and tears slipped down her cheeks. She reached out and took my hand and spoke softly. "Joseph, come in I have something to explain to you. We must talk privately." "Please hear me out without passing judgment." "It is not what you think."

She told him all the details of Gabriel's visit. That this same angel had visited Elizabeth and Zachariah and told them they would have a son in their old age and it has come to pass. She told him how she immediately went there and stayed until just before their baby was born, a son, just as Gabriel had told her.

"You can go there and verify all of this."

This was all so difficult to make sense of...my head was spinning! "Mary, I need to go and have some time to think and do some soul searching." My voice quivered.

"When I return in few days we will think this through and do what we must do." I left!

What more could she say? All she could do was pray. After he had gone she dropped to her knees and prayed and wept. "Lord, I know this is your plan and it will come to pass. I don't know what more to say to Joseph!" "Open his eyes to see the truth!" "I place it all in your hands." "Give me strength Lord, as I face this community; help me hold my head up." "My faith is in you." "Protect mother and my family from this shame I know will be aimed at them, and of course, Joseph too." "It is all in your hands, Lord."

Deborah waited until Mary had fallen asleep. Then, came into her room and held her and rocked her in her arms as she sobbed in her sleep. A sob that breaks a mother's heart. Tears slipped down Deborah's cheeks as she held her precious child.

Joseph's encounter with Gabriel

(But, God had already prepared! Gabriel, Gods messenger angel was sent to Joseph and he was visited in a dream too. Mary had told him of her encounter with Gabriel and he had a difficult time believing that. This was all so over-whelming, he could hardly remember her words.)

Joseph went into the woods to find some solitude and to think. He knew the law. If he were to deny her and expose her as unfaithful, she would be publicly disgraced and humiliated. She could even be stoned to death.

"Lord God Almighty, show me what to do!" "You know all things. You know my heart and that I do not want to hurt her or disgrace her." "Your will be done. Father God."

Joseph was exhausted as he arose from where he was praying. He went home and fell upon his mat and fell asleep.

In the middle of the night a dream / vision, covered him. It was so real! The voice said, "Joseph, son of David, do not be afraid to take Mary as your wife." "What she has told you is true. " "I am Gabriel, the messenger angel of God." "The child she is carrying is from the Holy Spirit." "She will give birth to a son and you are to give him the name Jesus, because he will save his people from their sins."

When Joseph awoke he did as the angel Gabriel had said. He knew this was more than a dream. He too had a visitation. He went quickly to Mary and of course, Deborah, was there with her.

When he had his own visitation, with this same message, he knew it was truly of God.

Joseph told her of the visitation of Gabriel coming to him. All the things he had said would come to pass. What a time of rejoicing we had!

Around the town all the gossip is flying. We must come up with a plan. A plan that will honor God and put all this gossip to rest. We will hold our heads high. Hold our tongues and not quarrel or answer back.

We agreed we would have a quiet marriage ceremony with only our close family, as not to cause a stir in the community. We knew the truth and that was all that counted. This union was so orchestrated by God, we all vowed before God and each other and the witnesses, of our love for each other and our God, this special child we were privileged to raise and nurture. We vowed also that there would be no physical union until after the child was born. Joseph vowed to love him and teach him as his own and give him the name Jesus as Gabriel had instructed.

That wedding was small, but powerful, as the presence to the Hoy Spirit orchestrated it all. The whole of Deborah's living-room where the couple exchanged their vows to each other and God, was bathed it in a Holy Light. There was an aroma of sweet incense filling the room, yet there were no flowers or incense in the house! We all knew the Lord God had prepared this entire ceremony and gave it His blessing.

Mary and Joseph go to Bethlehem

The powers that be, in Rome, had issued a decree that all the head of households were to return to the place of their ancestral line to be counted and taxed, as if we were cattle. To do less would be arrest, imprisonment and possible death. We Jews walked a fine line to be safe in our own country.

Shortly after we were married, I took Mary, our donkey, to carry the few supplies we would need and set out for Bethlehem. Mary's time was near delivery, so this trip wasn't easy for her. She did not complain but exhaustion was registered in her face.

The closer we got to Bethlehem where we were to register, the scene was crowded and out of control, with all the pushing and shoving. I found a safe niche in the wall were I left Mary, the donkey and our few belongings while I jostled with this sea of humanity to find a room for us. I prayed Mary could hang on that long......

The Inn Keeper

"I remember that night well." "O yes! Remembered it well!"

"When Caesar Augustus decreed all the Jews return to their home city for taxation, all complied, but mostly because we understood the consequences. Not only did we hate the Romans for the occupation of the land God had given us, now they had the audacity to demand each family to be counted and taxed, like sheep in the stockyards! Yes, there was nothing to do but comply."

"We had been degraded and disgraced, from a nation whose proud heritage and joyful celebrations at our feasts, our liberty in our God; to submission to a foreign, conquering tyrant, seated on his throne in Rome! Squeezing the life blood from our people!"

"O why hasn't the Almighty, Jehovah, sent the Messiah?" "Overthrow this madman and return us to rule our own country?"

"Yet, in a strange way, because of this law, Bethlehem was bustling. Bursting at the seams, with travelers returning to pay their pole tax; which in turn allowed every inn keeper and store owner to become very wealthy. It was crazy, like a love/ hate relationship! We were no better than the tax collectors hired by the Romans in Jerusalem. Yet we had a certain respectability. We could sympathize with the citizens; and yet each of us could charge all the traffic would allow."

"Inn keepers such as I, that at one time were courteous and highly respected, now charged outrageous prices for deplorable accommodations. We justified our actions because we were overworked; and we were. There were simply more people in Bethlehem than could be properly accommodated. They came in a steady stream. As some moved out there were twice as many vying for the space."

"The night this young man, Joseph, appeared at my door, seeking any kind of accommodations; his wife very near her delivery. They had searched the city for hours looking for a space, to no avail." I told him, "No Vacancy!" "But something about his disappointment and sadness made me a little more compassionate than usual. It wasn't much, but they could take shelter in the barn, " I told him. (At least I offered then that, a bit of shelter from the cold.)

"I suppose the fact my daughter was pregnant and near delivery made me a bit more thoughtful. However her situation was much different; we were well able to see to it she lived quite lavishly, for a citizen of Bethlehem."

"They were grateful and I felt a bit guilty,(I did offer them something.) Of course they still paid a steep price for that shabby barn. Joseph came into my Inn twice that night. Once to secure a room; and once seeking a midwife. I did not help him out on that one either."

"Later, in the middle of the night I did go out to see if his wife had delivered. She looked so young, and I am not sure how she had managed, but they had a beautiful baby boy, wrapped in strips of cloth I assumed to be torn from her garment. The baby and his mother were sleeping on some straw. I had a woolen robe about my shoulders, I spread over them as they slept to keep them warm, exhausted on the straw."

"For a brief moment I was caught up in the excitement of the birth of this baby, and off my greed. It felt good! I stayed and visited with Joseph a bit, finding out a little about them, before returning inside to my comfortable bed."

"I did notice how very bright the moon seemed that night. More brilliant then I had ever remembered. I shrugged it off."

"I was a bit giddy, from all of the excitement of how well I was doing financially, and this baby born in my barn! (I was later to realize the brilliance was the Star the shepherds said they had followed to find this baby.) It all began to add up. This was no normal night. I had been given the opportunity to participate in the grandest event in history and I had failed!"

"Yes, I did offer them my barn. O that I would have offered him my best! But this I did; I came to believe in Him. I was one of the 120 in that upper room as the Disciples waited for the promise of the Father in Jerusalem!"

THE MAGI

THE ACCOUNT OF THE MAGI, following the star that marked the place of Jesus birth, doesn't give us much background on who they were; or what their interest.

We do know they traveled from the East. So my mind began to imagine who they might be.

I think it would be plausible, they were descendants of Jews that went to Babylon as exiles in the time of the prophet Jeremiah.

I can imagine the people of Jerusalem and Judea; they were a rebellious lot! Jeremiah pleaded with them to repent, turn back to their God. He told them if they did not, King Nebuchadnezzar of Babylon would have them overrun, and taken captive to Babylon.

They were not willing to heed God's warning. They had mingled with the peoples around them, mixing the worship of foreign idols and the God of the Jews.

The women told Jeremiah they would not stop baking cakes and pouring out drink offerings to the Queen of Heaven, because when they did the foreign god blessed them and they had plenty. " "It was she who blessed them." They said, "it is with our husband's blessing we do this. They gather the wood and tend the fires to assist us."

Nebuchadnezzar army did come! He did conquer them and carry them off into exile, just as Jeremiah had said.

It seems Nebuchadnezzar was favorably impressed with the intelligence of these Jewish people. He chose 4 of the young men to be schooled in all the learning of the Babylonian empire. He was so impressed he kept them in his service and treated them very well. Daniel, his friends, Hananiah, Mishael, and Azariah, their Jewish names. The king of Babylon renamed them; Daniel, Belteshazzar; Hananiah, Shadrach; Mishael, Mechach; and Azariah, Abdenego. It seems obvious they were impressed with the Jews as a people, as in the Book of Daniel there is no mention of trouble between these four and the king.

The king made Daniel a ruler over all the providences.

After seventy had passed; Daniel, realizing their time of exile was ending, according to the prophesies, was so troubled by the sins of his people, he was praying and repenting, interceding for his nation and seeking the Lord's favor again. The angel Gabriel came to him and told him many things for a much later date, and assured Daniel of God's favor.

It was during Darius and Cyrus kingships that the Jews were allowed to return to their home country. They were so favorably impressed with this people they helped them with goods and protection.

During those seventy years, the people of Judea and Jerusalem must have settled through-out this land, built homes, farmed the land, grew in numbers and had a good life under Daniel's authority as a ruler.

When it came time to return to their own homeland, many were pretty comfortable; settled and did not desire to go home. To a couple of generations this was home.

By the numbers of the returnees, it seems clear, many must have stayed in the East.

This brings us to the Magi that followed the star. Many of the Jewish people that stayed in the east, must have been from all walks of life; including scholars of their faith. Scientist who studied the Scriptures and the signs prophesied in the sacred scrolls. They believed all the signs that pointed to this long awaited King of the Jews. The Anointed One! This group believed the bright star was a sign to find the birth place of the Messiah, God's anointed deliverer.

These travelers stopped in Jerusalem to seek information as to where they would find this new born king.

What it did was trouble Herod! He questioned the Magi as to when the star had appeared. I imagine he also wanted to know how long they had been traveling? How many miles they made in a day? This would give him a good idea how old this boy would be.

This was very troublesome to Herod who ruled over the Jewish occupation of that day. So troublesome, he called in the Jewish leaders of the synagogue of that day, about this awaited King.

Calling these traveling men back into his presence, he told them; "when you find this king, return and tell me, so that I can go and worship him too. (But God warned them in a dream not to do this. After they had found the boy, they went home another way.)

When they found him, Mary, Joseph and the boy, they were living in a home. At this time they were not in the stable, nor was Jesus a baby. They presented him with precious gifts of gold, and Myrrh and Frankincense and worshipped him. They did as they were told in the dream and went home another way.

When Herod realized he had been tricked, he ordered all boy children, 2 years old and under be slain. All these things had been prophesied hundreds of years before.

Joseph was warned in a dream to get up and flee into Egypt, as Herod was ordering all the boys be slain. They obeyed quickly, and stayed in Egypt until they were told Herod was dead and it was safe to return.

There must have been people of Jewish descent scattered in among nearly every nation in that area of the known world. These Magi were the believers who studied the prophets and the signs: they must have been waiting for just such a sign and believed this was that fulfillment! I also noticed they returned home. That country had been home for so many generations, their families must have numbered in the thousands. It was home!

It occurs to me, we are a strange people. We, as believers, study the O.T. and the N.T., claiming to believe it is all so, yet deny that God speaks to us in dreams. I know this is so. I've often heard from Him many times in dreams, but I have had many people argue this does not happen today. From Genesis through Revelation the Bible is filled with dreams and visions. (Acts 2: 17-21: Joel 2:28-32)

NICODEMUS AND JESUS

I MUST TELL THE ACCOUNT JOHN gives in John 1:1-6. These words set the scene for the whole of the New Testament.

It is the story of Jesus birth; his ministry, and his sacrificial death. All the stories I tell are based upon this.

John spelled it out as to Jesus identity. We know of Mary, Joseph and baby Jesus birth in Bethlehem, but its beginning is back much farther; to the beginning in Genesis 1:1-31. (John 1:1-6)

"In the beginning was the Word. (remember all that was, was spoken into being; into existence.) "Through him all things that were made, were made by him. Without him nothing was made. In him was life and that life was the light of men. The light shines in the darkness, but the darkness had not understood it."

Just as that darkness and void was made visible when God spoke light into that dark place.

"Light be!" And it was! This first chapter of the Bible, of God's creation, speaks of all three, that make up the Triune God. They all had a part in this creation, and they still do. God the Father, God the Son, God the Holy Spirit.

(God came into our lives as God the Son. When Jesus was born all three are there, then and still.) John 1:1-6

In explaining this in Luke's Gospel; hear what he says.

Mary was over shadowed by God the Holy Spirit, and Jesus the Son was planted in her womb. He is the Son of God.

John is explaining all this in John 1:12.

"As many as received him, (believed him) to those he gave the right to become the children of God."

This offer is made to all, but we must choose to receive this gift.

V.13, "children born not of natural descent, but born of God." John told all in v.14. "The Word was made flesh and lived among us."

(John and the other Disciples walked with him during those 3 ½ years of his public ministry and could verify all the things they had seen and heard. They were Eye witnesses.)

John went on to state, "we have seen his glory." "He is the Son of God; full of grace and truth."

A Pharisee named Nicodemus came under the cover of darkness to ask Jesus to explain these things to him. He needed to know more of Jesus than the rumors he had heard circulating about him. He knew there was something special about this man and the things he was doing. He could not speak of this to his fellow Pharisees, as they hated and feared him. They were plotting ways to do away with Jesus. To go to visit Jesus in broad daylight would most likely bring about his ex-communication!

(Let's listen to their conversation.)

Nicodemus: "Rabbi, we know that you are a teacher come from God, for no one can do these miracles you do unless God is with you."

Jesus: "I say to you Nicodemus, except a man be born again, he cannot enter the kingdom of God."

This must have been quite a surprise to Nick. After all he was a Rabbi; a ruler of some authority at the synagogue. He was among the "go to people," who made the rules, and saw to it all complied! Now Jesus is telling him he isn't ready?

Nicodemus: "How can a man as old as I, be born again? Can I enter again into to my mothers' womb and be born again?"

He is so confused! He has never heard of such a thing. He cannot picture how this could be, and by now, his own mother had probably dies long ago!

I can imagine Jesus smiling, knowing all that was going on in this man's thoughts.

Jesus: "Nicodemus! Nicodemus! Don't even try to figure all this out naturally. This birth, is a Spiritual birth." "That which is born of the flesh is flesh. That which born of the Spirit, is Spirit."

"Marvel not that you must be born again! You look very confused, my friend."

"Think of it like this."

"When the wind blows, you hear it. You see its energy in the trees and other foliage as it passes by, but you can't actually see the wind." "You cannot actually see where it comes from or where it goes. You see only the direction of the things in its path, as they sway. So it is with the one who has been Spiritually born."

(Nicodemus shook his head and wondered out loud how these things could be?)

Jesus: "You are a teacher of the Law: A rabbi of Israel; how can you not know these things?"

"Truly I speak the truth to you. I speak of what we know and have seen, such as the wind the trees. If you don't understand the natural things, how can you hope to understand the heavenly things?"

"You and your fellows in the synagogue won't receive my witness. If you won't receive the properties of the wind and don't believe; how will you received these things you have come to ask me about?"

"No man has ascended up to heaven but the one who came down to you. The Son of God."

"Just as Moses lifted up the bronze snake on a pole in the wilderness; the Son of Man must be lifted up, that everyone that will raise his eyes and believe in Him, shall have eternal life. (Jesus knew Nicodemus understood that story of Moses and the Hebrews as they crossed the wilderness. (After all, he is a well schooled Pharisee; a student of the Torah.)

It was to Nicodemus Jesus first spoke these most repeated words in all Christendom. John 3:16 "For God so loved the world that he gave his only begotten Son, that whoever believes in him should not perish but have everlasting life."

Many have speculated about Nicodemus over the centuries, but it is my belief Nicodemus became a believer right then; on the spot! He came seeking Jesus; wanting to be taught by Jesus. (Even though it was a very dangerous thing to do.)

All through the Gospel's, Nicodemus is the one to voice objecting to the things this body of the Pharisees are plotting, to trap and kill Jesus. He very well could have been Jesus inside man to keep him informed of all they were up to.

It was Nicodemus and Joseph of Arimathea who boldly went to ask for the body of Jesus to give him an honorable burial. They carried Jesus body to a new tomb in the garden.

He must have been expelled from the office of a Pharisee and his place in the synagogue. He was most likely disowned of his Jewish heritage.

I suspect he joined himself to the group of believers who waited in that upper room for the promise of the Father on the day of Pentecost. We have no further record of him, but he must have taken the message of Jesus to the far flung regions of the known world. After all it was to Nicodemus Jesus explained the Spiritual birth. He was the first one to hear God's plan of Salvation, directly from Jesus. He was the first who loved Jesus enough to risk all to give him a proper burial. John records it all in the account he wrote.

I can imagine he might join Paul's missionary journeys, as they were both ex-Pharisees!

There were probably others that joined, but these are the only two recorded in the Bible.

PETER, MY HERO

O F ALL THE PEOPLE I'VE met in the pages of the Bible, I identify more closely with Peter. It would be nice if I could say, Mary the mother of Jesus, Esther, Ruth, Mary or Martha. Maybe even Sarah or Rachael. All would seem so much more honorable. I guess that just isn't in my DNA.

Peter was quick to believe, and quick to speak; sometimes loudly and brashly. I've been known to speak up when others are afraid too, (or have been smart enough to keep quiet.) I kept talking when I should have been listening.

Jesus must have seen something special in Peter, as he was in the inner circle; Peter, James and John! Maybe that was so he could keep an eye on him and stop him when he was a bit over the top!

I am learning there is a wonderful lesson in "Jesus opened not his mouth." Many times our best answer is no answer at all. As many times those listening don't want to hear, but if they do, it is only to find something to accuse us of. "Jesus knew their hearts and their motives."

It had been a long difficult day....emotional day. We got the news; Herod had John the Baptist beheaded! I don't have to tell you, all of us were frightened! That is, all but Jesus. His concern was for Elizabeth and Zachariah, John's parents, and Jesus Mother Mary. Mary and Elizabeth were related by blood. He and John were blood relatives.

At this news, Jesus withdrew to a solitary place, as he often did to pray; to commune with his Father. For Jesus to find that time and place was difficult. Everyone wanted a piece of him. All clamoring to hear him...to be healed...to be delivered! Crowds scrambled from all the surrounding area, even across Lake Galilee. It was a difficult journey for most, but they were desperate for their Messiah. Even though they probably didn't term it that way, it was what they all sought. God would somehow deliver them from the Roman occupation. Seeing them, he had compassion on them; set aside his own need to rest and commune with his Father. Jesus was calm.

Jesus went down the mountain to teach them. He had been speaking and teaching and it was getting on into evening. The disciples noticed the situation and wanted Jesus to end this meeting and send the people away. They must be famished.

I can imagine the disciples put their heads together and formed a plan. They appointed a spokesperson, and I think it was most likely Peter, as he spoke most often, even when he had his foot in his mouth. Peter would remind Jesus of the situation and get him to dismiss this crowd.

Peter: "Jesus, look at this big crowd." "We are a long way from any village, and it is almost dark. Send the people away to get food and rest before night falls and they riot." (I doubt they were ready to riot, but it sounded impressive.)

Jesus: "They don't need to go away. YOU feed them."

Peter: "What! Jesus, don't you see the size of this crowd? There must be 15000 people here! All we have is a little boy's

lunch of 5 small barley loaves and a few fish, and they are tiny."
"You can't be serious!"

Jesus: "Bring those loaves and fish to me."(A little smile must have curved up at the corners of his mouth and a twinkle in his eye.)

Jesus: "Peter, have the disciples direct this crowd to sit down in the grass in groups of fifty, in an orderly fashion." "Group them so you can see they all get fed. My Father loves order."

Jesus, looking up into heaven, speaking to his Father, said; "we offer up these to you, Father; these people, and these loaves and fishes. Do as you will, that all may witness and bring you glory and honor. I know that you hear me. My desire is they know you hear me. You hear and love and you answer! Thank You for this love feast!"

The disciples had the people sit, not having a clue as to what Jesus was up too. Jesus had told them, "All those who have empty baskets, pass them forward." The disciples must have felt pretty foolish, since they had nothing to put into them! But Jesus told us to gather them, "so, OK. I don't get it, but OK!"

Scenario #1.

He blessed the bread crumbs and fish fragments scattered among the 12 baskets! He handed them to the twelve disciples, and motioned with his hand to start passing them among the crowd.

Such fear and trembling gripped the 12. (When that basket, now empty, was passed to the second person they would riot! Maybe a lynching! Mob mentality would break out.)

Scenario #2.

Jesus asked the disciples to bring him the empty baskets and ....He took the baskets in one hand and as he passed to the other hand, and to the disciple waiting there, it was filled to overflowing! The baskets were passed in an orderly fashion to the expectant people. As each basket was emptied, it was taken back to Jesus and he refilled it. Just by touching it! On and on until each person was satisfied. Completely satisfied!

The most astounded ones of all were the disciples! They had no idea how Jesus was doing this. (There is nothing in the narrative that says the people were surprised.) They must have come with expectation or they would not have followed Jesus there. They heard and saw Jesus and they believed! Believed there was no limit to what Jesus could do for them.

The thing I love most about the story is this. Those who came hungry were satisfied, and Jesus made sure his beloved followers, the ones he had chosen, were provided for. There were 12 baskets full of left-over's. One for each of them!

Did you catch that? Even though they were probably hungry and tired, they served others first; Jesus made sure they were rewarded with great bounty.

Yes, they were blessed with more than enough!! When we follow Jesus; do what he asks, no matter how foolish it seems, he takes care of his own. Often in ways we cannot imagine! Praise God!

Immediately, Jesus made his disciples get into the boat and head out, to go on ahead, to the other side of the lake. He dismissed the crowd, and went to the place where he could commune with God, as he did when he first arrived. (His plan for himself, he interrupted for the others.) He did not abandoned the plan, only delayed it. He was now alone with his Father, a good place to be!

I can imagine they spoke of the mission he must lead. Probably spoke about John and the part he had played in it all.

They spoke of Elizabeth and Zachariah, his mother Mary; all the grieving family. Speaking of the reunion they would have again someday.

Part 2

Jesus went up on the mountain that night to pray, he told his men to start out across the Sea of Galilee without him. They were probably feeling pretty good. They had 12 baskets of goodies for the trip.

They did as Jesus said, but there suddenly came such a storm. High wind and huge waves, so bad they feared for their lives. All of a sudden the "happy meals" were of no comfort.

They worked hard, but hardly made progress. (If you've ever been out on a large body of water with no more than muscle power, you know this is a serious situation.)

During the fourth watch, (between 3: and 6: am) Jesus went out walking to them on the water, and they were terrified. Thinking they were seeing a ghost! They cried out in fear! But Jesus immediately said to them: "take courage. It is I." "Don't be afraid."

"Lord if it is you," Peter replied, "tell me to come to you." Jesus said, "Come!"

I notice impetuous Peter was the only one who spoke up and stepped out. The other 11 disciples in the boat neither had the faith nor the get up and go to step out. They didn't even give Peter a word of encouragement.

Can't you see them? Those 22 eye balls peering over the side, like the seven dwarves in Snow White. Wide eyed in fear and surprise when they first saw her.

I can hear them whispering. "There he goes again. Making a fool of himself!" "Why in the world did Jesus call him to be one of us anyway?" "Surely he will drown, and then how are we going to explain that?" "Couldn't Jesus just let Peter drown, and who would know the difference?" "Or maybe we could just say, "Peter was so afraid when he thought he had seen a ghost he jumped overboard and drown, and we never saw him again." "Then when we get to shore we can hold a memorial service. Toss a few flowers into the lake; shed a few tears and say what a great guy he was and move on." "Yes we are better off without him!"

Isn't that what we do most of the time? We don't make a choice until we see how it goes, then jump on the bandwagon? If Peter had drown, they would say, "what a fool! We all know you cannot walk on water?"

If Peter had successfully walked all the way to Jesus, they may have all jumped out saying, "We believed immediately!" Who would have thought the other members of the inner circle would not have stepped out too?

Moving on with our story: Peter did step out, and started walking on the water toward Jesus. He was fine as long as his eyes were on Jesus. I am sure the voice of the accuser was whispering, "Peter don't you hear those howling winds and see those gigantic waves?" "Your friends have more sense than you do." "They stayed in the boat." "Who do you think you are?" That is always what the enemy does. He does not want us to trust Jesus. He reminds us we are flesh and blood. But guess what? Jesus told us plainly our rebirth is Spiritual! (Remember Jesus conversation with Nicodemus? John 3:1-8)

Peter took his eyes off Jesus and considered the natural and he became afraid; lost his faith for the moment and began to sink.

We seem to focus on Peter becoming afraid and beginning to sink, but the best part of the story is Peter's reaction. Who did he call on when he was afraid? Matthew 14:30, says, "But when he saw the wind, he was afraid and beginning to sink, cried out, "Lord, save me!"

Jesus immediately reached out his hand and caught him. Notice, he answered that prayer and saved him! Then he said, "You of little faith.""Why did you doubt?" This was a teaching moment. He was illustrating that doubt and fear interrupt faith.

Most of the teaching I have heard about this story focuses on the rebuke, directed at Peter. I can almost feel the embarrassment and hurt, in front of all those others. When I read it as it is written, it does not come off that way. Jesus saved him and told him what the problem was. It was a lesson to all 12, and all of us; down to this day.

John 10:10 "The thief comes only to steal, kill and destroy; I have come that you may have life and that more abundantly."

That thief would try to steal our faith, Kill our joy and destroy our Salvation. He has nothing to give, all his promises are lies.

The other 11 in the boat were probably saying. "I am glad I didn't get out of the boat and make a fool of myself." I wonder if these men relived this many years later in their memory and thoughts? Now thinking, "I should have believed Jesus and stepped out of the boat, knowing he would have never let me drown. He said, "I will never leave you or forsake you."

Again it was Peter who stepped out, took the risk at what seemed like a failure and rebuke. Some of the others may have been thinking, "See what happens when you take risks, speak up or jump out too quickly?"

The night Jesus was betrayed, Peter, James, and John and all accompanied Jesus to the Garden. Jesus told them all to watch and pray. Three times Jesus came back to find them sleeping. The other 8 must have been nearby, as it says at the arrest they all fled. We know Judas was there; he was with the mob. We know Peter was there as he drew a sword and cut of the right ear of Malchus, the servant of the high priest. Luke 22: 50-51, tells us that Jesus touched his ear and healed him! (I've always wondered if Malchus became a follower. It seems he would. He came into that garden with the army and the accusers who arrested Jesus, and went home healed by Jesus touch of mercy.) He must have gotten the message of "Jesus loves and seeking to save," more easily than most.

It seems Peter and John followed Jesus at a distance into the courtyard: where the mock trial took place. That was where Peter denied knowing Jesus 3 times, as Jesus had prophesied, after their last meal together.

It also said John may have had some connection to the Jews who held this court, as he gained entrance inside. Since it says these disciples followed at a distance, one guiding the mob that left 8 unaccounted for. They must have been the runners! (Accounting for the facts, Judas was with the them and he was the one who identified Jesus, and he ran trying to undo the awful thing he had done, giving back the thirty pieces of silver, then in remorse hanged himself.

All these accounts tell me all of these were just ordinary people such and we, with our same weaknesses and faults. It is good to know these are the people Jesus chose to walk with him. They were not powerful, learned or faultless people. Just plain folks! No wonder we can have hope!

This same, often blundering Peter, who denies Jesus out of fear for his own life, hid behind locked doors with the rest. After his encounter with the Holy Spirit on the day of Pentecost; he was so forever changed that at his first sermon, 3000 people believed, were saved, and baptized! Now that is some kind of a revival meeting!

He became the leader of that pack of Apostles who changed all the known world, reaching us still today.

These men, who ran in fear of death, now ran boldly to carry Jesus message, joyously, even though they faced death daily.

Biblical and historical accounts of those Apostles actions tell us they were so emboldened, and fearless, they risk their lives unto death. Gladly unto death!

Peter speaks up, only now without fear, planting the early church and it is said he was crucified upside-down in Rome for his faith.

John at an old age was sent to the penal colony on the Island of Patmos, at hard labor in the marble mines. It was a death sentence! But there God revealed to John the Book of Revelation. He survived and was pardoned by the incoming Caesar Nerva, who came to power after the assassination of Domitian.

Jesus knew what he was doing when he chose those most unlikely prospects. That is why we can believe he chooses and uses the likes of us! I am glad, aren't you?

This account of Jesus, ever near and presence!

It was this story in Matthew 14: 22-31 (walking on the water) that grabbed my heart when I got the colon cancer

163

diagnosis. I kept my eyes on Jesus. Each time the enemy would come against me, trying to dislodge my gaze from Jesus, I would say..."No, I have my eyes on Jesus!" When some medical procedure, or treatment would threaten, I would smile and say..."Lord, I am out of the boat here. I have my eyes on you!" And you never disappointed me! It became our little secret. The enemy could not break it.

We walked and talked all the way through the chemo, radiation, surgery, and more chemo. The dehydration, and the diarrhea; and over all those IV's.

When undergoing and the radiation therapy, they would situate me on that lead table so the radiation was directed at the four dots marking the spot. (You didn't know I had 4 little tattoo's, did you?) After getting placed just so, everyone would leave the room and a man behind a heavily glassed in room would talk to me. A little red light would come on and a buzzing sound that lasted only a few seconds. All four positions; the same process. As each little red light came on, I would smile and say, "Lord, I am out of the boat here!"

What did I learn? I know that, I know, that I know; without a doubt, Jesus will never leave me or forsake me! I've said this and believed this, confessed this many times over the years. But.... It is when you walk it out, that you know, that you know, that you know! I would not exchange this for all the tea in China!

That hope is still just as valid today and near to us as it was when Peter stepped out of that boat!

Mary and Martha...Part 1

WHO ARE THESE PEOPLE? WHY did Jesus consider them such good friends?

God created each and every one of us as he willed. Not accidental or by mistake. He has a plan for each of us; a plan for good and not evil, to give us a future and a hope. Jeremiah 29:11. No matter what version you read, it means the same.

Why is it so difficult for us to believe that it is for all? He loves us all the same.

It is about choice! We all have a choice to make: Life or death...the choice is ours. Life, to the plan we are created for, or the choice to go our own way. "No Lord! I will do it myself." That is the prodigal attitude in all of us. Of our own choosing!

The Lord is so good, and his love so deep, we are all given moments to repent. But then again, that is a choice.

ALL THIS TO TELL YOU THE STORY OF MARY, MARTHA AND LAZARUS.

I am attempting to fill in the gaps and put some flesh and blood on their humanity. They were real people, each with their own history of how they became so endeared to Jesus. The Bible does not go into detail. We just know that he was welcomed to drop in anytime with this large group of men. I don't see these disciples as all that refined! In fact the picture painted of them is quite the opposite, but Jesus loved and chose them. That was good enough.

Lazarus, Mary and Martha lived just outside of Jerusalem a few miles. Jesus was welcomed here as he traveled in that area. He was safe there from the powers in Jerusalem that opposed him. He stopped there often to rest and be refreshed in a way only friends can do.

This place was a safe haven to Jesus and his followers. To stay in Jerusalem was a dangerous place. That would give him many opportunities to stop to visit these trusted friends. He must have come that way often.

This family at Bethany loved him and he loved them. They all had their issues. They knew Jesus had forgiven and restored them, and they were grateful.

1. What was Lazarus issue? I believe he was healed that was healed of leprosy. He lived in the right place. Often when Jesus healed he said, "your sins are forgiven." People were healed!

The Bible tells us this disease of Leprosy was such a dreaded disease, they were shunned by all people. They Lived outside any contact with others and cried out day and night of their condition, to warn anyone who might come into accidental contact with them. It ate away at their flesh. A rotting, walking, corpse; until death consumed them. No touch of human compassion, at least until Jesus came by. It was probably on one of Jesus many trips down that road to Jerusalem, Jesus encountered Lazarus. Lazarus knew the truth of this healing. At the touch of this love he became a forever friend of Jesus. There was great love in this family and don't you know how glad Mary and Martha welcomed Lazarus home healed! (I can imagine, during the time of his abandonment they left food and clean garment out for him, giving what comfort to him they could.

2. One of the stories recorded in Scripture, tells us Simon, a Pharisee, gave a banquet and invited Jesus. We don't know what they were celebrating, but this woman came in and anointed Jesus with very expensive perfume. (We also have another account of this sister of Lazarus named Mary had also done this. I believe this is one and the same.)

The Pharisees among them whispered. "If this man Jesus was a prophet, he would know what kind of woman this is, and he would not allow her to touch him." (It must have been common knowledge of her reputation.) Jesus told them to leave her alone, "she had done this to anoint me for my burial and this will be an everlasting memorial to her." Awe! That was her moment to publicly give testimony for the things she had been forgiven, and this anointing, in great love and humility was hers!

3. That leaves Martha's story. Jesus could have come in the night with his band of believers. Did this family say, "go sleep in the barn and we'll talk about it in the morning? We need our sleep!" No! They got up and received this special group of men gladly. They were provided water so they could wash up form their dusty travels. I can see

Martha, coming with an arm load of bathrobes, saying. "Here put these on and give me your dusty garment and I will have them all clean for you by morning." She took those clothes away and probably called one of her servants to see that this was properly done.

Returning to the room, she said; "come let's have a snack and visit, and tell us all the things you've been up to since we saw you last." To Martha it was a snack, to that group it was a feast!

Martha never did anything half-way. "We are so glad you are here." "Thanks for bringing your friends with you. We are all one in you, Jesus."

The next morning she set out a continental breakfast. Martha must have stayed up all night. Now she began the preparations for a banquet that would have rivaled those of Herod and Pilate's palaces. All fit for a king, and that is who they knew Jesus to be!

Lazarus sent out word to his neighbors, "Jesus is here! We are having a Meet and Greet. Come visit him and eat with us!" Knowing what a spread Martha could lay out, none refused. Martha was known for her skills at planning and following through.

She was a multi-task specialist! She sat on every committee in town. Toast-mistress, of the toast mistresses of Bethany. School board and election board chairman. And the local Sunday School superintendent. This was the "gitter-done lady." She had no rivals in that place. She was a delegator; and knew how to delegate. She prepared a well thought-out shopping list; demanding only the best of all the produces and cheeses would do. She sent off her trusted maids to see to it.

The bread was already in the oven and things in that kitchen buzzed! Even Martha's anger! This was to be the meal of all meals and she was busting her buttons, and there sat her sister Mary at Jesus feet, taking notes on her sheep skin scroll!

"What is it with this girl?" "I think I liked her better before she was forgiven." "At least then she was of some help!" "Now she is worthless, can't get a thing out of her when Jesus is around." (Those who are forgiven the most, love the most.) The more she thought about it, the more steamed she got! Jesus was her friend too, and after all, it was for him she was doing all this work! It was work, but Jesus was worth it.

The bread baked, the fruits and veggies were at the peak of freshness. The cheese trays were beautifully set out on the finest serving platters. The barbequed lamb was done to perfection. This was truly a masterpiece of a dinner! Time was running out and Mary's help was needed now!

Martha moved into the great room where Jesus was teaching. All of the guest sat spell-bound at Jesus words. Their attention was riveted on him. Martha took a deep breath, gathered her composure, to ask Jesus if she could speak with him. (She knew Jesus well enough to know she could not speak in anger, or if any inflection in her voice was accusatory.) She must sound respectful!

"Jesus, will you ask Mary to come into the kitchen. I need her help. She has left me to do all the work."

I can see Jesus smile. As sweetly as Martha said it, he was not fooled.

"Martha. Martha, you are so busy and concerned over so many things. Mary has chosen the best and I will not deny her." "I know how hard you have worked and how perfect you desire your hospitality to be." "Don't you remember how the 5000 were fed? The 3000? And they were all filled and with more than enough?" "I would rather you come sit by me peacefully and listen." "I love you all!" "I desire your heart."

What Martha needed was a deliverance from, her own pride and efficiency. It is often credited to our goodness, but sometimes it is the hardest to recognize as something we need deliverance from.

She had shelves full of award and recognitions; trophies of her accomplishments. Service can become a god to us. It is a talent from God that can easily become pride and self-righteousness. It is saying, "I don't need any help, I am using my God given talent."

The voice of Jesus was explaining all these things to her, in his loving, compassionate way. Now she gets it! Yes, she too needs forgiveness and restoration. The love of Jesus compelled her to take an honest look at her motives and repent!

With tears glistening in her eyes, she moved close to Mary, sat down and gave a loving squeeze to her sister's shoulder. Yes, they all had received the forgiveness and cleansing they needed. Sitting as Jesus feet does that to the heart. There is no better place to be.

MARY AND MARTHA...PART 2

THIS BRINGS US TO THE second story in the lives of Jesus beloved friends of Bethany. Still as always, Jesus go to place when he was traveling through.

Lazarus was sick unto death! Mary and Martha knew it! All the citizens of Bethany knew it! The girls sent word by messengers to Jesus in Jerusalem. "Come quickly. Your dear friend Lazarus is near death!"

Problem being; this great crowd that mobbed Jesus! This gathering was massive. Jesus was tightly bound in on all sides. A wall of humanity! All wanted to touch him with their needs. His fame had spread like wild fire. "Jesus is the healer!" "He cares for us common people!" "God has not abandoned his people!" "Jesus is among us!" All made every effort to touch him.

The messengers arrived, gave Jesus the message and the crowd immediately closed ranks around him again. He had acknowledged he heard them with a nod.

Wasting no time, we called out; "Jesus your friend is near death!" "Come quickly!"

They headed back home, knowing to come back without Jesus; Martha would give them a good tongue lashing. The old

Martha would have fired them on the spot. The old Martha would have said, "you cannot do anything right!" "Not even delivering a simple message!"

This Martha is a changed woman. She will forgive us. Slowly we headed for home. One always wondered, will the old Martha or the new greet us?

Stories flew! The whole of Jerusalem was buzzing. A man blind from birth had just been healed! Never had such a thing been heard of! This was taking place as the men came to give them the message about Lazarus. Again Jesus delayed!

Jesus healed a man blind since birth. It was astounding!

Jesus didn't ask him if he wanted to be healed. (He knew he did!) This man had never seen a sunrise or a sunset; Even his own reflection. Nor even the face of his mother and father; the beauty of a mountain or a lake.

It seems people of that day assigned blame to such an illness, as to their sin or the sin of the parents. If you have ever heard this; Jesus puts that to rest. "Neither this man or his parents sinned, but this happened so that the work of God might be displayed in his life."

Jesus made a paste of mud and spit, rubbed it in the man's eyes and told him; "go wash in the pool of Siloam." He did and his sight was restored!

This caused quite a stir. The neighbors that had known him from birth were puzzled. "Could this be him? Hasn't he begged all his life to exist?" Some said "yes; some said no, it can't be." Never has such a thing happened. Even though the man said, "yes, it is I. I am that man!" He told them the story over and over. Yet they still didn't believe and asked again.

The city was in an uproar, so they brought him to the religious authority of the day. The Pharisees! Since it was a

Sabbath, they were enraged. The law was very clear. No work was to be done on the Sabbath!

"This man is not from God! He does not keep the Sabbath!"

Some said, "If Jesus is a sinner, how can he do such miracles?" Great arguments divided the people.

The Pharisees turned to the man, "What have you to say?" "It was your eyes he opened."

The man replied. "He is a prophet." (This did nothing to endear him to the Pharisees.)

The Jews still did not believe and sent for his parents.

This saddens me more than anything in the story. This man's parents were so afraid of their own position in the religious life at the synagogue, they would not speak up for their son. They replied, "He is of age. Ask him!"

They sent for the man again to question him. "Give the glory to God. We know this man is a sinner."

(Don't you just love this guy?) He is so convinced of Jesus authority over even this blindness from birth, he stood fearless before these people; the whole of society these people feared so much. He answered them with confidence. "Whether he is a sinner or not, I do not know. One thing I do know. Once I was blind, but now I see!"

Again they asked him, probably trying to trip him up. "What did he do to open your eyes?"

"I have already told you and you did not listen. Why, do you want to become his disciple too?"

In great anger they hurled insults at him. "You are one of his disciples! We are disciples of Moses! We know Moses heard from God! As for this fellow, we don't even know where he is from!"

This former blind man gives one of the greatest speeches of faith recorded. "Now this is remarkable! You don't know where he comes from, yet he opened my eyes. We know that God does not listen to sinners. He listens to the godly men who do his will. Nobody has ever heard of opening the eyes of a man born blind. If this man were not from God, he could do nothing!"

Their answer to him? "You were steeped in sin from birth; how dare you lecture us!" and they threw them out of the synagogue.

Some time it is a good thing to get thrown out!

Of course all this drew greater crowds to follow Jesus and get his touch. The press was greater and greater, as these miracles grew.

The woman healed of 12 years of hemorrhaging.

"Did you hear about my neighbor? She spent all she had on doctors and quacks and she is none the better. Even worse! This hemorrhage has plagued her for 12 years. I don't know how she has lasted this long."

"All of us neighbors have done all we can to help her." "The ladies in the neighborhood cook meals and carry over to her. We clean her house; do her laundry. Our husbands and sons split the wood, mow the lawn and try to keep the house from falling into disrepair. We do all we know to do."

"Well I just heard she had somehow gotten through that mob!" "I don't know how she did it. Just getting out of bed has been near impossible for her. Well, somehow she did it! She managed to get just close enough to Jesus, from where she fell, to stretch out her hand and touch the hem of Jesus garment! She was healed instantly! That hemorrhaging completely stopped! She knew it instantly! She felt that life giving flow. Her color spread until she had the most beautiful healthy glow! Jesus knew it instantly too! How, I don't know? It was only the lightest brush against his hem."

Jesus said; "who touched me?"

Peter spoke up. "Lord how can you say, "who touched me, in the press of this crowd?" "We are all getting jostled about."

"I felt the power of life giving flow go from me." Jesus replied.

"Anna, my neighbor, bowed at Jesus feet, sobbing for joy. Giving thanks and praises to God, said, "Lord it was I!" "I knew my only hope was to get to you and I would be healed!" Jesus smiled, took her by the hand and raised her to her feet. Hugged her close and said, "Daughter, your faith has healed you."

"Now this wasn't done in a corner. Hundreds saw it. So many of us knew how long and how debilitated she had been all these years. We saw the color of life arising! Not a one of us will ever forget it!" "We were there! We saw and we believed!" "Surely God is among us!"

Jesus smiled…He seemed to smile at everything and anything, as if nothing was impossible. Then he turned away and continued laying his hands on the people.

Peter seeing this entire exchange said, "Lazarus is dying!" "Lord, don't you understand, they said Lazarus is dying!"

Jesus finally, most casually said, "Lazarus only sleeps."

"Lord, that is a good thing. If he sleeps he will get well."

Jesus again smiled at Peter. "You don't understand, it is the sleep of death." "This is for the glory of God." "I am glad we were not there, so you my friend, will believe." "Truly believe!" Then Jesus and the 12 lingered there a few days more.

Abruptly, Jesus said, "Let us be going."

No one dared say a word.

As they arrived on the outskirts of Bethany, they stopped in the place of shade, where they often met with the family.

Guess who was the first one to find them? Martha! Mary was still in the house surrounded by mourners. (As Jesus had said, Lazarus was indeed already dead.) The mourning process fully engaged, as was the custom. Family, friends and hired mourners. This was the proper protocol of that day, so the mourning could continue night and day for a specified time. This was a respected family in that area and this mourning would be an elaborate affair.

When Martha reached Jesus she said. "Jesus, had you come when you were sent for, my brother would have lived!" "I know even now, God will give you whatever you ask."

"Martha, your brother will rise again."

"Yes, yes, I know that!" "He will rise in the resurrection at the last day." (She is thinking; he is not listening!)

"Martha. Martha! I am the resurrection and the life. He who believes in me will live and not die!" "Do you believe this?"

"Yes Lord, I believe you are the Messiah! The Son of God! You are the Lamb of God who came to take away the sin of the world!"

Martha got up quickly and ran to get Mary.

"Mary, the teacher is here! He is asking for you."

When Mary heard this she ran from the house to meet Jesus.

When she arrived she said the same thing as Martha. "Jesus had you come when we sent for you, Lazarus would not be dead!" "Why didn't you hurry? You could have healed him."

When Jesus saw their sorrow, and heard the wail of the mourners, he sighed, and was deeply moved. "Where have you laid him?"

"Come and see Lord."

Jesus wept.

Why are we surprised to hear this? "Jesus wept!" We should be more surprised if he didn't weep. This same Jesus was so grieved by the sorrow of our sinful condition he chose to die for us. The prodigal son's Father saw him as he turned and started for home; ran toward him with outstretched arms, tears streaming down his cheeks. How God must have wept when Adam refused to repent. We are created in God's image, with all the same emotions. God gathers our tears in a bottle. Tears are precious in his sight! The Holy Spirit can be grieved. When I am so wounded I grieve; I cry! Of course Jesus wept! He knows all about grief.

The watching mourners said; "see how much Jesus loved his friend?" "Could he who opened the eyes of the blind not have healed him?" They were puzzled.

Jesus, Mary and Martha, and all those who followed, came to the cave where Lazarus was entombed.

Jesus called out loudly, "remove the stone from the entrance!"

"But Lord," Martha cried out, "He has been dead four days! In this heat, the odor will be unbearable!"

"Did I not tell you, if you believed in me you would see the glory of God?"

The keepers of the tombs rolled the stone away.

Jesus looked heavenward and prayed loud enough for all too hear, "Father, I thank you that you hear me. I know you always hear me, but I am saying all this for the benefit of all these standing here, that they believe you sent me."

"Lazarus! Come out!" He spoke directly to Lazarus, the dead man! Four days dead! Guess what? Lazarus came out! His hands and feet bound with strips of linen and with a cloth about his face.

"Take away the grave clothes and set him free!" Jesus told the grave keepers.

John 11:4-46 speaks of the reaction of those who saw and heard all that was done.

Some believed on Jesus. Some ran to tell the Pharisees and other enemies of Jesus.

Isn't that something? Some saw this mighty miracle and ran to report to the very men who were plotting to kill Jesus.

Some rejoicing and some were angry traitors. Choices, choices, choices!

Of course the Pharisees called an emergency meeting of the Sanhedrin. The vote? "We must kill this man, and have Lazarus assassinated!"

Lazarus was now on their hit list also. "We cannot have him running all over the country telling this story!" "That would be devastating." "The media will be all over this." They will follow him, calling press conferences to quote everything he says. Radio and television talk shows! Book deals offered; we have to stop this, now!"

"The probing reporters will ask; "What was heaven like Lazarus? Did you see Moses and Elijah? Were the colors and the sounds beautiful? Are there any sick or lame there?" "No, this thing has to be discredited and stopped now! "Our power would be lost!"

Another dinner party would be given. Not with a guest speaker, but to hear first hand Lazarus testimony. Those who came saw and heard all this family had experienced of Jesus. They all had stories to tell. Jesus had touched their lives many times.

Martha served the guest with a whole new attitude! Mary helped with the serving with singing and great joy!

Don't you know this family was a part of the group of 120 waiting in that upper room for that Pentecost experience! This wasn't a quiet prayer meeting! There was music and dancing. They were each sharing their personal testimonies. Who could sit quietly? This was a celebration. (Paul, later said; "everything must be done decently and in order."(1Cor.14:40), So Martha organized that. Her gift!

WOMAN CAUGHT IN ADULTERY

J ESUS HAD GONE TO JERUSALEM and as usual, the Pharisees used every opportunity to set a trap for him. To accuse him of some sin, that would bring a death sentence against him. Jesus had a bulls-eye on his back! In their eyes the most hated enemy! An enemy of their religious practices that dated back many generations.

This system of faith and social law dated back to Exodus, When God gave the pattern /plan to Moses in the desert of Sinai. The Tent of Meeting, all the utensils, the Priesthood and their functions. God's perfect form of government; perfect law, that blessed everyone.

The Priest was to always be from the line of Aaron, Moses brother. This was the all encompassing rule over all the affairs of God's chosen people.

As they wandered through the wilderness; after 400 years in slavery In Egypt, slavery had become such a fact of existence it was the normal. All they had ever known, and a bit reluctant to leave. The farther they got into the wilderness the more reluctant they got! This reluctance turned to outright anger and rebellion. They rejected Moses,

Aaron, and Miriam, the very family God chose to deliver them out.

Just as today-people can be led like sheep by a few manipulators and discontents. Murmuring picks up speed and size, as surely as a snowball rolling down the hill. Over the many years this perfect government would be eroded into their own human will, now ruled with the iron hand of their religion. Truth forgotten and a lie believed.

Adam and Eve listened to the serpent; became suspicious of God's motives. Planted an evil thought and nurture it, it too picked up speed until truth was soon forgotten. When lies had robbed them of their innocence and oneness with God, they blamed each other, the deceiver, and even God.

The perfect plan, the perfect dwelling place, traded for a bite of juicy fruit was a sham as was Esau trading away his birthright for a bowl of stew.

Seems ever since, man has used his gift of choice to pick and choose what suits himself, his greed now has rule over him.

Over the 1500 years or so between Moses, to the prophesy of the Messiah, to Jesus coming, their waiting became forgetfulness. Most were busy carving out lives and cares of the day.

The perfect system of law for the "church" and their civil law became corrupted and self serving. The Pharisees, the Priest, the Sanhedrin; all the leaders of the synagogue, ruled with complete control and without mercy.

Did they believe a Messiah was coming? Yes! But not as they had expected! The one they looked for would be of their power structure and a military man. A man who would overthrow this Roman occupation! Until then, they would have this workable relationship with Rome, and so far it was a pretty good arrangement. We would appease them and they would live and let live. Peace for both!

Had this Jesus been the one, God would have told them! They, after all they were the chosen people! This Jesus must be stopped, at any cost! The power, their peace with Rome depended on it. He was leading people stray!

(When Jesus was crucified, they believed they were doing God a favor.)

People who may have desired to see Jesus need be careful. The Pharisees and leaders of the synagogue kept their eye on anyone who might be suspect of spending time with Jesus. They would be excommunicated from the faith. Shunned, or found guilty of a capital offense.

This Jesus must be kept under control lest civil unrest would bring the ire of Rome down and their quiet existence would be met with the fierce anger of the Emperor in Rome.

They could not risk the Emperor being challenged. (The powers that be at the synagogue played this card to the max.)

Now we have the back ground for this story of the woman caught in adultery.

We don't know her name or what brought her to this pace in life. So, her personal story is purely fictional. Everyone has a story as to why life came to be what it was. She was no different. Let us name her Bethany.

Bethany was born in the community of Bethany, to a loving husband and wife. So named for the place they called home. An only child and most adored. She was beautiful inside and out. They had no relatives, but this daughter made their life complete and good.

Sadly both died very close together leaving Bethany orphaned. Since she was nearly grown and engaged to a man who loved her dearly, life went on. How happy they had been. After two year her precious husband was tragically killed in an accident. She felt her world had come to an end.

In that time, a woman left without family, husband or children; and no resources was in dire straits. She went to Jerusalem where she thought she might find work.

She had no one to seek shelter with. No money, only the sadness and despair that filled her heart. After three days of not eating, she was desperate. The only thing left to do was beg. It was humiliating, but that was the only choice she could make.

The only one who took pity on her was a well dressed man, about the age of her late husband. He stopped and asked her, "what are you doing here?" "You are a beautiful young woman." "Come with me and we will have a fine dinner and see if we can't figure out something." The only kind words she had heard. (He took her to his home, and it was as beautiful as the clothes he wore. (He called a servant girl and told her to take Bethany to a room where she could bathe and change from her dusty clothes.)

When she came downstairs she looked even more beautiful than he had envisioned. She was stunning! Hair as black and shinning as a raven's wing, with eyes to match. Her skin so flawless and olive toned with roses in her cheeks. WOW! But he was the perfect gentlemen and he treated her with respect. They had a lovely dinner, the likes of which as she had never had! She felt she must be dreaming! Only a few hours ago she despaired of life. No hope she could see, and now being treated as a queen, at the home of a handsome, wealthy man.

After dinner he asked if she would consider living here until she could find her way forward. How could she turn that down? Surely his motives were pure as he had not done one thing suspect the entire evening.

Well, now we know what led her to this place.

This kind man allowed her to become so indebted to him, she willingly became his lover. Nearly a year went by and he asked her if she would do anything for him? She really did feel she would.

"I have a very influential man coming to town tomorrow. He is a quality person of some wealth and I would like you to entertain him while he visits Jerusalem. He has connections and to show him a lovely time would be of great importance to my business." It all sounded so innocent and it was important to him. How could I refuse?

Well, I am sure you have it figured out by now; my friend was a very high end pimp! I had traded my dignity and good name right into his hands. I could see it plainly. I could play this high stakes game, or be thrown back out into the streets.

I went along with it. After all I was well cared for. I had luxury surrounding and beautiful clothes. I lacked nothing.

I was in his "employ" for another year and I could see the hand writing on the wall. I had but a few years left and I would begin to fade and be of no use to him, and he would replace me with someone younger that would innocently fall into the trap I had.

I began to form a plan.

I had stored away some of the money from the clients, and from my clothing allowance. The men who came to me were all wealthy and important people. I was loyal and would not name names or seek revenge, so they trusted me.

I did all that was in my power to keep my looks and clothing immaculate. A woman that looked dignified.

Sooner than I had anticipated, I was told I must move on. I had been replaced. I made no fuss, and because of my loyalty, he gave me a very generous severance package.

I had enough money to buy a very nice house close to the Jews Temple and not all that far from Rome's palace. Ideal! I had already gotten acquainted with many important people from both camps.

Jesus had gone unto the Mount of Olives, most likely to pray, as he often did. Whether he prayed all night or very early in the morning we do not know, but according to John 9:1, it says, "Jesus went unto the Mount of Olives. And early in the morning he came again to the temple, and all the people came to him and he sat down, and taught them."

Notice the location of her encounter with Jesus. The Pharisees and assorted accusers were at hand. Seems Jesus went right up to their door to teach and the people were coming to him to be taught.

Highly indignant, these self righteous men dragged this women, who lived so close to their synagogue where Jesus sat teaching. They knew he would be there and they knew this woman would be home and with a man. Could it have been a set-up? One of their own?

("You make an appointment with her, and we will come at just the right time and arrest her. Don't worry, we will let you go and it will be anonymous. No one will know who her client was.")

This was an early morning raid and lynch mob! All in close proximity to the halls of their religion and power. She was known to these people. Why hadn't they cleared out her kind long ago, if it was the adultery they were so upset about? NO! It was a trap they purposely set for Jesus. More than likely some of this group was her clients too. She was recognizable and so were they!

On this particular morning, amidst Jesus teaching session, the men from the local synagogue, dragged her roughly into the center of this place and threw her down and made their accusations. "This woman was caught in the very act of adultery!"(How could this be? If she was caught in the act, there must have been an adulterer there also.) Hummmm.

They said the Jesus: "Now Moses in the law commanded saying, such a one should be stoned to death." "What do you say?" "Is this true?"

Some of it was truth, but a half truth…therefore a lie.

Lev. 20:10" And the man that commits adultery with another man wife, even he that commits adultery with his neighbor's wife. The adulterer and the adulteress shall be put to death."

All this time Jesus is kneeling and writing in the dust with his finger, as if not even listening.

We have all heard much speculation as to what he wrote, but no one knows for sure. My thoughts lead me to the O.T. Scripture. "He knew the hearts and thoughts of man that were continually evil." Gen. 6:5 (These Pharisees were students of Moses and they knew what it meant!)

Jesus raised up, looked at each accuser. He knew all things. His eye paused on each face. Not with a look of hate or revenge, but with sorrow. He had come to save them, but they would not! Jesus allowed his recent memory to recall how he had wept as he looked out over Jerusalem. "O Jerusalem, Jerusalem! You who have killed the prophets and stoned those sent to you! How often I would have gathered your children together as a hen gathers her chicks under her wings, but you would not allow it." "Your house will be left desolate."

Yes, Jesus loved those he came to save. O what sorrow! He came to seek and save! The lost sheep! The lost coin! The lost son!" But they would not choose him. Because of their self-righteousness they were blind. There were like watching a loved, wayward child going down the road to destruction, refusing to listen. Heart-break! Jesus felt the stab of pain for these.

So when they continued asking him. Demanding a response, he said still searching their eyes and hearts. "He who is without sin among you, let him cast the first stone."

Without looking back at them, his stooped and continued to write in the sand. This message could well have been, "He who has been forgiven much, loves the most."

Each of the accusers, their conscience convicting them, went out one by one, from the oldest to the youngest. Letting their stones slip easily into the soft sand. Thud..Thud...Thud; until they were all gone. Jesus raised up and saw only the woman was left. "Woman where are your accusers? Does no man condemn you?"

Bethany said, "No man Lord."

"Neither do I condemn you. Go and sin no more."

Did I hear that right? Did he really say; "neither do I condemn you?" "How can this be?" "Everyone is Jerusalem know my reputation.""I am a high priced call-girl." She knew it! They knew it! Certainly all the women in Jerusalem knew it! Surely Jesus knew it too!

When Jesus looked into her eyes he said, "neither do I condemn you, go and sin no more." Those eyes said you are forgiven. Your slate has been wiped clean. You have great value, a precious daughter of the kingdom." I knew I was forgiven and cleansed. I knew, that I knew that I knew!

I arose from the dust. Brushed of the dirt from my torn dress and softly said in a barely audible voice, "Thank-you." I went home, closed and locked my door. "Never again would this be a revolving door!" I did not know what I would do, but this I did know. I have to find out all I can about this Jesus. Who he is and why he cared for me. The first time since coming to Jerusalem I felt clean and had worth.

It was a long night. I could not easily fall sleep. I kept trying to imagine my future, whatever that might be. I knew whatever, it would be honorable. When I drifted off to sleep it was so peaceful and most refreshing. And I had a plan! I would go out to find Jesus or people who knew him and find out all about this one who forgives so much!

My first thought. "Go back to the beginning. Go home and there you will start over." Where did that come from? I don't know, but I will follow! I will go to Bethany, my name sake. The land of my family, and the happiest moments with my husband. I will return and start afresh. A new beginning!

I saved money and had some valuable treasures in my Jerusalem home. I can sell them and buy a small home in Bethany.

I was so excited of all the possibilities for a new life, it all rushed through my thoughts! I could hardly wait to get started!

Bethany being only a short distance from Jerusalem, didn't take all that long.

The beginning of a fresh start!

By now hunger and thirst was a necessity. A good place to start was at the community well. I remember this place. The coldest most refreshing water ever! It was known far and wide. The reason the city was built here. The reason people were reluctant to leave. Of course the problem now at hand, I had no bucket or ladle.

A servant girl had come to draw water for her mistress houschold use. She looked pleasant enough, so I took the chance and asked; "When you are finished, would you be so kind as to draw a cup of cold water for me?"

The young lady said; "of course!" "My mistress of the house would be very un- happy and disappointed with me if I refused you."

At this she offered me the most refreshing water I could have hoped for.

The girl arose, finished her task at hand, turned to me, saying: "Please accompany me home and meet my lady of the house." "I know she would love to meet you."

We started for her home and talked all the way as if we had known each other forever. I told her my history and my plan, and she told me how she came to be a servant girl and how blessed she was to be in such an employ. I was so starved for the companionship of other women and didn't even realize it until now. There was a time when talking all things over with my mother was such a strength and wisdom to me. O how I missed her!

Since I had told her I was looking for a small house and a fresh start, she said; "I know if there is any property for sale my Martha, whom I serve will know of it."

Hannah and I were on a first name basis and I helped her with carrying water home. As we approached this home, I could not believe my eyes. It was beautiful and near being palatial! How could I have been led here? My heart was pounding. This is the best day of my life! I heard within me say. "No it is the beginning of your new life in me!" Where did that come from? What could that possibly mean? Then, I immediately knew, I was home!

As we neared the back door we were met by a tall, handsome women: Wisdom and efficiency written all over her. Yet, joy, love and wisdom evident in all she said and did. "Hannah, who have we here?"

"Martha, This is Bethany." "We met at the well."

"Nice to meet you Bethany." "I am sure you already know this community bears your name." "You must have been named by some loving parents who loved this place." "You are most welcome here."

"Thank you so much; Hannah has told me I would be welcomed."" Hannah has been so kind." "You must be very glad to have her as a member of your household."

"Yes, I surely do! She is most loved and trusted." "Come in, come in; lunch is nearly ready." "Come eat with us and let us get acquainted."

My, did they all have stories to tell! They knew this Jesus I was seeking and not only was he all I had imagined, he was their best friend! Surely I have been led here! This is no happenstance!

Their stories were amazing! They told me how Jesus had delivered them all of the things they needed delivery from. How Lazarus their brother had been delivered from leprosy, and later from the grave after four days of death! They told how often he came with his men and stayed with them and received their hospitality. All the blessings he had brought them!

This family, the best people I could have ever found to tell me about Jesus.

Hannah had her Jesus story too. It was wonderful. The entire household, O so close to Jesus! I had no doubt I was led here. All of this could not have just been random. Never in a million years!

Martha: "How rude of us. We could go on and on about Jesus, but we want to know about you." "It is evident you have been guided here."

I could hardly believe my good fortune. I blurted out my story. From the beginning, to this moment. From being orphaned and widowed and all alone.

How I was enticed into prostitution. All of it. How I was at fault to let it go on this long. How I had been shoved aside for a younger more beautiful women. How I struck out on my own to carve out a life and livelihood with the richest and most prominent men of power and prestige in Jerusalem. How the Pharisees and leaders of the local synagogue dragged me and threw me at the feet of this man Jesus and demanded I be stoned to death for my sin! Jesus challenged them of their own sin and how they stole away. How he so lovingly forgave me and said. "Neither do I condemn you. Go and sin mo more." How I felt so clean and freed! Forever set free!

I came here determined to find out who this Jesus was, and why he would love and forgive me? He led me to you! By now, tears of joy and gratitude streaming down my face, dripping from my chin. As I raised my eyes to Hannah and Martha, they were weeping too! How I knew beyond a doubt I was led here at this very moment to meet the people who could tell me all the things I needed to know.

Martha:. "You must go back to Jerusalem, gather your things and return to us as quickly as possible." "I will send servants with you and carts to carry your belongings. You will return to live with us." "God will show you what you must do."

When Martha spoke; things happened! We immediately headed off to Jerusalem.

We packed up my things, and I had decided to leave some of the valuable pieces behind as they would take up so much room on the carts.

I begin to think about how to sell the house. "I guess I will leave that for another day and another trip", I thought. While contemplating these things a very wealthy looking man enter the house. "Excuse me." "I see you are moving, would you be interested in selling your home?"

"Well, yes but I have not gone so far as to find it's worth and put in on the market."

He said, "I will make you and offer."

I was so taken back by the suddenness of it all I was tongue tied! This offer was astounding.

He said, "If this is to low, maybe we can settle on a higher number."

I recovered my sense and said. "No, that offer is most generous; I am a bit confused."

"Are you thinking of selling all these beautiful pieces?" I said, " I am."

He said, "I will add a generous amount and buy them too."

I nodded in agreement and he pulled out the largest amount of money I had ever seen, and believe me I thought I had seen big money. He paid me in cash for it all. I wrote him a bill of sale and it was done!

I turned to look at the servants Martha had sent with me and they were as astounded and wide eyed as I! I kept saying to myself. "This must be a dream." "This can't be happening." But it was!

We arrived in Bethany trying to relate all that had happened to Martha and Hannah. I was talking so fast, I am surprised they understood a thing I said. The servants, who had traveled to help me, still in such a state of shock, all they could do was nod in astonishment.

As I related these things, through my sobbing with joy, I again head this voice audibly, yet I knew it was in my spirit. "Beloved daughter." "You were lost and now you have come home!"

"I know, that I know, that I know that I know! Jesus will never leave me or forsake me!"

When I recovered, somewhat, I asked Martha. "What shall I do with all this sudden wealth?"

Martha: "Put it in a saving pot. You have received it for a purpose." "When there is need in Jesus ministry you will have funds available to support it." "There will be need to assist other believers."

I asked her: "What do you do with yours?" She said, "we do the same."

"O Martha you are so wise; can I put mine with yours that it may be administered with wisdom?" "I am so very new at this and I have so much to learn, and I am sure I will, as you teach me."

Although I was so new, I just had to kneel and pray in my stumbling way," O Jesus, may generation after generation be blessed by these means you have blessed me with." "Continue to lead me and bless me with the things you would have me do.""I am a grateful child, an orphan that is no longer an orphan. Now I am home, never to be orphaned again"

"This family so blessed me. Taught me, daily I was learning how wonderful You are. Jesus. I can't say enough. I am so earnestly awaiting your returning by this way so I may worship at your feet!"

Martha; "Bethany, you don't have to wait. He sees you and hears you. He knows your every thought of gratefulness and love for all he has done for you." "You can speak to him at all times, just as you are doing now."" Continue to commune with Jesus! He is always with you! Hallelujah! I give praise to God for bringing you to us!"

"My faith soars!"

Bethany

THE RICH YOUNG MAN

THE ACCOUNT OF THE RICH young man who came to Jesus to inquire what more must he do to inherit eternal life. Obviously a good Jewish man that kept all the strict laws; dietary and customs of their faith, but feeling he had a lack of the understand of eternity; a lack of teaching.

(Since we know nothing more about him, I will put imagination to work again.)

We know this was a real person and not a parable. Recorded in Matthew and Mark of the encounter with Jesus and the disciples as they traveled. (This was a teaching moment for the man and the disciples.)

Since he was a rich Jewish man, we will ascribe his heritage as from one of our best examples; Joseph, who was sold into slavery by his jealous brothers. Wrongly accused and sent to an Egyptian prison. A dungeon of despair. Seems only a Godly intervention could arrange a release from this place.

This gifted Jew was a man of faith. Honorable, even in these circumstances, gained favor in the prison; later in Pharaoh's court. I have chosen to name this rich young man of our story Joshua Joseph Ben Judah

According to Strong's concordance.

Joshua...Jehovah saves

Joseph...Let Him add

Ben Judah...Son of Judah. One of the seven names of Israel

Joseph an honored name, then I followed the line through his son Ephraim, as that name means...God has caused me to be fruitful.

Joseph's first born son was Manasseh, as his name means, "separation from his people." A name that would tie him to his past and here we must move forward.

I believe throughout world history all have known the Jewish people to have astuteness for business and invention as no others.

No doubt about it! And Joseph had a double measure.

I am a firm believer that our names have meanings that follow us all of our lives.

Be careful what you name your children! A girl named Delilah or Jezebel will be marked for life, unless we confess our error and rename the child.

Our daughter's middle name is joy and she has lived up to that! My husband's nick name, given to him at birth, stuck. Barney! And that he was. The Biblical equivalent of Barnabas, means one who assists, helps. Son of Abba, host, a friend, a teacher. Consoler. That he did! He felt compelled! "You need anything done? Call Barney!"

To my surprise, the name Barabbas was a form of that name! That was before I gave him a redemption story. (Everyone I have asked, said they were taught the same as I. He was a bad guy!) This should not surprise us. Our Father is in the business of restoring broken lives and saving them! The thief next to

Jesus on the cross, saved at his final minutes! The Roman soldier who drove the nails into Jesus; forgiven in Jesus final breaths. After all, he came to seek and to save!

Before I was aware of these things concerning the names; we called our two boys "Dennis the Menace and Dangerous Dan." Praise God they out grew it! It was spoken in fun; but ignorance is no excuse.

Joseph heard from God in dreams. This is recorded throughout history. O.T. and N.T.

Joseph knew very well these dreams came from God. Even though the dreams he had of his brother's got him into trouble in the first place.

Now we have the background. On with the story!

Joshua Joseph Ben Judah; so named, to reflect the family hope and heritage.

Every generation desires their children exceed all their accomplishments. This man was no exception. He held great promise and was most likely told often of his abilities. He came from a long line of very successful businessmen in Jerusalem. He grew up in the family business. Paid attention and learned the family trade. Special attention given to quality and customer service, never taking them for granted.

He researched constantly, how to do it better and in a more efficient way without sacrificing quality.

He was in the clothing business and he hired only the best seamstresses and tailors. He paid them well, and hired them as much for their character as for their craft.

Joshua far exceeded his father and his grandfathers in the industry and at an earlier age. They were all so very proud of him.

One of his major innovations that had direct bearing on this success, was to divide his business into separate, stand alone arms.

One business made the sturdy working man's clothing. For the carpenters, stonemasons, fishermen's line and etc.

Another, for the common class, of house wives and children. Clothing that was not only useful, and sturdy, but still colorful and attractive. Garments that could take the hard use and many washings. Clothing that lasted, but on the other hand could be easily mended. This line was so successful, as he realized how hard working these people were and every coin spent must be spent well. Every woman deserved to work hard yet look her best for her husband and family. Joshua valued these people. This was his busiest area of business.

Another division was the elaborate garments for the leaders of the synagogue. The Pharisees, the Priest, the Levites, all the workers that kept the most sacred of places in Jewish society; clothed in the finest garments. Crafted from the very best linen.

All made to the specifications and qualifications of the Torah. God had given all these special instructions to Moses in the wilderness. However, it did seem these modern day officials wanted something a little more elaborate. There were special garments for sacrificing the animal. There were garments for the ones that burned all the offerings and gifts. There were bakers, and oh so many different kinds of work that went on there. All made perfectly, of the finest quality of workmanship for each duty. Since this was his faith, he was pleased to offer such services.

Service offered not only for the synagogues and Temple in Jerusalem, but all the surrounding land of Judea.

The next arm catered to the Roman captors who ruled over them. This was a very lucrative business. The Roman governors, kings, all their household servants; the slaves that kept this whole place running. All the wives, children, mistress; all must be dressed fit for a king. Even The Emperor in Rome would occasionally order. All these people wanted the best and they were delighted to pay the top end price.

There was even a division, within the division to make, mend and repair the Roman soldiers clothing. The Emperor wanted no one in the world to out-class his army!

These people of Rome must far out class the subjects they ruled!

One of his inventions to serve all these, was something he called. "sales calls." He had teams that had regularly appointed routs to call on their customers. They would take orders, even special orders. Review any complaints, and if there were some, address them quickly, to the stores satisfaction. It made for great relationships. They always carried swatches of the newest and latest fabrics from around the world.

Joshua took pride in his Jewish roots, his honesty, and the workmanship of every division of his business.

All in all, Joshua was a very rich man, and in his travels about, began hearing more and more about this Rabbi Jesus, and his disciples. Joshua was intrigued. Seemed the whole citizenry was speaking of these things.

Joshua kept all the commandments, gave liberally to his synagogue. All the things good Jewish men did, yet he felt there was something missing. Something he couldn't quite put his finger on. There was some talk of eternity, but there also seemed to be much disagreement among the authorities. The teaching was sketchy at best.

What he was hearing seemed to be everywhere he went. This man, Jesus, spoke to great crowds about it. He spoke there was a "here after" beyond this life. His message was unlike anything anyone had ever heard.

Joshua being a student of all he did; wanted to search this out. Maybe this was that missing piece within him.

He was taught the ancient history, The Torah, The Ten Commandments.

All the laws and statutes, they all seemed in agreement among them, but "eternity," a place after death stirred arguments among the authorities. Some said "yes" and some said "no." The arguments on both sides were pretty shaky. Not wanting to find himself with any disagreements with his customers, he just didn't go there. All his wondering he would keep to himself. It was better for business that way.

The more he heard being discussed among his customers and workers the more intrigued he became, secretly of course. Soon his intrigue gave way to a serious doubt about his own faith. Maybe this was the thing. Maybe this was the thing he was seeking to fill that lack he felt. He knew something very important was missing from his life.

All this he cataloged in his mind for further study.

Since he was traveling for business, he would no doubt run into this man, and talk to him privately. It would seems like an ordinary sale calls and above suspicion. The Jews were used to him calling on all people, even the Romans. After all, his business brought much money into their coffers.

Actually he was looking for the Teacher, and word had it this man was a Rabbi! Still he must take care as to be seen doing business and not seeking to become a disciple.

Jesus wasn't hard to find! Crowds gathered to listen and ask questions. The healings, the importance of forgiveness, and this new subject, "the kingdom of God is at hand! The kingdom of Heaven! The kingdom to come! The kingdom of heaven, coming to earth!" This was the perfect opening to start a discussion with Jesus.

Seems a session was just ending and the people were starting to disperse. It was getting into the evening. Joshua approached him just as the last person was departing.

Joshua approached carefully. He even had his fabric samples in his hand. (He might have fooled the crowd, but Jesus could read his heart.) Jesus knew he was a true seeker of truth, and he loved him.

The gospel of Mark place this encounter as Jesus was purposely going to Jerusalem where he would be arrested, tried and crucified. Still he had time to hear this young man and speak with him.

Joshua sort of blew his cover when he knelt before Jesus and ask, "Good Master, what must I do too inherit eternal life?" Can't you just see him tossing all those fabric samples to the wind? If any of his synagogue acquaintances were close by, he had a lot of explaining to do! (I doubt he would be excommunicated, or whatever the Jewish term for that was. He was a rules keeper and kept them all perfectly. His tithing on that kind of income would not be easily replaced.)

He had gotten right to the point. No small talk, no chit-chat. "What must I do to inherit eternal life?"

Can't you just see Jesus smiling? "Why do you call me good?" "There is only one good and that is God!" "You know the Ten Commandments. shall not steal, lie, defraud anyone. You do not commit adultery. You Honor your father and mother. Keep the Sabbath. All the things God commanded Moses."

Joshua answered. "Yes Lord, all these things I have kept since my youth."

(Jesus knowing how wealthy he was, even though the man had not mentioned it). "There is still one thing you lack." "Go, sell all you have and give it to the poor and come follow me. Then you will have treasures in Heaven."

At this, Joshua walked away grieved, as this was the one thing he could not do. It was his identity, the whole heritage of generations of his ancestors. It was honorable, and he certainly was not stingy with his blessings. It made no sense! Why would Jesus ask such a thing of him?

Did you catch it? This man had unwittingly made his wealth his god: His pride in his ability to gather wealth. And he didn't even know it!

Jesus knew it and he was grieved to see this precious soul walk away. He looked around at his wide eyed disciples and said. "How difficult it is for a rich man to enter into the kingdom of Heaven." "It is easier for a camel to go through the eye of the needle, than for a rich man to enter the kingdom of Heaven." "For with men it is impossible. But with God all things are possible."

At this the disciples were astonished and most likely it was Peter who cried out what they were all thinking. "Lord, we have left all things to follow you. What are we to expect? We have left family, our homes, our fishing boats and business; all the riggings. Will we have anything here or is our reward only in eternity?"

At this Jesus smiled as he looked into the eyes of each one and said. "I tell you the truth, anyone who has left any of these things for the gospel's sake will receive a hundred fold now, with persecution. In our eternal lives, we will have everything. That is our destination. What we have here will pale in comparison."

Peter. "How will we know if we are making a god out of things in this life?"

Jesus. "Peter, anything you could not give up for me and this good news we carry, that is your god."

Jesus, taught on wealth and the dangers there of. It is repeated three times in scripture. A warning repeated three times is, "This is important! Listen up!"

Here, Matthew 6:19-20 and 1 Tim. 6:10.

After Joshua Ben Judah left Jesus presence, he went to a solitary place to pray and think. "Why had Jesus asked me to give up all my hard earned fortune?"

"I had noble and honorable motives. I have always acknowledged all I have, God has given me. I've used my God given talents and intelligence to His glory."

"God has placed all this in me, as he did my name sake Joseph!"

"All Jewish society has benefited from this business. I've been fair in all my dealings with customers and employees. I've been fair with every social class; not given any undo advantage to any over the working poor; from the least to the greatest."

"I've honored my faith, my family and my ancestors."

"Lord, what more do you want of me?"

Hours of seeking and searching; struggling with conscience and tears, he fell asleep. It was a deep sleep but with troubling dreams. He was seeing himself more deeply than he had ever gone. Never had he felt the need for such self examination. It seemed the struggling with conscience had no end.

Then, a small light, as one at the end of a long, long tunnel, slowly began to grow, larger and in intensity. "I felt transfixed! It seemed I was dreaming, yet I saw it so clearly as if I was wide awake."

"When my vision became clear, I recognized Him! It was Jesus!"

Dressed in a long white robe with a golden sash about his middle! There was a brilliant aurora surrounding his head. That smile, those eyes; that love and understanding that shined forth. I'd know him anywhere! Just as I did when I had spoken with him!"

He motioned for me to sit with him and he spoke to me as a friend. I knew I had nothing to fear.

He said to me; "I know you are an honorable man in all your dealings"

"But you have allowed pride to creep into your life. You already know this, don't you?"

"I asked you to give up the only god that stood between you and eternity."

"A choice is set before you." "A choice everyone must make."

"Do you love me more than anything?" "Even life it's self?" "Keep an open mind as you listen to me. I have something to tell you. After you have heard me out, then you must think on it and make a choice."

"Some of these things every Jewish man knows because he has studied the Torah, and practiced his faith, faithfully.""This is Truth and it is God's Word."

"Do you know all this and believe it Joshua?" "I know you do."

"Joshua, you know God; He is triune. All three, in perfect oneness, from the beginning."

"In the beginning, the earth was without form and void and darkness covered the face of the deep. The Spirit of God moved upon the face of the deep."

"The whole of creation was spoken into existence. In their order, and perfectness. First the light; my light. Nothing can exist without light. Each of creation in its order! When all was ready; God said 'Let us create man in our image.' In the likeness of God, man was created. It was so and God's creation was complete, and the sixth day was ended. The seventh was a day or rest. Established forever to honor God. And all of nature, man and beast were to rest. It is an act of worship."

"Joshua, I Am! I Am! God the Father, God the Son, and God the Holy Spirit. I was always. All things created have my fingerprint on them!"

"In the beginning was the Word, and the Word was with God, and the Word was God. All things that were made, were made by Him, and without Him was nothing made."

"In Him was life, and that life was the light of men. The light shinned in the darkness and the darkness comprehended it not."

"Joshua, I am He!" "I came to the Jewish people; my chosen people but they would not receive me." So I turned my grace to the Gentiles and all who would receive me; to as many as would believe, I gave power to become the children of God."

"One of your own, Nicodemus, came to me by night seeking, just as you, to learn of this. Because of centuries of poor teaching he was confused. He was taught to look for the Messiah, but they were looking for a warrior who would free them from Rome, not the One to ready them for the Kingdom of God! I told him words of life that will ring out through the ages, and by them millions will come into the kingdom!"

"For God so loved this world and all who live here, that He sent his only Son, that whoever believed him would never perish but have everlasting life."

"Nicodemus was slow to get it, but he did! He is a secret follower, an agent on the inside. Misunderstood, chided, but the final act he will do for me, and he will. A very brave thing to do; as it will expose him to the Jews, and the consequences; could be expulsion at the least, or death at the other end of the scale."

"Joseph of Arimathea and Nicodemus will one day boldly ask for my body to give me a proper Jewish burial. A very bold thing to do!"

Jesus related to me the entire story! It was clear he wanted me to make the right choice! I sat mesmerized as Jesus spoke the gospel message to me! As he spoke my understanding was opened and I saw it! We Jews were looking for the Messiah and Jesus came. He came to give us that eternal life I was so fervently seeking. Since we Jews refused Him, He opened the way to the Gentiles.

Yes! Our Father God is the Creator of all and, yes, we are chosen by God to uphold his standards high for all the world to see. But much of the time we failed because of our pride. We have been blessed and much of the time refused our Father's way to go our own path. Justifying our choices and walked right into our own exile. Still God did not dessert us. He sent prophets to us time and time again. Some we honored; most not! If we didn't like the things they spoke, we abused them; sometimes stoning them to death.

As Jesus spoke I knew he was speaking truth. Our leaders for so long were ruling out of pride. (Seems all nations so blessed fall by pride, taking credit for the things God has done.) We all claim he is God, but we go right on hating, justifying our refusal to help the helpless. Hearts full 0f unforgiveness. O yes, we do a lot of good, but so often excuse ourselves of so many things.

We have become man made leaders, many times without pity and without justice.

Jesus slipped away quietly, as his light dimmed and then was gone. I am convinced his presence was here and he was speaking to me personally; even though he could slip away as easily as he appeared. All without my sense of understanding how this could be. Then I remembered; "nothing is impossible with God."

I fell to the ground sobbing; not tears of sorrow but tears of joy! I knew I was saved for as he spoke I believed him! I had made the choice when I believed him! I am eternity bound! I wept with joy until I fell asleep; a lovely, peaceful, restful sleep.

When I awoke I knew what I must do. I must go home, speak to my wife and family, telling them of this encounter and that I am a new man; a new creation. I must give away this fortune I have amassed, because I realize I have made it my god. I must do as Jesus asked and give it all to the poor and follow him, where ever that leads. I knew full well they would not understand. I surely didn't, when Jesus first told me that is what I must do!

Well, I did exactly that! They were wide eyed and troubled, thinking he must have lost his mind! Seemed everyone was talking at once. Some were arguing, some weeping; all in some phase of disbelief.

I told my highest manager to begin the process of dissolving the business and getting things in order. Begin clearing the way to disperse the funds to the poor and needy.

I was serious! (There must have been talk in whispers, behind my back of having me committed to a mental institution.) I was realizing we are all judged this way when we step out of the usual and into following Jesus. It does look crazy to the natural.

In our culture, my father, the oldest living relative; the most honored among his family, stepped forward. Raising his hand, for quiet and attention. This is our tradition, giving him honor by complying. Having the Torah in his hands, turned to a grandson of 13, telling him to unroll the scroll to Genesis 22:1-19. There my father read aloud where Abraham was told by God to sacrifice his only son. The long awaited son of promise; his most precious possession. With a heavy heart, Abraham started off to do as God had told him. He took the boy a three days journey into the wilderness. His son said, "father, I see the wood and the fire, but where is the sacrifice?" He told him, "son, the Lord will provide." Can you imagine the pain in Abraham's heart, yet he was willing to do as God instructed. (How much more precious Isaac was than any fortune!)

As he bound the lad, lay him on the altar, and began the downward thrust of that fatal plunge, an angel stopped him! A voice called out; Abraham, Abraham.!" He answered, "here I am Lord." (he recognized God's voice.)

"Lay not your hand upon the boy!" "For you have proved yourself faithful; even to the giving of your most precious son!" Abraham needed that confirmation for himself, that he would follow God, no matter what.

Tears of joy streaming down his face, he raised his tear dimmed eyes and there, in the thicket was a ram caught by his horns. Yes, God did provide. They made a sacrifice of the ram; a sacrifice made by fire unto the Lord.

At this Joshua's father rolled up the scroll and handed it back to the young man. At this I knew my father understood; what I understood. This was as old as the Scripture: To be willing to give that which was most precious.

The Lord God loves me and all my people, but I had set my heart on the god of wealth. My pride in myself, my ability to grow a fortune, my good works, my ancestor worship; all these things became be a trap.

"Lord, now I am willing to lay it all down. I don't want anything to come between you and me." Use me Jesus as you will, not my will but yours." Giving it all up with a new attitude of the peace and assurance I had been seeking.

At this, I went into a private place, where I could commune freely with my Lord and my God; to give him the honor, and the glory due him. I wanted no distractions as I gave him praise. After all who am I that my Lord would love me so much he would personally visit me, telling me all these things? As I was deep in worship I again heard his voice. "Joshua, I have heard you. I have seen how honestly your desire is to follow me. You faced the ones you love, at the risk of losing their love and respect. Even to the point of being ridiculed as crazy."

"Just as the Scripture your father read; as Abraham had spared not his son, I rewarded him, so I reward you."

"All the fortune you have amassed I give back to you!" "Steward it well!" "Keep me first, with no other gods before you. I love you and you have found the eternal life you sought."

We all know this is so. How often when we hang onto something so tightly, we feel if it is gone, we cannot go on. When we finally believe and do as ask, the Lord gives us something more wonderful to replace it. This time around we are more aware of holding it loossely and not allowing it to become a ruler over us! After all, the devil prowls around like a roaring lion, seeking someone to devour. He has not changed. "He came to kill, steal and destroy. Jesus came that we have life in great abundance." Praise God! Both now and in eternity!

JAIRUS' DAUGHTER

JESUS LIVED AND SPOKE; SOMETIMES in parables, sometimes not. Many times it was the story within a story, mingled in time. It was one miracle merging with a following miracle. Jesus life seemed to move this way.

This is one of those times. Another story unfolding right in the middle of the one they were living.

Jesus was once again surrounded by the multitudes. Pressed in on every side. Everyone wanted a touch from Jesus.

Stories flew! The crowds were buzzing!

These events took place in the region of Lake Galilee. Some distance from the center of the rule by the Synagogue in Jerusalem and the center of rule by the conquering Roman over the whole of Judea.

Jesus home towns of Nazareth and Capernaum are in this area. The area of which the rulers in Jerusalem said, "can anything good come out of Nazareth?" Neither were these cities their choice or interest.

This is also the area where Jesus did most of his ministry. The sermon on the mount was here. The Beatitudes; The feeding of the 5000. Jesus taught his Disciples the Lord's Prayer here. On and on! The crowds grew bigger and bigger!

Jairus had probably been newly graduated from the seminary school of the Leaders of Synagogues. This out-post was more like a sentence. If one sent here and survived it, maybe a slight chance of upward mobility. Most not! Sent away to these places and forgotten.

We don't know how long Jairus was in this section, but long enough to have seen and heard of the mighty miracles of this man Jesus, who walked among the dying, poor, sick and lame.

His twelve year old beloved daughter fell ill and was near death. Jairus ran to find Jesus. He knew full well, to seek Jesus would put his chances of advancement in jeopardy. A promotion for Jairus now was not likely! He didn't care. This little girl was his life! He would sacrifice all for her!

Jairus went seeking Jesus to come, lay his hands or her and heal her!

He got to the masses surrounding Jesus; fell down before him, crying out: "Jesus my 12 year old daughter is near death! Come lay hands on her and I know she will live!"

Jesus started out with this grieving father, but the press of this crowd hemmed them in. Everyone wanted a piece of Jesus. All had come to believe Jesus could provide what- ever the need was. They were delayed in the mob, as so often happened; delayed but not forgotten.

At the same time, men arrived to tell Jairus, "Don't trouble the teacher. Your daughter is dead." "Why bother the teacher further?"

Jesus ignored what they said. "Jairus, don't be afraid, just believe."

Jesus allowed only Peter, James and John to go with them.

When they got to the home, the customary mourning was in fully engaged. To do less would be disrespectful at that time and place.

Jesus: "Why all this commotion and wailing? The girl is not dead, she is sleeping."

At this they were offended and scoffed. They knew she was dead. For hours she had been dead! The customary preparation of washing the body, dressing her in her finest, laying her out upon her bed for viewing, was done. Yes! She was dead!

Jesus put them all out of the room except the parents, Peter, James, and John. All doubters removed from the room.

Jesus took her by the hand. "Little girl, I say to you, get up!"

Immediately she stood up and walked around. O the astonishment and the joy! I can imagine her parents falling on their knees in worship, drawing their beautiful daughter with them, in joyous weeping! This family now forever followers of Jesus!

"Get her something to eat and don't tell anyone about this!"

What? When they left that room and walked out through that crowd, the cat was out of the bag! The whole of that area would know it.

I can see the surprise and shock of those onlookers! There must have been a barrage of questions. All this family could do was smile and "Not open their mouths."

So many of these encounters! The disciples were as astounded as this family. Each one, as if it was the first miracle they had seen! It never grew old, and the band of followers grew, as most of these had been the beneficiary. How could you not follow the one who raised your precious daughter to life?

LAKE GALILEE

I HAVE READ MANY TIMES there are cities, even countries that are ruled by demon spirits.

Some are ruled by the spirit of alcohol and drugs. Some, the spirit of suicide." "Some by the haughty spirit of self righteousness; and some by the spirit of exclusiveness." (No new comers allowed!) I have witnessed these things are so.

But closer to our story, look at a map of the Lake Galilee area.

Most of the ministry of Jesus was in this area. The demon possessed man living naked in the tombs encountered Jesus there and was delivered of the legion of demons. He was called "Legion," as that many possessed him. The place was called Gadarenes. (Gadara)

Close by this area was the town called Magdala, the home town of Mary Magdalene. Jesus delivered her of seven devils. This woman knew the torture of being demon possessed. She was wild, feared and shunned. This deliverance was dramatic! She was forever changed. The scripture doesn't say when or where her deliverance took place, but it very well might have been near her home town. (Many have speculated.) What we do know, Jesus so often ministered there.

Bible history is set in this area. The O.T. and N.T. It was at Endor, the witch Saul had consulted when he disobeyed God, and he no longer heard from the Lord. Samuel the prophet had died so Saul did what so many do today. He consulted a medium. Strictly forbidden!

Yes there are evil spirits seeking a place to infest.

This is also close by the area where the last battle will be fought. In the valley of Megiddo; the battle of Armageddon. Demon spirits will be released to go draw the nations of the world to this place to fight the Lords return.

I am convinced every sin has its own demonic spirit. Whatever that area chooses to allow will be ruled by that spirit.

Self-righteousness seems to have been the demon spirit the Pharisees fell into. Anyone or anything that does not lift the name of Jesus high can fall prey to these demons spirits. The Romans ruling over this area worshipped their emperor as god. These are demon spirits.

When God said, in Exodus 20:1-3. "You shall have no other gods before me." It is the love of God, our creator to protect us. When we honor God in this way, we are covered all around and the enemy cannot touch us! Anything we add will be a snare to us. It is not God plus anything or anyone. He will not share his glory. Not even any good thing. It is good to do godly service, but we must be alert. Even this can become a trap.

Yes, there were demon spirits in this area, and these people knew they needed a Savior. It was in Jerusalem where the seat of religious and civil power was located. They watched Jesus trying to ensnare him. In the Lake Galilee area he was free to move about and the people came to him.

In the garden of Eden, Adam and Eve had the authority over that deceiving snake, but they choose not to use is. That authority is ours today. The commission we are given as followers of Christ is to heal the sick, speak of God's kingdom and cast out demons. The 77 Jesus sent did it, and to their surprise they saw these thing happen.

In this area he taught the multitudes: The Beatitudes, the Sermon on the Mount, where he chose his disciples. Feed the 5000, and the 3000. Many of the towns where his miracles took place where in this area. It was also the home and preaching of John the Baptist.

I am thinking the reason Jesus had such ministry in this area, they were receptive. They knew they needed a savior! Jesus came to them. His opposition was in Jerusalem where they sought to kill him. To trap him in some way to have him killed. He was a fly in their ointment!

No doubt this place had welcomed evil spirits, yet, they were people receptive to Jesus!

Had the Pharisees had any interest in these outlaying places, they would have been able to see all these things were prophesied in the Scripture they claimed to believe in.

When they said, "can anything good come out of Nazareth?" They would have already known, "Yes it can!"

LEGION AND MARY MAGDALENE

MARY AND LEGION WERE RAISED in this area. To the people who lived in this area, didn't give it a second thought. Such things as witchcraft and demon spirits were very acceptable. They all practiced it in one form or the other. To them they more than likely worshipped all sorts of things.

These two were not the only ones who had allowed themselves to be possessed!

We only know them because their lives were selected by the Holy Spirit to be included in the Scriptures.

John said near the end of his gospel," If all the things were written that Jesus did or said, were included in books; the world could not hold them all."

Believing that is so, we will attempt to bring life; flesh and blood to the bones of these people. Trying to imagine where they got to where they were in life.

Mary was a beautiful child, but like any, left to herself, with no godly instruction, she was easy prey to the evil spirits in an area where those spirits abounded. No different from most in the village of Magdala. Their games, stories, music all centered around the occult. So common, they were worshipped as we seem prone to idolize celebrities and sports hero's today.

Mary's favorite place to visit was Endor. For centuries this place was the center of witchcraft. Mostly she watched! She became intrigued. She saw mysterious things happening.

Mary's mother and all her friends and neighbors didn't mind, as they all dabbled in such things. It was parlor games to them. Their Wednesday night "bridge game" was Tarot cards and reading tea leaves.

It was during her growing up years the witches of Endor took notice of Mary, and carefully began to draw her in.

These witches took a special interest in a young man, we will later call Legion. He would be the challenge they were looking for. How far could they take his human body? How many demons could they draw into one body?

They had a plan! First they would befriend him with kindness.

He would be so starved for kindness, this would be easy!

After several trips to Gadara, taking care to speak to him, they would offer him work at their coven. They did and he took the bait! They found odd jobs for him to do. They paid him well and treated him well. He was a hard worker and tried hard to please.

After the passing of one full moon cycle, he trusted them and suspected nothing. That evening they offered him a permanent position! Pay, room and board! How could he turn down such an offer?

That evening they fed him a wonderful meal topped off with a goblet of spiced wine. It quickly took effect and this was the state he was in that first evening Mary of Magdala spied on him from her secret vantage point.

Mary sneaked close to watch. She saw the young man brought into their secret meeting room. He became so passive, and submissive.

Mary wasn't actually an invited guest so she stayed hidden to watch.

These witches preformed some elaborate ceremony. Offered animal sacrifices. Chanted as they danced around the slab of stone where the young man lay, so still, not flinching or resisting as though dead. Still Mary could see his chest rise and fall with even breathing. So strange! They burned him with candles and made cuts that seemed to have some design to them, yet he did not move! This strange ceremony went on and on. These women seemed as if in a trance like state as well as the young man.

Mary stole out of her hiding place, terrified and ran for home. Still she was drawn back night after night. Watching from her secret place, this went on for a space of one full moon to the next.

How could this man endure all this over this length of time? She had never seem him eat or drink, whimper or cry out. He simply lay there as dead! Seeing all this, she did not know what it all meant, but there was something terrifying, yet intriguing about it. This she did know, she had to know who this man was and why he was the subject of such ceremonies.

At the end of this month, this coven of the witches of Endor, secretly took him back to Gadara. He was still in some sort of a stupor. They left him there in the streets. Mary followed at a distance to watch.

He slowly gained consciousness, and when he did he was as a crazy man! He ran through the city damaging and destroying everything in his path. Mary thought him a wild animal more than human.

Men of the city captured him as a caged wild beast. Chained him, and took him across Lake Galilee to an ancient cemetery, where they tried to bind him to a large tombstone. He broke free! The chains dropping as if they were twine! These men, ran for their boat; fearing for their lives. They made it! Rowing as fast as they could, not knowing if he would chase them. And not knowing if he had this super human strength to swim after them. It was the talk of Gadara! No one would go near that place.

Mary followed secretly across Lake Galilee and watched from a safe distance. It was terrifying! This man was a wild animal now. Not the strong young man she had witnessed before he was drugged. What had these women done to him?

As Mary watched this man in the tombs, she was recalling how she had done her home work. She had checked out books from the local library. Took a few on line classes. The more she studied the more intrigued she became. All this time she spied on the strange ceremonies these women were doing. She felt something strange arising in her mind, beginning to control her thoughts. She had to stop this! She had witnessed what had led to the condition this young man was in! Yet she felt compelled to stay there and watch!

She noticed a correlation between her reading and studying, a war was going on within her being. She was having trouble sleeping. Frightened of things she had never feared before. She purposed to rid herself of all this stuff. She realized she no longer had any control over this thing. She no longer washed her face or combed her hair, and she just didn't care!

In the general area was an expanse of hillside where the hired men of the swine ranchers grazed their herds. They stayed far away from this mad man, but close enough to see the rage and raging of this man; often cutting himself with pieces of sharp stone. (They kept the community informed about this creature.)

She stayed in her secret place where she could watch this man. She felt she was a kindred spirit with him in some way. How she longed to have some deliverance for herself and this man, if this was possible! She was hoping to see him getting better and his sanity return. If he was somewhat better, maybe there was hope for her.

Rumor had it around the community, stay away from that area, as this was a violent, uncontrollable man!

The swine herdsmen in the area had witnessed from a distance, how he had snapped chains, living among the tombs naked. Yes, he was crazy but resourceful. He had plenty of water from Lake Galilee. When we desired meat he would kill a swine with his bare hands, drink the blood and eat the meat raw. Who was going to stop him? The herdsmen ran from him and hid! Stopping him was way above their pay grade, and as hard as it was to get anyone else to go this close to this area was next to impossible. They had no worry of being fired from their jobs! As long as they kept their distance, this man would leave them alone, and they were glad to have that arrangement. When it came time to take the swine to market, they would drive the herd a much greater distance to a remote beach, where they could raft the herd across the lake without crossing this man's territory.

Mary never forgot what she had seen or never gave up her quest to find out who this man was and why the witches of Endor chose him for whatever purpose this was. She was afraid! Afraid to tell anyone, even her mother. Knowing her mother would laugh and dismiss it. After all she dabbled in all this stuff too.

Legion meets Jesus!

One afternoon a boat load of men came, beached the boat beneath the graveyard. (As if they purposed to be there! Purposed to see this man!) No one dared get this close to him! But they did!

(Mary sneaked closer, to get a better view and to hear the conversation.)

No one looked her direction; yet she felt they knew her whereabouts. This one man seemed to be the leader.

The demon possessed man called him Lord! How could this be?

The men with him called him Jesus!

Jesus said to this madman, "What is your name?"

The man answered. "Legion."

Jesus. "Why do they call you Legion?

The man answered: "Because, I am possessed by a legion of evil spirits."

This mad man seemed to be speaking, yet it didn't seem it was he. It was like something inside of him. Beyond his control.

He garbled. "Son of God, do not torture me!"

For Jesus had demanded the evil spirits to come out of him.

At this, it seemed as if he was seized and thrown to the ground! Violently, writhing in the dust, screaming!

Jesus said, "Go!" "Come out of him!" "I command you to come out of him!" "Do not trouble this man anymore!"

(A herd of swine was grazing on the hillside close by.) The demon spirits begged Jesus, "Let us go into those pigs!"

Jesus answered calmly. "Go!"

At this the demons went into the swine and they ran violently down the hillside, jumped off the cliff, throwing themselves into the sea and were drown.

Mary sat there stunned! "Who is this man that delivered this demon possessed young man?" "There he sits quietly and in his right mind!" "Calm and completely changed from moments ago?" "Who is this Jesus?"

"I need to know him!" "I need this deliverance too!"

The men hired to keep watch over this herd of pigs, ran to town to report all these things! What they had witnessed was astounding!

The people of the village came quickly! They saw this crazy man healed and in his right mind! You would think they would be happy to see this man delivered! No! They were angered! These swine were their livelihood. They demanded Jesus leave immediately!

The delivered man ask: "Jesus, can I go with you? Can I follow you?"

Jesus: "Go back to your home and tell of all the good things that God has done for you!" "You are now my missionary in all these parts; to all these people." "The fields are ripe unto harvest and the workers are few." (Jesus is still saying this to us today.) "You are my disciple here!"

Jesus and his men hugged this man, got into their boat and left. It was as if this was their specific purpose, to meet and deliver this young man.

The delivered man immediately set out for his home town of Gadara.

Mary followed at a distance. "I must find him. Talk to him, hear his story from his perspective and tell him what I have observed."

I need him to tell me who this Jesus is and what I must do! I need to find this Jesus!

Going into Gadara, Mary made herself as inconspicuous as possible. Which was easy, as no one took notice of any strange behavior. These people had no moral compass. Any kind of behavior was acceptable.

Mary learned as she listened. This man's mother and father had died young, leaving their son an orphan.

In that society, no one took compassion on him and he grew up in the streets. Doing what work he could find and eating what he could scavenge or steal. Still he grew big and strong.

The witches of Endor were welcomed in all the villages. Gadara had a spirit of witchcraft over it. Most all the citizens were involved in one way or another. These women were as welcomed as the butcher or the baker.

(Mary did find Legion and secretly watched and listened.) He had not stopped telling everyone what this man Jesus did for him.

At first few listened, but the numbers begin to rise. Most all had seen this man before he encountered Jesus and had to admit something miraculous had happened to him.

Legion began to realize the power and authority Jesus had given him when he spoke in Jesus name. People were healed! Delivered! The ones who had shunned him as a child came weeping, confessing their sin of not caring for him, asking forgiveness. And forgive them he did! They immediately felt that heavy burden of grief lifted: Replaced by a most freeing peace. An unimaginable peace! Under Legions preaching and love they found and received Jesus and were truly set free!

A wave of believers sprang up all around Gadara! The enemy's strong hold was being broken! Legion was joyously overcome by this love of Jesus.

Mary made herself known to him. She told him her story. Filled in all the gaps for him, as to how these witches had cast spells over him and filled him with demon spirits. She had watched it all! She had followed him at distance back to Gadara; from the tombs on the hillside above Lake Galilee. All of it! She saw Jesus and his followers come, as if they were there just to find him and deliver him. She saw and heard his salvation and deliverance!

Mary said: " I have to find this Jesus!" "I have to know him." "Please tell me who he is and where he is that I may find him!"

They became friends and met often. Legion witnessing to her the Salvation message. He answered all her questions. She followed him and watched his ministry of witness at Gadara.

"Legion, I too need deliverance." "I need this Salvation!" "I am conscious of these evil spirits who have also taken up a lodging in me!" "I don't want them."I want Jesus to set me free!"

Legion: "Mary you are on the road to Salvation and deliverance!" "You are aware of the sin that has captured you and desire to be set free in Jesus." "That is turning and repenting." "Would you like to invite Jesus to save you right now?" "To deliver you?"

"O yes! Yes! Yes!" she cried. They prayed and she asked, "Jesus come into my life and be my Lord and Savior!" (Another life saved and her name written down in the Lamb's Book of Life! Hallelujah! Heaven celebrated!)

Legion: "Mary, Jesus knows all about you. He has known you even before you were. He loves you and will come to you." Only he knows how, where and when, but he will." "Go home. Fast and pray for three days."Mary, be forever blessed!"

Mary did as she was told. She went to Magdala; found a very private place in her home, where she would not be disturbed and began her fast and prayer session. Not knowing what to expect, just believing.

At the end of that time, a knock came at the door. She opened it to see a smiling Jesus! She recognized him, even though she had not seen his features before; only seeing him at a distance at the tombs. Only Jesus could have those eyes of such love and compassion!

She opened wide the door and asked him to come in! As he stepped in, she fell at his feet and began to worship him. Jesus lifted her to her feet. "Mary, I have seen your journey!" "I've seen your longing and your search for me." "I saw your Salvation and deliverance I gave you!" "You are one with me and all the believers." "I know your heart, and you will never leave me." "You will never turn away!" "Bless you my child!"

"Lord, what am I to do?" "Do you have a plan for me?" "A plan like you gave Legion?"

"Yes, but my plan for you is unique, as I create all to be unique!" "You must come, follow me and the large group of disciples that move about with me." "There are many and I have chosen you to be a special friend and daughter to my mother." "There is a large group of women who all have unique and diverse gifts, all for the glory of God.""My grace covers all!" "Mary, will you follow me?"

"Yes, Lord, Yes!"

Immediately she ran to wash her face, comb her hair and put on her best dress. As she passed by her mirror, she gasped! That look of young innocence was back! Those wild terror filled eyes were now soft and loving. "Yes! I have been delivered!" "I have stepped out of the darkness and into his wonderful light!"

Well, the rest is history! It was Mary who followed Jesus all the way through!

That awful abuse as he carried his cross to Golgotha. It was this Mary who held his mother close and comforted her as she witnessed all this cruelty heaped upon her beloved son. As they stood, tears streaming down their faces as he was nailed to that cross. The abuse he endured and yes, the forgiveness he gave! Salvation to the thief on the cross next to him and the Roman soldier who had driven the nails through his wrist and feet! She heard and understood as Jesus asked John to be a son to Mary, his mother; Mary to be John's mother. Even at the end, caring for his mother and friends.

Mary Magdalene was the first to go to the tomb that first Easter morning to find the stone rolled away! The first to see Jesus was not in that tomb! The first to see the risen Jesus! The first to speak to him, and he to her. He said, "Go tell my disciples, and especially tell Peter, I have risen!" "I will go before them, to meet them on Lake Galilee!'

(Yes, Jesus told her she would have a unique ministry. A unique place in this ministry, and did she ever!)

She was one of those 120, still close to Mary, Jesus mother, as they waited in that upper room for the promise of the Father, that fell from Heaven upon them on that day of Pentecost; baptizing them with power and fire to take this message to the ends of the earth!

She would be the first to tell us, "Come you have a unique place in this ministry! It was placed in you at creation! Come follow Jesus!"

NAIN

N AIN, A SMALL COMMUNITY IN the Lake Galilee area.
Jesus loved these people!

This brings us to this a funeral procession in Nain. The body of a young man; the only child of a poor widow.

Not only has he died, but is followed to his tomb by his broken hearted mother. This very well was a death sentence for her too.

Her husband had died. When he was alive, they never had enough. With just barely enough food could they scrape by. He worked hard but things just didn't change. He was a good man. They loved each other in this most humble home. They had one child; an only son, born in their old age.

He would care for them. He was their hope!

Well, plans just didn't go as planned. Shortly after her husband died this son fell ill. She stayed by his side night and day caring for him as best she could. Sleeping little and crying much. Forcing as much fluid down him sip by sip.

She had heard of this kind man who went about healing the sick and doing good, but how could she find him?

More tears; but her precious child did not survive another night. After weeping until there were no more tears, she raised herself up in sorrow, stepped out, to face her neighbors. They were all in the same situation as she. They also had nothing. They would help if they could but they were all in the same boat.

That evening they gathered at her home, to try to figure out how to take her son to the tombs outside the city.

From the wood scraps they could find, they made a makeshift bier, wrapped the body in his only quilt; and lay him on a hand cart. Two men that lived close by would pull the cart. This woman and the neighbors would follow weeping.

As Jesus was passing by, coming into the city; saw the funeral procession coming out. Out of respect, they stepped aside, heads bowed; all except Jesus, that is! He held up his hand stopping this procession. With eyes of compassion resting on this lady, said in a powerful yet compassionate voice. "Stop! Weep not!"

By this time the funeral procession, the Disciples and the by standers were all in a state of shock!

"How can he call this to a halt and tell this lady not to weep?"(I am sure the Disciples felt as if they were about to be stoned!) This makes no sense! No, it doesn't. But Jesus didn't come to make acceptable sense of all these things. He came to heal the sick, raise the dead, heal the broken hearted, and certainly this lady was broken hearted!

Jesus reached out his hand touched the bier, and said, "young- man, I tell you to arise! Sit up and live!" "Come down from there!"

As Jesus took him by the hand, his eyes opened and the light of life was there! He smiled at his mother; swung his legs over the side of the cart; Jesus presented him to his mother, alive, alert, and smiling. What a stir it caused!

First he sat, looking around as is to say. "What is all this fuss about?" Soon having seen his wide eyed weeping mother and neighbors, he remembered. I was so sick, I died! I saw the whole thing! I saw my mother weeping as she held me as long as she could. Weeping as she closed my staring eyes of death. Kissing me is great sorrow one last time.

Gathering all the courage she could muster, stepping out her door weeping, to tell them all, "he is gone." Yes gone! Even in death, I was aware. Life in this sphere was past and gone.

The Disciples were probably the most surprised. Even though they had seen so many amazing things, the next one still nearly over whelmed them. Again and again it had happened.

From the friends and neighbors who came to support this grieving mother, to all the bystanders of that place: A shout went up! Never had such an amazing thing happened in that poor village!

Jesus held up his hand to quiet the commotion. They all stilled, wide eyed and at total attention.

Addressing the mother, Jesus said to her. "The God of all creation loves you. He has seen you tears and felt your grief and he has given you back your only son"

At this a great fear and excitement fell upon all those who saw and heard. They began calling out; "Teach us! Teach us all these things! We will listen! We will hear! From what our eyes have seen and our ears have heard, we believe!"

The whole area sat at Jesus feet. Revival had broken out, right on the spot! Jesus words to them was as pure gold. That entire area became believers and the blessings of the Lord fell upon them. The very atmosphere changed to one of hope.

The demons that had oppressed this place began to flee. They cannot stand in the presence of Jesus. These people were witnesses!

Neighbor began looking after neighbor! This city became a regular stopping and refreshing place for Jesus as they passed that way. He would lodge with this widow and her son.

Those tears were seen and heard all the way to Heaven and moved the heart of God! They still do! Praise God!

BARABBAS

I AM BARABBAS, ARRESTED AND in prison for murder and insurrection!

I call myself a freedom fighter, who did not believe in being passive under this Roman occupation, as the Pharisees, Sadducees and leaders of the local synagogue were.

They were actually pretty comfortable. They obeyed the Roman rule and the Romans would leave them alone. In fact, it was a pretty good arrangement for them. They turn their back and they are left alone by the Romans. They would comply and keep control and obey their captors. A pretty cozy arrangement!

Imagine for a minute if we were over taken by some other foreign enemy and the church submitted by secret arrangement to live and let live regardless how ungodly they were. There would be such an uprising, from without and within the sanction of the church. We would rebel and try to drive these foreign occupiers out!

This was who I was! I was hated by both the rulers of synagogue and the Roman occupiers. I was an enemy of the church and the state. In my eyes I was a patriot!

I led a street gang, if you will! During the street riots I must have been involved in killing a Roman soldier during hand to hand combat.

I was subdued, arrested, thrown into a Roman jail, chained; awaiting my execution. This was the price you paid for resisting Rome, and the church, turned a blind eye.I knew this was the price I would someday pay and I was willing to die for the cause. Trying to free my people and they didn't even care what it cost. They considered me the enemy to their way of life.

The prison was insight and ear shot of where Jesus mock trial was held. The crowd whipped into a riotous mob, calling for Jesus crucifixion.

Pilate, trying to find a reason to release Jesus; as he found no offence worthy of death. Since it was the Passover season, the custom was to release a political prisoner. Pilate said,"shall I release to you Jesus?" The Jewish religious powers that be, coaxed the people to cry out, "crucify Jesus" "Give us Barabbas!" "Release Barabbas!"

How could this be? None had ever lifted a finger to help me before, as I crusaded to free them from Herod's rule.

When the guards unlocked that cell gate and the chains, I was told to go. "You are free!" I feared I would be run through with a sword before I reached the street.

During my imprisonment I had been treated brutality and most hated. I was an enemy of Rome!

Once I hit the street, if I made it that far, surely I would be beat to death by the mob. There would be no friends waiting to protect me. They had all fled!

With fear and trepidation I slinked out onto the street, making myself as invisible as possible; I melted into the mob. What a wild scene!

All the attention of hate and anger was turned on Jesus. No one even seemed to notice me.

In full view of the leering crowd, Jesus was stripped of all but a loin cloth. Chained to a post and flogged unmercifully with a cat-of-nine tails. Even a hardened criminal such as I was appalled at their cruelty!

Jesus looked so frail and helpless, weaken by the abuse. He was marred beyond recognition. Streams of blood flowing freely out of his abused body. Other earlier wounds encrusted in dried blood and mud.

I followed at a distance, watching the horror of the torture. The rough hewn crossbar of his crucifixion cross seemed to weigh more than Jesus. He was weakened, so weakened; forced to carry this heavy rough timber on his raw, wounded shoulders. He staggered and struggled and fell from his weakness and the weight. He would attempt to get up, stagger and fall again and again. Guards would beat and abuse him, and pull him to his feet. Jesus made a few more staggering steps, falling again. This was a horrible sight to behold. I watched and cringed.

When the Roman soldiers were afraid of the punishment they would receive should they delivered a dead man to the site; forced a bystander to carry the crossbar the rest of the way.

Still I followed at a distance. The thought began arising in my mind…..."This man has taken my place!" I was trying to push the thought down and keep it at bay, still it came. It became louder and louder and ate at my soul. Yet, I could not turn away.

Reaching Golgotha, a large mob gathered. (Crucifixion always drew a crowd.) The crowd was most festive: A few mourners. Cruel guards who saw it as a job to be done and without compassion. The religious, self righteous Pharisees, and other officials who felt they were doing God a favor, watched to make sure it was carried out.

I could not dismiss this thundering voice beating in my head! "This man, Jesus, is dying in my place!" "I am set free because he is dying in my place!"

Jesus is roughly handled, slammed to the ground upon the cross, too weak to help himself. Nails pounded into his wrist and feet; too much to watch, even for a criminal such as I. I would turn away for a moment. The sound alone was excruciating. I cringed with each hammer blow. Jesus is too weak to even cry out. The hammer seems to be spelling out the message; "Dying in my place! Dying in my place!"

Jesus mother and a few friends are weeping as they watched. What a terrible thing for a mother to witness. Her friends seem to be unable to comfort her as she sobs. Tears streaming down her face, dripping from her chin onto her dusty blood stained garment. Stained from the many times she tried to comfort him when he fell, as he struggled up the hill. Each time the guards, handling her roughly; shoving her away. I cannot help but feel such compassion for this soul wounded lady. Few seemed to care about her.

I wondered, does my mother know all the things that have happened to me? Do her friends scoff and condemn her because she has raised such a rebellious son? Would tears be streaming down her face if I was being nailed to that cross? "Thud! Thud! Thud!" "Dying in my place!: Dying in my place!"

As I watched, I see Jesus life ebbing away.

He turned his head toward a thief on his right, crucified along side of him. This man said to Jesus: "Remember me when you come into your Kingdom." What this man had seen and heard made a believer of him." Jesus replied: "Today you

235

shall be will be with me in paradise." How can this be? This man was condemned to die just as I was! He forgave this man at the last moments of his life!"

Jesus looked lovingly at his mother and friend/disciple, John. Jesus asked John to "take her home and be a son to her," and to Mary; " be a mother to John." Even at his death caring for the people he loved. The words I was most astonished by was, Jesus prayed for the very ones that nailed him to that cross! He said: "Father, forgive them. They know not what they do!"

Speaking his last words, saying, "Father into your hands I commit my Spirit!" "It is finished!" How odd! Jesus seems to have willingly given up his Spirit!

The black clouds roll in; the sky becomes as black as night. A cold breeze begins to blow. Thunder crashes almost before the electricity from the lightening has died away. It seems to repeat the message. "Dying for me!" "Dying in my place!"

The crowd disperses; runs for cover from the storm. I cannot move. Cemented to that spot! Saying to myself, "I have watched my own suffering and death!" "He died in my place for the sins I committed."

All is quiet now. The prisoners have died. The Romans guards break the legs of the two thieves crucified that day. Just in case there was a flicker of life left in them, so they could not escape. Coming to Jesus, seeing he is truly dead, they don't bother to break his legs. Instead they run a spear through his side. The last little pool of blood left in his body trickles out with the cardiac fluid that surrounds his heart. There is no pumping, it just slowly drains away. He is dead. Even the guards leave now. I am alone, still watching.

Two men come, take Jesus body down carefully, and lovingly carry him to a new tomb in the garden below. It is the eve of the Sabbath so they must hurry, as not to violate the Jewish law of the Sabbath. I follow; keeping in the shadows.

The two men do what they can, with what time will allow.

They wrap Jesus in a burial cloth after anointing him with a small amount of the traditional burial spices. They must hurry the sun is nearly down. They leave hurriedly, but I stay in my hiding place.

Guards come, roll a large stone in front of the entrance to the tomb. Sealing the tomb with the official Roman wax and stamp. They stay on duty, to be sure no one disturbs the grave as the Pharisees have requested. During the long night I fall asleep.

A noise awakens me! The Sabbath has passed! A woman is coming with spices to finish the burial preparations properly.

It is Sunday! I have slept through the entire Sabbath!

She is as surprised as I am! The stone has been rolled away and the guards are gone! She looks inside, backs out startled! He is not there! She is in great distress! Seeing a man she thinks to be the gardener, she cries. "They have taken away my Lord." " If you know where they have laid him, tell me and I will go get him." "I will take his body to his friends for a proper burial."

I am shocked! She does not recognize Jesus immediately, but I do! "This is Jesus, alive! I saw him die! I saw the last drops of blood ooze out! "He died in my place!"

When Jesus speaks her name, "Mary!" Her eyes are opened and she knows. She falls at his feet in worship and cries "Teacher!"

Jesus tells her, "Go and tell the disciples, especially Peter!" She runs weeping with joy! I can't hear all of their conversation, but what I did hear, I know she is elated. I look again and this man Jesus is gone. I follow this woman. I have to know what these people know about this Jesus. All I know is, "this man died in my place." "I have to know him! I have to know him!" "I have to find these friends." "I have to know this Jesus, and why he would take my place!."

All of this, of course is my imagination, but it could have been something similar. I am sure it is close. Barabbas was the first one who saw and knew for sure he should have been crucified, but Jesus took his place. "I was tried and found guilty, sentenced to death for insurrection and murder." " I am guilty as charged, but Jesus died in my place!"

If my account is in any way close, when he was taught the story by the disciples, he knew without a doubt. "This is the Lamb of God who takes away the sin of the world." " Yes, he did take my place and set me free!"

He must have been among the 120 that waited in that upper room for the promise of the Father; when the Holy Spirit fell, baptizing them all with power and fire on that day of Pentecost.

Aren't we all a Barabbas until we see clearly this Jesus who took our place and sacrificed himself for us, is our Savior? We must invite him into our lives! He lay down his life to save (ours) mine! What perfect love!

THE FIRST SUNRISE SERVICE

E ASTER. THE SEASON WE CELEBRATE Jesus resurrection from
the dead is a sacred date of remembering our Lord. The
suffering and what he went through to make this sacrifice for
us. How he willingly lay down his life and shed his blood.

Yet he agonized over it. Knowing the price he would pay.
It was no surprise. He counted the cost and did it anyway.
I have to keep asking myself; who am I that Almighty God
would pay this cost for me? It was love! Love compelled him!
Love for his children; his prodigal children. He came willingly
to seek and to save that which was lost. All have sinned and
fallen short of the glory of God. None of us can claim our
own righteousness. It is the Righteousness of Jesus. He coves
us with his righteousness, none of our own. He came to seek
and to save those who knew they needed a Savior. He came
to heal those who knew they needed healing. Give hope to
the hopeless.

Yes, Jesus willing went to the cross, carrying all the sin of
the world,(including mine), suffered, bled and died to pay that
debt in full. Even went into the bowels of hell that was meant
for all who had gone their own way. He paid it all. Death and

hell, all completely erased for all who would give him their lives. He knew it all going in, but chose to do it anyway. He agonized over it as he prayed in the Garden. But in the final analysis said, "Father, not my will, but your will be done."

Jesus was terribly abused and tortured. But he did not cry out against his cruel treatment. In fact, he forgave them. "Father, forgive them they know not what they do."

The Disciples could make no sense of it! They had followed him, saw the miracles, they had believed he was the Messiah! How could this be? That he could die by human hands? They were disappointed and confused. They were also ashamed of themselves, as most fled at the first sign of trouble. Only John and Peter followed from a distance. Peter denied he knew him after he vowed he would die with him, if it came to that. Confused, all confused, to say the least.

Now they hid out in fear for their lives. Their sorrow was overwhelming.

Jesus had told them plainly what would happen. He would die, be raised to life on the third day.

The third day came and not one was waiting at the tomb to see this marvelous miracle. Mary Magdalene went to the tomb that Sunday morning, not expecting to see a risen Savior, but to finish the job of preparing him for a proper burial. They just didn't get it. (The hindsight we have from our vantage point, we wonder, how they could have been so faithless? Yet we disbelieve every day. Funny isn't it?

The Tech giants announces a new product of their latest gadgets, phones, pads, tablets... and we stand in line for hours to get the first ones and pay a hefty price. Why? Because we believe they will do what they say! We even ignore the truth. That item we so passionately have to have will be obsolete in a heartbeat.

A wink of the eye, a newer version with more gadgets on it will be that " have to have" item, and we do it all over again.

They didn't even sneak out to take a peek, just to see if what Jesus said was so. No, these chosen people Jesus loved hid in fear.

An angel of the Lord told Mary," He is not here! He is risen; just as he told you. Come and see where you know he had been entombed! Go tell his disciples! You will see him!"

She ran back to the group and gave them this exciting news. Peter and John ran quickly, seeing where he had lain, but they still didn't believe!

All 4 gospels give an account and they still didn't quite get it after several visitations. Jesus came through a locked door and a solid wall. Showed them his wounds and ate before them. They simply didn't know what to do or believe anymore.

Peter said to the group, "I am going fishing." "Back to our old lives." It was the one thing he thought he knew how to do! Back to Lake Galilee they went, to pick up where they had left off 3 ½ years earlier. They had fished all night and caught nothing.

They saw a man on the beach near their camp site. Jesus called out to them."Friends, have you any fish?"

"No," they replied.

"Cast your net on the right side of the boat and you will catch some."

I wonder... was this so close to the scene and words, when Peter first encountered Jesus, it triggered his memory? When Jesus told Peter; "follow me and I will make you fishers of men?"

At this they recognized him! Peter jump into the water and swam to shore, the others brought in the boat, their nets so filled with fish, they nearly swamped!

They noticed Jesus already had fish on the coals. Breakfast was ready! Their Sunrise Easter Breakfast! (A good week or two, maybe more, after Jesus resurrection; It really doesn't say how much time had elapsed.)

What a reunion! As Jesus spoke, they put it all together. It had all came to pass, just as He told them it would.

By John's account, at this breakfast meeting, Jesus gave them their final instructions.

Three times Jesus asked. "Peter do you love me? Feed my sheep, my lambs."

Reassuring Peter he was forgiven of the three times he had denied him. To make sure he knew beyond a doubt he was forgiven. It is clear to me this message is to all of us who follow him; our forgiveness is sealed. We are restored. His love covers us forever! Love covers a multitude of sins!

No. there was no sunrise service on the grandest day in history. The day Jesus arose from the dead! I am not sure when this celebration was first celebrated. This first Sunrise Breakfast was more like their graduation class. Jesus was going back to the Father and he left the ball in their court.

They would never be alone, just as he told them in John 14:15-18. The comforter he was sending them would be living in them and he would tell them all things, teaching them all things. He would never leave them of forsake them!

Acts 1:1-5 tell us Jesus was still with them, instructing them. They must have gone back to that upper room in Jerusalem, as he told them not to depart, but wait until the promise of the Father he spoke of, had come. "For John (the Baptist) truly baptized with water but you shall be baptized with the Hoy Ghost not many days from now."

"After the Holy Ghost is come upon you; and you shall be my witnesses in Jerusalem, Judea and all Samaria, and to the uttermost part of the earth."

When he had spoken these things he was taken up while they were looking, and the clouds received him out of their sight... Two men dressed in white appeared and stood by them. They said; "You men of Galilee, why are you standing here gazing up into heaven? This same Jesus, who is taken up from you into heaven, will return to you in this same manner."

They did as they were instructed. A gathering out about 120 believers held a prayer meeting, waiting for this one who Jesus said was to come.

The OT testament feast of Pentecost, 50 days after the Passover feast. When this time was fully come; this promise of the Father came with a mighty wind and tongues of fire, sitting upon each one. They were empowered and emboldened, and this earth has never been the same. The church sprang up, and to this day, it is still going forth in truth and power.

These men who hid after the crucifixion, now covered all the known earth even unto death. As Jesus their Savior had, gladly giving their lives, as he lay down his! THE GREAT EXHANGE!

THE ROMAN SOLDIER'S STORY

THE TRIAL AND CRUCIFIXION, FROM the Roman soldier's point of view.

My name if Antonius, a Roman soldier assigned to Herod's jurisdiction in Jerusalem.

Our imperial forces scattered all over the known world. We Romans ruled over all the far flung countries and territories with strength and numbers that are mind boggling, at least to me.

We went into every battle prepared and without doubt we were the best equipped fighting force the world has ever known. Superior in every way!

To believe otherwise would be considered treason. The Emperor in Rome would tolerate no free thinkers. To question any of his decisions or orders would be swift and terrible. Many had been executed for less.

When the Emperor's troops over ran and subdued Judea and all its scattered peoples, we were a bit surprised by how little resistance they put up.

What we heard rumored about; they were pacifist and expected a long awaited Messiah to come rescue them; soundly defeating any who would get in his path. Well, he didn't show up, but they kept waiting, believing he would still come!

We simply walked in and took over! There were a few who tried to resist, but since they were not backed by their own ruling religious order, it fizzled away without much bloodshed.

Rome set up our ruling government order with a squadron of Roman soldiers to enforce Roman law. To resist Rome was high treason. Those who were found guilty were executed without mercy. After all, The Emperor claimed himself to be deity and who was to argue with that?

The religious rule saw how futile it would be to resist; made a truce to appease this Emperor. They would willingly comply with all Rome asked and in turn they could freely practice their religion. The Jews would pay taxes to Rome and respect their rule. Rome would allow them to practice their faith. A win, win situation that pleased both sides; and it seemed pretty workable to all.

Years passed and both sides fell into this seemingly peaceful routine. The synagogue liked it, but the people detested it. They simply didn't have a choice in the matter. As time passed the anger faded, and that is just was the way it was.

About this time I arrived in Jerusalem.

Many of the Roman squadrons, who elsewhere fought difficult battles; with great loss to both sides. In the end Rome won. The Emperor proclaimed himself God, and no one would challenge him.

I considered duty in Jerusalem a picnic. Of course occasionally someone would commit a crime punishable by death and we would carry it out, but for the most part, it was peaceful. Some of our soldiers even married Jewish young ladies.

There began some rumblings of a radical in the area of Lake Galilee. A few times I was sent as an escort to the Roman King Herod's caravan, as it traveled through the area, this raving mad man would follow along shouting insults and accusations at the King as he passed. This man, in no uncertain terms, called the King out for adultery with his brother Phillips wife! (It was true and we all knew it, but who could have the nerve to challenge Herod?)

I have wondered why Herod did not order him beheaded? We were under order to carry out any command he would give. It seemed Herod had some kind of fascination with this man.

Crowds followed this man, John the Baptist. Seemed he feared no one. He preached loudly and forcefully of repentance and baptism.

The ruling Jews had a riff with him, but Rome was willing to let them tend to their own religious matters. The storms seemed to gather as the crows grew. (Perhaps the Jewish leader feared an uprising that would unseat them.)

The next rumor that filtered in was of a man from the outlying communities, the crowds were saying could be the Messiah. The puzzling thing about him was he had no plans for raising up an army. His message was peace; the kingdom of Heaven. Healing, goodness to others, There was even rumors of some great miracles.

His crowds were out-growing John's, and many of John's followers left him and joined themselves to this man, Jesus. We considered him a nut case and the Jewish leaders considered him a threat. He did nothing to be a reason for his arrest. There was nothing to bring an accusation against him by the Jews or by Rome. How can you arrest a man who speaks peace and good will? He was encouraging people to seek forgiveness, justice, helping the poor, the widows and the orphans.

The rumors of the healings were soon to be no longer a rumor. Many were attesting to these miracles openly. Blind eyes opened, deaf and mute began hearing and speaking. The lame walking and the lepers healed. These large crowds of thousands were being fed with no visible evidence of a source of supply. His message was of a kingdom beyond this earth. It seemed his was a message of offering the people an invitation to life.

None of the powers that be, knew how to deal with him. The Jewish leaders wanted him assassinated, and the Romans wanted to ignore him. The Jews leaders needed to trap him into speaking something against the Word of God but the Romans were not interested their religious squabbles.

Trying to entrap him into speaking against Caesar, they asked Jesus; "Is it lawful for us to pay taxes to Caesar?" Looking at a coin, Jesus answered them; "whose image and inscription do you see on it?" They answered; "Caesar!" Jesus said: "Pay Caesar what is due him and the Lord what is due him."

They finally got their opening. A disciple of Jesus had offered his services, for a fee of thirty pieces of silver, to betray Jesus; delivering him into their hands, where they could arrest him away from the adoring crowds that followed him.

They would and bring false witnesses against him in a late night kangaroo court.

It worked as planned and Jesus was arrested. He was tried in a mock trial; with hired false witnesses. They needed something to force Rome into doing the actual execution, as the religious body had no authority to put a man to death.

The charge they brought was this: They accused Jesus of challenging Caesar as being God. They claimed Jesus said he was God!

Herod and Pilate tried to get Jesus released as they knew this was not true. The religious leaders, whipped up the mob to demand Barabbas, convicted of murder and insurrection be released, and Jesus executed. Shouting," We have no King but Caesar!" At this Roman felt duty bound to act!

After the Jewish leaders had him abused and humiliated, he was turned over the Roman soldiers to administer all the torture humanly possible.

At this we were trained masters. Whipped with the dreaded Cat-of-nine-tails, that tore the flesh of his back to shreds. He was beaten until he was nearly unrecognizable. Then to march him up the hill to his crucifixion; carrying the raw splintered crossbar to his further torture. This place, a hill called Golgotha. (The place of the skull.) where the actual crucifixion would take place.

The detail I was assigned to was driving the spikes through his hand and feet that held him to the cross, then help to stand it up right where he would hang until dead.

I tried to detach myself emotionally, as we were trained to do. Even though I had been told his weeping mother stood near.

(My personal opinion of these things I saw and heard, caused me doubt, as to the legality of it all. But we were not allowed personal opinions. It certainly would be a disobedience to a direct order.)

As I positioned Jesus to drive in those first spikes, he looked directly into my eyes. It was not a look of hate, anger or fear, but as if he understood the orders I had been given, and the look was of forgiveness. I was trembling as I finished the task. I was too stunned to even speak! Do you know how difficult is it to drive spikes into one who looks directly into your eyes with such a tender look?

The upright of the cross was roughly slammed into the hole dug for it. What a jarring pain that must have been.

I watched as the insults and abuse continued. His mother, a Disciple, and her friend stood weeping uncontrollably. I could not make eye contact with them. The day wore on and I wanted death to come quickly and end the pain I knew he must be suffering. It didn't happen.

The Jewish leaders watching, wanted to make sure is was done in the most torturous way. The Roman soldiers on duty with me; without mercy, gambling for his robe. I wanted to run! I wanted to intervene in some way! But I didn't do any of these things. I just stood there hating every minute of this and shame nearly overwhelmed me.

When Jesus and the two crucified with him were nearly finished, one of the men said; "Jesus, remember me when you come into your kingdom." Jesus answered; "this day you shall be with me in paradise."

"Did I hear that right?" "He took his fleeting breath and forgave that convicted man! He was sentenced to die; but Jesus assuring him, he would be in his kingdom!"

With great effort, he turned his head toward his weeping mother and her friends. "John, take my mother into your home and be a son to her." "Mother, dear Mother, go with John and be a mother to him."

He had no concern for himself. His last wishes were to see his mother cared for.

Then he turned slightly and looked at me, without any remorse, and said: "Lord, forgive this man and those, who had to carry this out. For they knew not what they were doing."

I received those words he spoke in prayer, into my being and felt a weight lifted from my soul. I didn't understand it, but I felt free! In my spirit I said, "Surely this man is the Son of God!"

Then this man, Jesus, said; "It is finished." He willingly gave up his spirit and died. How could this be?

We finished the task we were assigned to do. We broke the other two prisoner's legs, just in case they were not quite dead. But when we looked at Jesus, we knew he was dead. One of my comrades pierced his side with his sword. I cringed at this, hoping my fellow soldiers did not notice. Such emotion would not be acceptable of a Roman soldier.

At that moment an earthquake rattled violently enough to knock us to the ground. Then a black, black cloud rolled in, causing the sky to turn day into night. A cold wind and rain struck with a vengeance.

Our work done, we fled back into Jerusalem and our barracks.

My comrades stopped for some after hours refreshment, but I could not bring myself to go.

I took of my uniform, put on my civilian clothes, walked out of that barracks not looking back. I could do this no longer. It hit me like a ton of bricks! I have been forgiven!

I walked away from my military life. I knew I would be a hunted man, and when found, I would be given the same sentence as Jesus. It would be the worst sort of disgrace to Rome and the brotherhood of the soldiers. I would be a deserter, AWOL and treated without mercy.

I must find Jesus followers and go into hiding. If my presence brought harm to them, I would flee to a foreign country. But what I must do was learn all I could of this teaching and tell it wherever I went. Even if it cost me my life! I am willing!

To God be the glory,
Antonius

MARY'S MEMORIES - PART 1

WHAT A LIFE I WAS called to live! I had no Idea of all the surprises; all the facets and turns I was to take. I knew God had something in store for me, but my understanding of it was small. It has been a roller coaster of emotions I've lived out.

Jesus was no ordinary child! In some ways much like his neighborhood friends. They laughed, played ball, climbed trees and got dirty. He was fun loving and good natured with a wonderful sense of humor. He was a loving son that always had a smile and a hug: Never ashamed to walk along side me with his arm around my shoulders. Loving me and protecting me.

Joseph kept the promises he had vowed before God and that small group of witnesses as we exchanged our wedding vows.

(He promised to raise this child with love, all the guidance in all the things of life and faith. He vowed to teach him his trade as a master craftsman. All the things a boy learns from his father. He did that and more with a level of love beyond explaining.)

My memory has never lost a second of the day we were married in my mother's living room. It is forever etched in my mind. Our God's presence so strong the atmosphere was charged in an incredible way.

I remember how serious Joseph was as he spoke with such determination, as if it was a powerful moment between himself and his God. (And it was!)

Yes, Jesus learned all the things a boy could learn from a father. Respect for others; all people really; even those who might disagree with him. He never argued in anger, yet holding to the truth. Jesus was passionate about his Jewish faith, eager to study and learn the teaching of the Torah. At age 13, upon graduation, the family celebrated his Bar-Mitzvah. His learning and understanding was amazing.

Jesus loved working with his hands, doing all the creative things his father taught him. So very good, in fact, Joseph made him his apprentice on the jobs he contracted. The quality they turned out was in great demand.

O yes, Joseph was so proud of him! We were a blessed family. Joseph was such a tender teacher to each one of his sons. A special love for the girls in the things they can only learn from their fathers love.

Joseph had only lived long enough to see Jesus Bar-Mitzvah. He passed away suddenly, soon after. It didn't make sense then or now, but I trusted God knew what he was doing, and that it was time to call his faithful servant home.

We were a large family! We had averaged a child every two years. Five boys and two girls; each one as welcomed as the first. Jesus 13, James 11 (I was pregnant with James when we fled to Egypt to escape Herod's wrath.) Joses 9, Simon 7, Judas 5, the twins girls Salome and Suzanna, 3.

Each was such help and I relied on them as I grieved for my beloved husband.

I am sure Joseph was handpicked for this assignment, to raise the Messiah, just as I was to give him birth. Every time I tried to think it through, I marveled! "Why us, Lord?" "Who are we to be so blessed?" I have no answers, just a grateful heart. I have seen your hand upon us all along the way. Not only upon Joseph, Jesus and I; but your hand also upon James, Joses, Simon, Judas, Salome and Suzanna.

My hands were full; but such a blessing I did not have the times to be selfish and dwell on the past. Joseph had been a wonderful teacher to the boys in the carpentry shop. Jesus and James soon became the teachers to the younger boys. Each one of them quickly becoming very good at carpentry in his own rite. Since Jesus already had such a good reputation by his workmanship, his customers trusted him with more additional orders than we needed. That humble shop became an assembly line with all the sons working. All the orders filled and to rave reviews. We never lacked for anything; never missed a meal.

The older boys helped me care for the younger ones. Each were so good to help with the twin girls. Ours was a home filled with love and laughter.

As time marched on, one by one, all the boys had gone through their own Bar-Mitzvah ceremony. Each grew into a fine young man and master craftsman. As they grew up, married and started families of their own, my family grew. Four lovely daughters-in-law, and new births in the family line came often. O my, the grandchildren!

The twins were the last to marry. Jesus, his brothers and I gave them a beautiful double wedding to remember! All the customs and traditions of the Jewish people, and I believe Jesus and I invented a few more. He had a wonderful time. Since he had finished all the schooling necessary, he was a Rabbi, and he took great interest in performing this very special ceremony for this two little sisters.

Jesus stayed home working in the shop; enjoying his father's trade. He was such a devoted son to me and all the family.

One morning, he said, "Mom, it is time!" I didn't have to ask what that meant. I knew this day would come, and when it did, God would tell him. He didn't say "Gabriel has visited me." I knew he had heard from his Father: The Most High God, directly!

Yes, I knew what he was sent to do and he would fulfill his mission. I hugged him and said, "Yes son, I know. Go and do whatever you are sent to do. You have been called." "Keep in touch! Know that I love you."

"Mom, there is one last thing we must do as a family." "Cousin Andrew has asked me to officiate his wedding: A memory to be treasured!"

"I have one last journey to make before then, so I will meet you there."

I was delighted, having all of my family together one more time. Jesus said, "Mom, at this wedding a wonderful thing will happen and you and I will see God's miracle through me." "That will start the journey I was born to walk out." "At that time you and I will be the only ones to understand fully what this means."

There must have been a sparkle in my eyes as I anticipated all of these things.

Jesus said, "I must go to the Jordan River, near lake Galilee and be baptized by John." Then I will do battle against Satan, and after he is defeated, I will choose my followers;my Disciples.""When that has been done I will meet you in Cana for the wedding."

I don't want you to be sad, as you know this better than anyone." "After all, you were the one God sent Gabriel to visit first!"

"No matter what happens, stay close to God and trust in Him and do not be afraid." "This is what I came to do." "I could not have been sent to a more godly, loving, amazing family!"

"Thank You, Mom!" With that, he hung up his tool belt, and closed the door to the shop one last time. He gave me one last hug and kissed my cheek and walked away without looking back. I am quite sure there was joy in his heart and a tear in his eye he did not want me to see.

I had joy in my heart too, but many, many tears in my eyes. I would miss him so very much, yet I was excited to see him called to move forward and into his purpose. Not knowing how it would unfold, I would be as surprised as the next one. God's plan had begun to unfold and I was witness to this moment in history that would change the world, and only Jesus and I would understand it!

Jesus headed for the Jordan where John was preaching and baptizing. His strong preaching was drawing crowds. There was quite a commotion! Seems the Pharisees, and some Sadducees were coming to him also, but John saw through their motives. "You brood of vipers! Who said you could escape the wrath to come?" "Do you think because you claim Abraham as your father you can escape?" "I tell you no!" "If you have not laid down your self-righteousness and false humility, baptism will profit you nothing!" "God can raise up these stones to be children of Abraham!" "There must be fruit in your life that witness of your repentance!"

"The ax has already been laid to the root and every tree that bears no good fruit will be chopped down and burned in the fire!"

Jesus watched all this, listened and smiled. When the embarrassed crowd from the synagogue had fled, Jesus presented himself to John for baptism.

"No, I should be asking you to baptize me." John replied.

"We must do this John, that all be properly done and fitting for the fulfillment of all righteousness." Jesus told him.

At this Jesus submitted himself and John obeyed God's command.

As John completed this baptism, and Jesus was lifted up out of the water: The heavens opened and the Spirit of God, descended and came down in the form of a dove and rested upon Jesus shoulder, and a voice from heaven said, "This is my Son! My beloved Son! I am wonderfully pleased in Him!"

As Jesus mother, I was told these things by some of the men who had followed John. They also told me of Jesus being tempted in the wilderness area.

After Jesus had gone without food and water; fasting 40 days and 40 nights; the enemy, knowing he would be in a weakened condition, came and said to himself, "Jesus must be so hungry and thirsty he will do anything for a slice of bread."

"Jesus, if you are the Son of God, as you say you are, it would be an easy thing for you to change these stones into bread!" "That would prove you are who you claim to be."

Jesus replied: "Man does not live by bread alone, but by every word that comes from the mouth of God."

Then Satan took him to the highest pinnacle of the temple and said: "Jump Jesus! Prove yourself!" The Scripture says God will send his angles to lift you up and protect you from even stubbing your toe against a rock!"

Jesus answered: "It is also written:"Do not tempt the Lord your God!"

At this the Devil took him to the highest mountain peak and showed him all the kingdoms of the earth. "I will give you all the kingdoms of the earth if you will bow down and worship me!"

"Get away from me Satan! For it is written, 'Worship the Lord your God and Him only shall you serve!'" At this the devil left him and the angels of God came and ministered to him. This was a complete victory over Satan! Satan came to kill, steal and destroy, but Jesus defeated him by the very Word of God!

Jesus went about gathering his team. Many were shocked by these he chose. Some would say the most unlikely! Most would say a bunch of misfits! Not a man among them would they have chosen!

Jesus sent word to me. "I will meet you in Cana at cousin Andrew's wedding. We will have a great family reunion." (It would be the start of Jesus public ministry.)

A Jewish wedding is a marvelous affair: A mix of Faith, tradition and festivity that lasts for days. This wedding was no exception! The ceremony could not take place until the groom had prepared a home for his bride. He could not simply throw up a shack and call it a home. His father would determine when it was done. The workmanship completed to his satisfaction. The groom had been working on it through-out the long engagement. I suppose the family honor might be judged by it, as this was a family of carpenters. So it was undoubtedly a masterpiece.

(Years later when Jesus spoke to his Disciples the night before his betrayal, he told them he was going away. At that time they didn't understand it, he was referring to that Jewish wedding ceremony tradition.)

When he comes back to get his bride, the church, he tells them: "In my Father's house there are many mansions. If it were not so I would have told you. I go to prepare a place for you. When I return, I will take you to be where I am." (He is coming back for his Bride, the Church!) The Jewish wedding symbol! Only the Father knows the day or the hour.)

When Joseph and I married, the ceremony was small, but he had been working on our home during our betrothal; but our wedding was just of close family and the presence of the Holy Spirit had fully enveloped that room in my mother's house, no wedding could rival that.

Since we didn't get to spend many days there before going to Bethlehem, it sat unused until Herod was dead and it was safe to go home.

Back to Andrew's wedding.

It was most beautiful. The bride was radiant. There was merriment, singing and dancing. The most fun wedding I had ever attended. Even though I knew my position had changed. Now I must share Jesus with the world. I purposed in my heart to let go and let God!

MARY'S MEMORIES - PART 2

I T WAS AT THIS WEDDING Jesus did his first miracle.
The steward of the wedding said in my hearing to one of
the servants, "we have run out of wine!"

This celebration was only at the mid-point, so this was
a major disaster for the host family. I called to Jesus and
told him the situation. He smiled and said, in a teasing way,
"Mother, what has that to do with me?"He knew what I was
asking.

I motioned to one of the servants; "go ask Jesus what you
must do and whatever he ask, do it!" The man looked puzzled,
but delivered the message.

Jesus told him, "Fill those six large stone 30 gallon water
pots to the brim with freshwater." "Now dip out a ladle full
from the pot and take it to the wedding steward to sample."

The man went and did as Jesus had told him.

The steward, in great surprise said:"Where did this come
from?" "This should have been served first and the lesser
last!"

Seeing this, the newly appointed Disciples were amazed
and put their trust in him.

Only the servant, Jesus and I knew! The first recorded miracle! I knew his ministry had begun and now we would share him with the world

Yes we did, and the crowds were so big that followed him, we had very little access to him. (I must say, even knowing it had to be this way, I felt a bit selfish.)

When the wedding celebration ended, Jesus and his Disciples headed to Capernaum.

Little did we know what he was about to do. News reached our ears that he had gone into the synagogue; read the section of the Torah that speaks of the Messiah, in Isaiah 9: 2, 6-7. The coming Messiah, and declared it was he!

From that day on the Pharisees, Sadducees and other leaders in the synagogue began plotting how to rid themselves of him! It must be carefully done as the masses believed him, and a riot may break out. Should this happen the powers of Rome would step in, their anger would be upon them.

We, his family, were puzzled at what all this could mean.

I would hear occasional news of Jesus from people who had seen him as he traveled about.

We had heard he was coming our way, but the crowds were so massive, I had little hope of getting close to him.

My other children and I thought "maybe we can get a message to him to meet us and we can have an hour or so alone with him."

A strong, fast, young son of James agreed to deliver the message. He would be our best bet to get to Jesus. All the nieces and nephews wanted to see their favorite uncle. Well he didn't quite make it, but passed a message on to another that seemed to have discovered a way through the mob.

After some time the message reach Jesus. "You mother and your brothers and sisters, and their families are outside wanting to see you."

Jesus, looking around at the people said: "Who is my mother, brothers and sisters?" "It is they that do the will of God!"

I was disappointed, of course, but understood the mission. His brothers did not, and were angry? A divide was created between them that day that only time would heal.

Jesus call was to all that would hear and believe. As many as received him he gave the right to become children of God.

He had offended his brothers who said, "if he doesn't want to see us, why are we wasting our time!" It hurt me, but I also understood their disappointment.

His brothers were feeling the effects of Jesus bold preaching in their pocket books also. Some of their best customers were refusing to give them contract work. If they were found doing business with the brothers of Jesus, they could be expelled from the synagogue. The gulf between Jesus and his brothers widened.

All during these 3 ½ years of his ministry, we would hear stories of many miracles. We also heard the stories of the Leaders of the synagogues and their hatred, with plots to kill him.

The celebration of Passover was quickly approaching. Jesus sent the Disciples on ahead, saying he would not be going this year.

His brothers saying; "We think he has gone mad;" They sent word to him to go. "Go do some of your miracles, if you are so anointed! Show yourself and we and all will believe you!"

The others would not go, but I could not stay away. I knew deep down something terrible would happen.

Just as I had thought, Jesus would go also, alone. I followed him.

The city of Jerusalem was filled to overflowing. Jewish people from far distant places came to offer their sacrifices. The Temple courts were set up with tables and stalls of livestock for the sellers to sell; and tables for the money changers to exchange all the foreign currency to that used in Jerusalem. (And, at a great profit.)

A lot of the travelers could not bring their own animals to be sacrificed, because of the distance, so they would buy what was need there.

The Temple courtyard was a zoo! A literal Zoo!

The Passover celebration was the high point of the Jewish festivals! The celebration of their people being delivered from 400 years of Egyptians slavery.

Pharaoh had refuses to let Moses take the people out of Egypt. God had provided a series of miracles; even some very severe miracle did not move Pharaoh. The last, most bitter one, Moses had told Pharaoh would come, was the death of the oldest son in every household, from his palace to his lowest slaves, even the first born of all the animals. Still Pharaoh was not moved!

God had instructed Moses to prepare the Jews to sacrifice a lamb, use the blood to paint over the door and side post of their homes, with a hyssop brush. Be dressed and ready to go!

Eat the Passover lamb with the bitter herbs that night, and when He sent the angel on death, that angel would Passover all the homes with the blood above the door.

This was a national festival and all must go; an everlasting ordinance. Many still followed that tradition; therefore the streets were full.

Jesus was so upset how the temple had been desecrated to be a market place! With a whip of cords he turned over the money changers tables, scattering the coins everywhere; driving the livestock into the streets! "You are making my Father's house into a market, a den of thieves!" he cried.

At this he was challenged by the Pharisees. "Who gave you the authority to do this!" The gauntlet had been dropped! Jesus days were numbered.

After going up the mountain to pray he sent some of his Disciples back into Jerusalem, to an upper room where he had instructed them to make ready for their Passover dinner.

By this time, I and a group of his other followers had joined ourselves to them. Jesus must have known we would be there, as the room was set up to accommodate us.

One long head table where Jesus would eat this with his 12 Disciples; and many other tables set up for the rest of us followers.

This ceremonial dinner was a very moving experience. Each table was served just as theirs. I did not understand exactly what Jesus had instructed Judas to do, but he left suddenly and the dinner proceeded.

After dinner Jesus got up removed his outer robe, tied a towel around his waist, took a basin of water and washed each of his Disciples feet. (In this culture, it was the duty of the lowliest of servants.)

Peter protested! "No! Lord we should wash your feet!" "I am not worthy to have you wash my feet!"

"Peter, if you don't allow me this, you have not part in me."

"Lord, wash all of me! Not only my feet, but my head and my hands, all of me!"

"If I, Your master have washed your feet, you ought to lower yourselves to wash each others feet."

(We then remembered he had told us, "I came to serve, not to be served." "Do not think of yourselves more highly than you ought." So many of his words came back to us.

In that room we were all participants in this whole evening.

After hours of teaching, it seemed he was trying to tell us all the things we would need to know. Time was running out.

He spent a great amount of time telling us he was going away but he was sending his very Holy Spirit to live within each one of us. Until now, he had been with us; from now forward, he would live within us! Leading us, teaching us, guiding us in all things, even the words we are to speak.

It was getting very late, but he told us his time had come.

We went with him to the garden of Gethsemane. There he took Peter, James and John a little farther and asked them to stay awake and watch while he prayed.

Kneeling down among some old twisted olive tree trunks he began to pray fervently. In great agony of spirit, knowing what was so come. He knew every lash of the whip, the insults and humiliations. The nails that would fasten him to that cross: all of it! In his humanity, faced it as you or I might have. Praying his Father might find another way. Yes, his agony was real.

I and the other Disciples, a bit farther back, could see his suffering as he prayed. As a mother, my heart broke. I would have gladly traded places with him, yet knowing I had done my part in this plan of Redemption, and he must do his. It didn't soften my sorrow though.

I remembered the day we took Jesus to the Temple for the required circumcision of every Jewish male. We were met by an aged man named Simeon, who had been told by the Lord, he would not die until he had seen the Lord's Messiah. Taking Jesus into his arms, spoke some words that troubled me. Not understanding what they meant until now.

"Let, now let your servant depart in peace, according to your word.

My eyes have seen your salvation, which you have prepared before the face of all people: a light to the Gentiles; and the glory of your people Israel." With those words spoken he blessed Jesus and I, then added; looking directly into my eyes, "Yes, a sword shall pierce your own soul also." I would suffer great sorrow seeing what my son would endure.

Twice Jesus arose from his knees to find his closet friends sleeping. "Could you not watch with me one hour?"

The third time he prayed he was in such agony. His sweat fell as great drop of blood. "Father, if there is some other way!" Being met with silence, he said: "Not my will but yours be done."

This last time he awakened them, he said, "Come, it is time! My betrayal and arrest is at hand."

At this a mob from the Pharisees camp and some Roman soldiers came with his friend, Judas. He moved quickly toward Jesus and kissed him on the cheek as if in greeting. At this the soldiers grabbed him and held him fast.

Jesus said."It is me you want. Let these others go." Why this secret raid?" "I was with you teaching daily in your very presences." "You could have arrested me then." "Were you afraid of the crowds that followed?" A servant of the highest Pharisee stepped forward in a threatening manner, and Peter, being Peter

Reached for his sword and cut off this man's right ear.

"Peter, Peter this must be done. Put away your sword! Don't you know he who lives by the sword will die by the sword?"

At this Jesus touched the man's ear and instantly healed him!

This fellow was greatly astonished and fell back into the crowd. I can imagine he began his journey toward Salvation that very instant.

MARY'S MEMORIES - PART 3

FROM JESUS ARREST THROUGH THE crucifixion, and resurrection; what a time of turmoil and emotions. I marvel I made it through this horrific time. Only the comfort of the special friend, Mary Magdalene and the fellowship of the Holy Spirit, was it possible. I have no recollection of how we got from Golgotha back to that upper room.

I've been told Mary Magdalene put to me bed and sat by my side until she was sure I was in a deep sleep. Sleep does allow the body's healing.

When I begin to stir, my memory came back, and could begin to see clearly all the horrific things I had witnessed were all of a part of God's plan. People needed to see clearly the agony of sins consequences. Sin is death; eternal punishment. Not of God's choosing but by of our choice. Praise God! My son took all the punishment of everyone's sentence; of those who would trust in him.

Yes, it was the sword that pierced my own heart, just as Simeon had spoken to me, the day we took Jesus to the temple for his circumcision.

Now all the things along the way had come to pass and needed to be; to complete this Journey Jesus had come to do. In a dream He has shown me: He took hell so we won't have too. He took all the evil Satan could throw at him; for our sake. He suffered all the pain in our place. The shame, abandonment, the humiliation: All of it in our place! We can now be free to enter that kingdom, pure and clean without blemish, spot or wrinkly, as a bride adorned for her groom. All the soil of this earth that has soiled us, gone! All by the Grace and Mercy of God! He took us from the pit and cleansed us in the blood of the sinless One. Removed our tattered, soiled rags and covered us with his spotless righteousness.

All these things rushed through my mind, I opened my eyes. As all this revelation came upon me, I begin to smile. I arose from that bed of suffering into everlasting joy.

I got up, dressed, washed my face and combed my hair. As I stepped into the room of my down casted friends, they simply could not understand my change. Mary M., guided me to the breakfast table, thinking I must be about to crumble. I assured them I was fine and my joy was real. I had many looks of disbelief and pity, but I knew they would soon understand. I was cuddled and coddled as if I were some basket case, but inwardly I knew they would soon understand my visitations from Jesus. Right now, they didn't get it.

When Jesus visited them, they thought they were seeing his ghost. The eye contact Jesus and I made, told him I understood.

It was after Jesus met them on the shores of Lake Galilee with their final instructions did they realize; yes, it is true and he is risen!

They came back and reassembled as Jesus instructed them. Told us the story of the coming "promise of the Father," and how we must wait there in that upper room for this.

We did, and there with us many followers who had been touched in one way or another; about 120 of us waiting, joyous believers; so happy to be included.

When that promise came, it was almost beyond explaining. We heard a mighty wind, sounding so fierce, as if it could rip the building apart, but it didn't! Instead a holy flame of fire appeared and separated into individual flames and sat upon each one of us.

At that moment each one of us was changed and we knew it! We had received a boldness beyond knowing that gave power to our words and actions that would change the world.

People from all the surrounding area's were hearing these people who had this upper room experience, speaking in their native tongues! "What is this they cried?"

Peter answered, saying this is what was spoken by the prophet Joel.

"In the last days, I will pour out my Spirit on all people. Your sons and your daughters will prophesy, your young men will see visions, and your old men shall dream, dreams."

"Even on my servants, both men and women, I will pour out my Spirit in those days, and they will prophesy."

"I will show wonders in the heavens above and sign on the earth below, blood and fire and billows of smoke. The sun will be turned to darkness, and the moon to blood, before that great and glorious day of the Lord."

"And everyone that calls on the name of the Lord will be saved."

Peter, who and denied Jesus, then hid, now was the boldest speaker imaginable. He rose up, and spoke to the amazed crowd, explained what they were seeing and hearing. A sermon the world will never forget. Before he could even conclude his words, people were weeping and crying out in repentance. "What must we do? What must we do, to be as this that has happened to you?"

He gave what we now call, an altar call, so powerfully, 3,000 souls were saved and added to our numbers that day. I was as amazed as any there!

From there we began to scatter, because of the persecution from the Pharisees and leaders of the synagogues. This was meant to wipe us out, but it only spread the Word, through-out all the known world. Everywhere we went a body of believers would spring up. It was a dangerous life, but so exciting.

Over the years, John started a work in Ephesus where he preached daily, to greater and greater audiences. He provided Mary Magdalene and I nice quarters. We were often given liberty to tell our story and many came to believe. John loved to share his pulpit with all who had a story of Jesus. He seemed to have no problem allowing women to speak.

I lived in this lovely compound until the day of my death. I was now old and ready to move on to paradise. I was surrounded and respected by all. John had truly kept his promise to Jesus that day as he took me in and cared for me, and I for him. It was a wonderful arrangement.

Mary Madalene, companion to Mary, Jesus mother. Mother of Jesus the Messiah.

Postscript: It was my pleasure to be the personal companion of Jesus Mother. We gave her a beautiful funeral of great honor to a great lady. She had blessed all of our lives. Many come forward to tell of some memory of her kindness.

All would agree, the Lord our God knew what he was doing when he hand- picked Mary to be the one to bring the Messiah into the world. She was a most wonderful wife, mother, and friend to all.

Lest you would think any of these other children in her family never returned to faith, let me tell you! They did come along! His brothers became some his most powerful supporters. They had seen their error of putting their personal gain above their love. They repented and ask God's forgiveness. Forgiven they were, and they took their testimony of the truth of Jesus everywhere. James became one of the powerful leaders in the Jerusalem headquarters. He gave his life willingly, and was martyred for his faith.

A most grateful daughter of the King!

Mary Magdalene

EPILOGUE

THIS HAS BEEN A LABOR of love, yet for an uneducated, first time author, it has been hard work. Yet, the most rewarding thing I've ever attempted.

In the process, all the things I thought I knew, and didn't, have been amplified. I see it all the more clearly as the events I've followed, came into places with people I have come to know, as friends. They have become so personal; I feel we could sit down and visit over a cup of coffee in each other's kitchen.

When we meet Jesus we are changed. That change comes as rapidly or slowly, depending on how willing we are to be changed. Most usually we all have things we don't want to change. The older we get the less all those things we so stubbornly cling too, seem so useless. The Lord does not force us to make those choices, as He is so loving and patient; longsuffering, awaits us to chose Him. How glad I am! How good He is!

I had a hard time giving this work a title. Seems all the things that cropped up just didn't fit. As strange as it seems, the one I chose came to me in a dream. I've always been a dreamer and many times things I've dreamed, have come to pass. So this caught my attention. I was a bit puzzled and wondered how that "fit" into the stories.

Then I recalled a favorite Scripture I liked so much. Isaiah 49:15. "See, I have engraved your name on the palm of my hand."Some versions say tattooed, written, etc., all meaning the same thing. Written there; reminding me, I am ever before Him. He says I will not forget you! I also remembered somewhere in the O.T. it said we should not make marks or cuts and such on our bodies.

Then I was thinking what all this could mean? I recalled Thomas (the doubter) reaction when he first saw Jesus after the resurrection. The things that caused him to believe it was true, was these scars on His hands, feet and the spear wound on His side. He fell on his knees and cried out, "My Lord and my God." Those scars are a Testimony of what our Salvation cost Him. He bore the punishment our sins deserved. What did it cost us? Only that we believe Him. Those scars and our acknowledgement sealed the deal!

"In the Palm of His Hands," is the story of each one of us. Our name is written in those scars. Everyone who will claim them! The choice is ours. Think it over and ask yourself, "have I chose to believe and receive that most precious gift ever offered?" He has opened the way to Heaven for each one who will choose. That simple! He choose to make it simple; "so simple a child can understand it". It is man who has made it hard.

What is stopping us? I have found most people have had a bad experience somewhere along the line, and following those bad examples and joining them is not what they desire to do! Me either! The first thing I want you to know is, "Saying: YES to Jesus is not joining a church or a denomination. It is not about accepting church charters and doctrines, and rules.

It is simple becoming one with Jesus. It is making a choice to receive his gift. He took the punishment for our sin. It is a gift, and the choice is ours. No one can take it from us! He took all the punishment upon his own body, nailed it to the cross, and paid the price in full! He even went into hell and defeated that last enemy, death. Arose and set us all free!

It is an easy thing to do! Simply ask Him! He still sees us, hears us, even if we have spent a life time ignoring Him. He is so happy to see you come home

That prayer does not have to be fancy. He hears our most heart- felt cry. Sometimes that cry we cannot even express with words. When Peter was about to drown, all he could do was cry out, "Jesus, save me!" and He did!

You can start by just calling Him Lord. (Fill the blanks with your name.)

If you would like to invite Him in Just say, in your own words something similar to this:

Lord Jesus, I ...., believe you love even me. I......... acknowledge I am a sinner, as the Bible tells me, "All have sinned and fallen short of the glory of God." That include me. I .... am so sorry I haven't come before, as I have missed so many of the blessings by waiting. Come into my life now, and be my Lord, my God, and my Savior!

NOW BEGAN TO PRAISE HIS NAME!

If you have any questions you can contact me at the address below.

Write or e-mail me.
AJ Cork
3180 N. Wabasha Pl.
Wasilla, Alaska 99654
corkaj@gmail.com

Know you are now a child of God, and let not that enemy tell you otherwise! He will try. But come against him. He is a liar! He came but to kill, steal and destroy. He desires to steal your new found faith. Run to Jesus and that Liar has to flee. He cannot stand in the presence of Jesus. James 4:7

About the Author

I AM A FIRST TIME author, at the age of 81 (almost 82.) I live in Alaska, the most beautiful place in the world. I suppose everyone sees the beauty of where they live.

I have three children; 8 grandchildren and 19 great grandchildren. And they really are blessings.

We came to Alaska from Oregon in 1976, intending to only stay for the summer construction season. We fell so in love with this land we stayed and never looked back. We loved it here. Our family is scattered from here to Oregon, Washington and Idaho.

The cover photo is of Mt. Iliamna on the west side of the Cook Inlet, as seen from the Old Sterling Highway. The drive from Soldotna to Homer, at the end of the road, is worth the trip to Alaska. These views are through-out Alaska. Of course that is why so many creative, artistic people are drawn here from the world over. The handiwork of God is evident everywhere.

There are exhibits of artist work at nearly every stop along any road system. The native art work is so beautiful and unique; many using the tools of many generations back.

I am sure I wouldn't have been writing if I lived any place else. It is simply an inspiring place to be.

Who knows; maybe I'll be inspired to write another book?

AJCork

CPSIA information can be obtained
at www.ICGtesting.com
Printed in the USA
FSOW01n1531020816
23360FS